THE MACABRE

STUART JAMES

Edited by Eve Hall.

Cover design by Thea Magerand.

bookvault
Publishing

ISBN: 9781804673829
Perfect Bound

First published in 2023 by bookvault Publishing,
Peterborough, United Kingdom

An Environmentally friendly book printed and
bound in England by bookvault, powered by
printondemand-worldwide

Sometimes the lights aren't the end of the tunnel.

THE INTRUDER

1

Marcia Graham lay on her side, facing the wall, with a thin white sheet covering her body. Opening her eyes, she peered at the alarm clock. 1.22am. Something had woken her.

She placed her hand behind, feeling for her husband, and touching his left arm. His presence comforted her. She moved her body backwards in the bed so she was able to feel his warm breath on her neck.

Closing her eyes, she breathed in the cold air of the room, and pulled the sheet to her neck, now feeling warmer.

A door opened in the distance. Marcia sat up, leaning her body against the soft headboard. She listened hard, waiting in the darkness—her body still and stagnant.

Someone was in the house. Fear washed over her as she listened to the groans coming from below, and her stomach began to cramp.

Gently, she pushed the sheet off her body, listening to it fold on the mattress, and angled her frame around the bed, facing the door. She dabbed her feet on the cold, wooden floor, circling them, searching for her slippers. Sliding her feet into them, she stood. Marcia considered waking her husband, but she freaked at the slightest noise, and when he woke, he struggled to get back to sleep. He'd be annoyed with her and sulk.

Maybe I'm imagining it, but I have to check, she thought.

Marcia held her arms in front of her, able to see the shape of the wardrobe, her fingers poking into the darkness, one foot in front of the other, careful, easy steps, feeling for the door handle. Sliding her hand slowly down the wooden door, grabbing the handle with her right hand, she turned it anti-clockwise. Marcia pulled it towards her, worried the slight creaking sound would wake her husband. He had an early start, often leaving the house at 5am. The commitment of being a London stockbroker showed no remorse.

Marcia stood in the upstairs hallway, closing the bedroom door behind her. She pawed her left hand on the wall and ran her fingers along the smooth surface, searching for the light. The sound of a delicate click and suddenly, the hallway was visible.

Her reflection in the hall mirror caused Marcia to jump. She smirked. *Get a grip. It's probably next door's cat or a fox.* She stared hard at her face, suddenly distracted, a ploy she often used to escape a bigger problem, tracing her finger over her soft skin and under her chin. Marcia was almost fifty but looked at least ten years younger. Her long blonde hair glistened, her hazel-green eyes were dazzling, and she hardly had a wrinkle, thanks to the odd botox session.

Waiting, she listened for another noise, movement, anything to clarify they had an intruder. She pondered calling out or whispering at the walls.

With slow, deliberate steps, Marcia reached the top of the stairs. The house was still. Hesitating, she dipped her right foot on the top step and glanced back towards the bedroom door. Marcia stood still for a second, vulnerable, scared. The darkness below was unwelcoming and hostile. She took a deep breath, her slim frame shivering in her night slip.

Marcia moved down towards the ground floor, her right hand gripping the thick railing, sliding along the cold wood as she moved.

Another noise, this time definite footsteps. They were heavy, cumbersome, moving below her.

Marcia froze; fear washed over her as she held her breath and waited. She backed up, too frightened to turn, placing one foot behind the other.

'Marcia?'

Spinning around, she saw her husband had opened the bedroom door and was standing naked in the hall. His eyes were swollen with tiredness as he peered at her.

'Call the police,' she whispered. 'Someone is moving around downstairs.'

'Come back to bed. I assure you no one is in the—'

A figure charged up the stairs, footsteps pounding loud in Marcia's ears. She screamed, a bellowing roar that filled the house.

'Marcia! Run,' her husband yelled.

The person swung a hammer, hitting Marcia hard on the side of the head.

Her world became dark as she fell on the stairs.

* * *

The following evening, Marcia woke, her eyes darting around the strange room, across the white ceiling, and down the bare walls, confused by the unfamiliar surroundings.

She was lying in a bed with an endotracheal tube

through her mouth and into her lungs, due to being uncon-scious when first brought in. The tube was attached to a ventilator to provide oxygen. She went to move, placing her palms flat on the mattress and hoisting her body upwards. The tube was irritating her, and she felt uncomfortable. As Marcia grabbed it, a voice instructed her to lie back down and get some rest.

Later, a torch was shone into her eyes to see how her pupils responded to light, followed by a tirade of questions; the nurse instructed Marcia to blink her answer, one for yes, two for no.

'Do you know where you are?'

Marcia blinked twice.

'Do you know why you're here?'

Again, two blinks.

With blurry eyes, Marcia skimmed the room; a haze of confusion filled her mind.

The nurse stood over her, tucking the sheet back, a kind smile on her face. 'You're a lucky woman. You received a nasty blow to the head. You're in the Intensive Care Unit. You need to rest.'

Marcia glared towards the array of machines, then closed her eyes. A few minutes later, she heard another voice. Deep, soothing.

'How is she?'

'She's conscious,' the nurse said, 'Which is a good thing. But she's uncertain of her environment. I tried to ask a few questions, but it's a little early. I don't want to frighten her. Confusion is common with head trauma. She was put into a medically induced coma to rest the brain and deal with the swelling.'

The voice was close now. 'Marcia. Marcia love. It's me, Daniel. How are you feeling?'

Marcia opened her eyes. She stared at the man in front of her, taking in his features. The cropped black hair, light green eyes, his chiselled jaw. He was so handsome in a rugged, washed up kind of way. He was tall, athletic and his face seemed kind.

Gently, he reached forward and stroked her cheek with his fingers, watching her wild eyes.

She pulled her head back as if recoiling. Concern adorned her face. She kept blinking as if instructing the man to move away from her bed.

'Marcia, you know me. I'm your husband.'

Marcia continued blinking.

He turned, pushing out a heavy sigh, then moved away from the bed.

'Why can't she recognise me?'

The nurse kept her voice low. 'It's possible she has retrograde amnesia and cannot remember anything before the blow. We have weaned the sedation, and she's now conscious. That's a good sign. She needs to rest. Time is a great healer.'

The smell of detergent filled her lungs as Marcia lay in the bed. The telly was on with the volume low, the picture was grainy, and she tried to hear what they were saying. She closed her eyes, struggling to recall something, anything of who she was, what she liked to do, memories from childhood, her parents, siblings, her past. There was nothing. It was like her mind had been wiped clean, a computer with its files erased, a shop ransacked and emptied during a robbery. She felt so scared and vulnerable. Her head ached, and her eyes felt heavy with tiredness.

The man who had come to see her claimed to be her husband, but to her, he was a stranger, a face in the crowd. Nothing he had said made sense. She felt frustrated. She wanted to get away from here and the unfamiliar faces prodding her, asking questions, treating her like a lab rat.

Turning on her side she wept until she fell asleep.

Marcia woke in the night. She could hear someone calling out from another room, a voice, scared, lonely, asking to go to the toilet.

A nurse dashed along the corridor outside her room, her eyes closed again. Later, Marcia heard a man whistling and the sound of a mop as it bashed against the skirting boards. She closed her eyes and dreamed of falling into a pit. When she hit the ground, her eyes opened. Someone was standing by the bed.

'Marcia. Marcia, are you OK?'

She opened her eyes, again, hazy, blurred. Blinking, a nurse became visible by her bed. Reaching for the tube in her throat, she began to cough, watching as the nurse spoke. Her mouth moved, her lips bouncing together, but Marcia was unable to dissect the words. Her brain was like a sieve, the sounds falling through and dispersing.

She closed her eyes and drifted back to sleep.

Over the next few days, Marcia continued to see the man with the deep voice. He'd visit, standing by her bed, rubbing her face, pushing her hair back, which was damp from the heat of the room, and running his fingers through it. He told her about them, how they'd met, what they liked to do and how they spent their time at home. Home, a place she couldn't picture. A life outside this hospital with a stranger stood by her bed. It was awkward. She wanted him to leave. The things he told her didn't register. Her hobbies, interests and programmes she liked to watch made no sense. She felt disorientated.

Marcia couldn't envisage being with him. A man she didn't remember wanted to take her home. To spend the rest of his life with her. How could she do that?

How can he expect that of her?

She didn't even know who he was.

* * *

Towards the end of the week, a nurse removed the tube lodged in her throat and she found that she was able to talk again.

'Now, that's better. How are you feeling?' the nurse asked.

'I can't remember anything.'

'You mustn't worry. Head injuries can be tricky and confusing.'

'I'm not confused. My mind is empty. I can't remember a single thing about my life. What's wrong with me?'

'You have amnesia. It's common with the type of blow to the head you suffered.' The nurse pulled a trolley to the side of the bed. 'Are you hungry?'

Again, the torch in her eyes, the blood pressure machine crushing her arm, the buzz as it squeezed tight. She imagined her arm bursting, the blood and tissue spilling onto the floor. More whistles from mop man as he glides the end over the hospital floor, soaking up the blood.

Marcia didn't answer.

'Come on. Easy does it. Sit up and eat something. You need to regain your strength.'

Marcia stared at the coffee and toast. 'Am I going mad?'

'Listen to me. You are so brave. We'll do everything we can. I promise. It's common for this to happen, but you need to fight, OK?'

Marcia smiled. 'OK.'

* * *

Once another CT Scan showed the swelling had gone from her brain, Marcia was brought to a general ward, where she would spend another few weeks. She mostly slept, went through rehab, and stared blankly at the man who came to see her every day.

Listening to him, she wanted to remember, to recognise the person she apparently married before the attack. Her brain was an empty vessel, and the frustration began to build.

Patients lay in beds around her, but she couldn't muster the strength for conversation. Instead, just nodding.

Where do you live? How long have you been here? Do you have children?

That last question stirred something in her mind. Marcia looked towards the old lady lying next to her, peering at the bandage on her right foot, the flowers in the vase next to her bed, the drip attached to her arm.

'I think I do. I remember a girl. I think I have a daughter.' As the memory of a child pushed into her mind, Marcia felt excitement. Comfort drenched her body, and her skin tingled. Closing her eyes tight, she clawed desperately into the void, needing to remember something. The harder she thought, the more empty her head became. She lay still; seconds trickled to minutes, and then she opened her eyes.

The man was standing over her again.

'Marcia, how are you feeling, darling?'

She stared right through him.

Again, he asked her how she was, and she didn't answer. She was suddenly scared.

A man she couldn't remember, claiming to be her husband, was standing by her bed.

Voices reverberated through the room. Police officers trying to take a statement from her, unable to answer their questions and patients lying in beds, chatting with visitors. The sounds were sharp, paining her ears; her mind was busy digesting words. Marcia's head began to throb, and she trembled with the pain.

Children's laughter echoed in the distance, the smell of detergent filled her lungs, and groans spilt from the patients next to her as their loved ones tried to make them more comfortable.

As she drifted to sleep, she heard voices. She recognised *his*. She kept her eyes closed.

'I want to take her home.'

'It's not recommended, Mr Graham; she's still recovering.'

'I understand. But she's frightened. You can see that, surely? If she's in a familiar environment, it may help her remember.'

'Well, possibly, but—'

'Look, she's able to walk, to talk; you said the swelling is gone; surely it means she's out of danger.'

'Mr Graham, a head injury can cause no end of problems. After what your wife has been through, there are lots of after-effects. She's at risk. She could end up with a bleed, blood clots; there's also the possibility the amnesia may last long term.'

'We'll take our chances.'

'I'd prefer her to stay here under observation. At least until we've done everything we can.'

The man reached forward, placed his hands under Marcia, and gently lifted her body. 'I'm sorry. I believe the best place for my wife is at home. It's been weeks. I will watch her; if anything happens, I'll call the emergency services. I'm aware there'll be visits, physio, ongoing rehab. That's good enough for me. But she's going home now.'

'I strongly advise you to leave her here to rest.'

The man turned as he helped Marcia dress. He could see Marcia's vulnerability, how she obeyed his instructions, her face a blank canvas. He held her, supporting her frame and began walking towards the door. 'And I strongly advise you mind your own business.'

The nurse watched as Marcia left with the man who brought her in, and feared something was very wrong.

'OK, we're parked on the ground floor. You can do this, Marcia. I'll take care of you from now on.' He linked her arm and guided her slowly towards the lift.

'Where are you taking me?' she asked.

'Home, honey. It's for the best, you hear?'

They stepped into the lift. Marcia watched as Daniel pressed the ground floor button, and the lift began to drop. The memory of the young girl spurred her on. This man had to be her husband. Why keep coming to the hospital? Why is he so concerned about her well-being? Marcia had no choice; she was alone, lost and had no one else to turn to. She needed to trust him. Maybe when she got home, she'd remember.

As he moved towards her, she backed up against the wall.

'There's no need to be frightened, OK? We'll get through this together. You're my wife, and I'm going to look after you. Marcia, you really don't remember anything?'

She didn't answer.

Outside, the cold air hit her hard. She tried in vain to recall any memory of this person. He'd said that she'd been attacked in their home. As they walked, she felt his strong arm gripping her wrist, like a prisoner being led to the gallows. Could she trust this person?

The man led her towards a large, black car. A badge stated the word Jaguar. Opening the passenger door, he helped her into the seat. Then he closed the door, getting in the other side.

She looked at the other vehicles, a small moped, the empty disabled bays. Then she started crying.

'Hey. Come on, Marcia. I won't let anything happen to you. I know it's hard. Christ, you've been through such an ordeal. But I'll be here every step. We'll get through this together.' He leant forward and hugged her.

'I'm so scared. Tell me again, what happened?'

'Are you sure?'

'Yes.'

He pulled out of the parking bay, drove up the ramp, and stopped at the ticket barrier. Daniel removed a small card from the dashboard and placed it into the slot. The gate opened, and the car pulled onto a busy road.

'That night . . . I woke up and you weren't in bed. I assumed you'd gone to the toilet or something. I got up, opened the bedroom door, and I saw the hallway light was on. You were standing at the top of the stairs. I heard footsteps moving towards us. That's when I shouted, and you were attacked. You fell to the floor. The intruder wore a bala-clava or something. I assume it was a man from the size and shape of them. He ran back downstairs and out of the front door.' Daniel placed his hand on Marcia's thigh, his eyes flicking from the road to meet hers for a second. 'It was horri-ble. I thought you were dead. I called 999, and the emergency services came within minutes. You were rushed to hospital.'

Marcia pictured the scene as Daniel had described it. Watching the busy streets fly by out of the car window, the sun reflecting off the shop windows, she should have felt at ease.

'You really don't remember anything?'

Marcia didn't answer the question; instead, she said, 'Are we happy?'

Turning towards her, he said, 'Of course.'

'How long have we been married.'

'Oh, coming up on six years.'

She watched his face, examining it, looking for any sign to say he was lying. She saw nothing. Marcia had to ques-tion him in the hope he'd put her concerns to rest. As they spoke, she began to have faith in him. 'Tell me about us, about me? What do I like to do? How do I spend my time?' Marcia recalled him talking to her in hospital. He'd told her so much of their life, but now she was more alert.

'Well, you work in IT, recently from home. You enjoy it, although you don't like any of your work colleagues. You said it was a blessing being able to wake, go downstairs and open the laptop without commuting to work. You like read-ing, you often run in the mornings, and you like your soaps of an evening. We also enjoy boxsets; that's how we spend most evenings.'

'Where do we live?'

'Camden. It's in North West London. It's a busy area, full of shops, bars, restaurants. You love it there.'

'Do we have children? While I lay in the hospital bed, I think I had a flashback. A girl?' She watched his face change. The smile was replaced by a fierce scowl.

Daniel turned towards her. 'It's just us, Marcia.'

She didn't ask anything else.

* * *

Daniel pointed. 'This is it.'

Glimpsing the huge townhouse from the passenger window, Marcia said, 'This? This is where we live?'

'Yes.' He parked the Jaguar in an empty bay on the road. 'This is home, baby.' Undoing his seatbelt, he turned to her, watching her bewildered expression, like a child in a classroom, striving to take all the information in and hold onto it.

Marcia undid her seatbelt, opened the passenger door, and stepped out onto the street. The noise suddenly hit her. Cars, buses, lorries; a horn that sounded close made her jump. She held her head as if it were about to explode. After a moment, she composed herself. 'It's incredible.' She gazed over the semi-detached building, the brightly coloured brickwork, the front door that looked like it had just been painted a fresh white colour. The windows were large, which would allow ample light. She peered along the side entrance, the gate leading to the back.

Nothing seemed familiar.

No memory developed in her mind.

Waiting for her husband's instructions, she felt like an intruder in this man's life, but she'd have to adapt, get used to life as it was before.

'Are you OK?' he asked. 'You don't need to be scared. You love this house.'

Marcia smiled. 'I'm sure I do.'

Daniel took her by the hand like he was leading her into an abyss, a dark, intimidating void where she shouldn't go. She was frightened, panic began to bloom in her stomach, and her head ached. Marcia felt the side of her face. The skin was sore.

Opening the gate leading to the house, Daniel reached behind, holding her hand as they climbed the steps.

She gazed at the back of his head, then towards the house. *So what, I'm supposed to fall in love again? Live with a person I don't know? Do I even love him?* Her mind raced with questions. *What is he like as a person? Is he kind? What if we don't get on, or I find I don't like things about him? How can I escape? Maybe that's what needs to happen. Maybe I'll escape?*

'OK?' Daniel said as they stood by the front door.

The voice brought her out of her thoughts. Marcia offered a smile.

'This is home. It will seem strange at first, but I'm sure with rest, it will begin to become familiar.

Daniel placed the key in the front door, battling to pivot the lock. The door opened, and Marcia instantly noticed the darkness.

Daniel reached to the sidewall and flicked on the lights.

Marcia stood, looking at the stairs, then along the hallway towards the back of the house. The walls looked solid; the floor was thick oak, so clean you could almost eat your dinner off it. There were rooms left and right off the hallway with sturdy-looking doors, and the ceilings were high. She glanced around, bewildered. Nothing was out of place. Marcia wondered if it always looked this organised.

She stepped forward, her body tense with anticipation.

'Is anything coming back? Memories, I mean?'

Marcia shook her head.

Turning, Daniel said, 'We'll get through this. You were viciously attacked; what happened was dreadful, a man coming—' He broke off. 'I'll be here for you. Whatever it takes.'

'I'd like to lie down. My head is throbbing. Sorry, Daniel. Just bear with me while I recover. I'm trying so hard to remember.'

He stepped forward and held her close, kissing her forehead. 'Come on. I'll show you to the bedroom.'

Marcia winced. She hadn't even thought of sharing a bedroom. 'If it's OK, I'd like to sleep in another room.'

'Excuse me?'

'I, I would just feel more comfortable at the moment. Please. Don't read too much into it.'

Daniel stared at her.

She was uncertain how he'd react. To Marcia, the man standing in front of her was a complete stranger. Someone who took her from the hospital and expected her to live with him, sleep in his bed, and make love with him. She wasn't ready for it. She wondered if she ever would be.

Upstairs, Daniel pointed towards a closed door. 'This is the spare room. You can sleep here temporarily.' He pushed open the door, and stood watching her as she looked around. 'There's an en-suite with a power shower, a telly, books. Why don't you make yourself comfortable? If you'd prefer, you can pay rent. How does that sound? I'll strike up a deal if you help to clean the place. I'll make it really affordable.'

'Daniel, please. Don't be sarcastic. I don't appreciate the tone you're using.'

'Look, get into bed. I'm sorry if I'm irritable. We've both

been through a lot. Get some rest. I have things to do. You won't be disturbed.' He stood watching as Marcia began to undress.

'Are you going to stand there staring?'

'What?' he asked. 'Oh, sorry. I'll leave you to it. Call down if you need anything. Sleep well.'

Marcia watched as Daniel left the bedroom. When his footsteps disappeared down the stairs, she removed her flat shoes, blouse, and skirt, clothes Daniel had brought to the hospital, and got into bed.

Looking over the room, she felt absent and misplaced. The walls were painted white, but no pictures were hung to personalise the room. The floorboards were exposed with no carpet or rug; the bed was small but comfortable.

The pain was almost unbearable as she placed her head on the pillow, so she turned onto her other side, pulled the blanket up closer to her neck and closed her eyes.

* * *

Marcia woke a couple of hours later. Sitting up, she leaned against the headboard. A gap in the curtain allowed a small amount of light into the room. She grabbed her phone from her handbag, holding it in the air. Behind the bedside unit, a charger was attached to a socket and plugged into the wall. Marcia had been desperate to look, hoping there'd be pictures, messages and contacts. She'd asked Daniel to bring a charger into the hospital, but it had fallen on deaf ears. Careful not to make any noise, Marcia pushed the charger into her phone.

It came on a few minutes later and the screen showed 1.15pm. She wracked her brain for any memories. She remembered Daniel taking her from the hospital and leading her to this house. She'd insisted on sleeping in the spare room. That's it. Nothing else. Her mind was an empty box: no childhood memories of her school days, or teenage years, and nothing of her parents or siblings. Tears began to fill her eyes. Was this it? Her life starting from the time of the accident? No depth, no personality, just appearing in a hospital bed and boom. Get on with it.

Tapping the camera app, Marcia was met with a blank screen. No photos to show. Her body tensed. *What is happening? Where are my pictures?* She closed the app and re-opened it—a blank screen. The photos were gone. She swallowed hard, frustrated, unable to understand how this could happen. Had someone deleted them on purpose?

She slid back down the bed, pulling the blankets over her face, then closed her eyes again.

A moment later, Marcia jolted. Throwing the blanket away from her body, she pushed her palms into the mattress, and forced her body up and against the headboard. She was certain she'd heard a voice. The distant cry of someone calling out. It wasn't possible.

Marcia remained still, listening hard. There it is again. It was a muffled sound, like a voice in a well or deep in a hole underground. Goosebumps appeared on her arms, and a shiver darted through her body.

Stepping out of bed, she searched for something to wear while in the house. Marcia flicked the bedroom light on and found a white dressing gown in the wardrobe, large, fluffy, and warm looking. Opening it, she felt its hefty weight, and placed it around her body. She pulled the belt tight and walked to the bathroom at the back of the spare room.

Marcia turned on the taps and splashed water on her face, dried herself and then left the bedroom.

Moments ago, she was certain she'd heard a muffled

sound, like someone was calling for help. Walking along the hallway, she found the main bedroom. This was the place she'd spent every night with Daniel. He'd pointed it out to her earlier. Marcia tapped the door with her knuckles and waited. When no one answered, she opened the door. The bedroom was empty. She felt like an intruder, walking around a stranger's home. Marcia stared at the white walls, decorated with large pictures in frames. Old, romantic-looking restaurants and bars. Others showed a couple in various places, walking hand in hand through the park, the rain heavy and a certain urgency about them—a meal outside with the sun on their backs. The pictures looked professionally painted. Marcia stepped forward and saw numbers on the bottom right corner. 1 of 5000.

It wasn't her or Daniel, and she wondered who these people were. Maybe anonymous subjects of a painting, or were they people dear to her?

Stepping towards the window, she looked out over Camden. Although it was cold, the sky was a clear blue. The traffic below was moving slowly, and people rushed along the pavements.

She stepped away from the window and out of the bedroom.

Walking slowly along the hallway and standing at the top of the stairs, Marcia found that she didn't know her place. Her function. What did she do? How did she spend her days? Does she go down and make coffee? Does she prefer tea, or iced water? Does she sit on the sofa in the living room and watch telly or clean the house? Her head was perplexed. *Go downstairs, say hi to Daniel. Ask him what he's doing. Offer to make a drink or a bite to eat. Be friendly.*

Bracing herself, Marcia began walking down the stairs. Reaching the bottom step, it happened again. A stifled bawl from deep in the house. It sounded like white noise, a background buzz or ringing in the ears.

Marcia gripped the handrail, frightened to move any further. *Where is Daniel? What are the voices in the distance?* 'Hello? Is someone there?' She held her breath, listening hard through the vast house. 'Is someone there?' Marcia reached the ground floor with delicate steps, then pulled the belt of her dressing gown tighter and called out again. 'Hello? Who's there?' Slowly, she crept to the kitchen at the back of the house. She stopped by the closed door and pushed it open. Empty. Turning, Marcia looked towards the front door. 'Daniel?' Her voice echoed through the walls. 'Daniel, are you here?' She'd left her phone upstairs. Marcia could call him, find out where he was. Then ask him about the voices.

She climbed the stairs two at a time, panting hard, holding onto her dressing gown. At the top, she walked into the spare room. Grabbing the phone, she held it to her face. The screen opened. She pressed the search button and typed the letter *D*. Names popped up in her contacts. *Diane Work. Debbie Gym.* People she couldn't recall. Marcia dialled Daniels's number and listened as it rang. When his voice prompted to leave a message, she hung up. She looked through the contacts; so many names, people from her previous life. She began tapping letters, looking at the list. The first name that showed was *Abigail Friend*. Marcia hesitated for a moment, then pressed on the name. Nothing happened. She went into the contact and found the phone number missing. She bounced the mobile in her hand, frustrated. She decided to try another number. *Bev School.* Again, Marcia found the number missing. *What is happening?* Quickly she picked another few names. Every phone number had been deleted.

Marcia slung the phone on the bedside table. *What the fuck is going on? How is it possible to have all my contacts erased? Who would do—?* Turning, she faced the bedroom door. Marcia was sure she heard the muffled cries again. *No, no, no. This isn't happening.* 'Is someone there?' She crept out of the bedroom and back down the stairs. Marcia stood in her dressing gown, her feet cold on the wooden floor. Reaching for the front door lock, she tried to pull it downwards. She was going to run. This person, this 'Daniel', was fucking with her. The door was locked. 'No. Don't do this,' she cried. She pressed harder, pushing her body against the lock and using her weight to force downwards. Marcia banged on the glass, shouting for someone to help her.

Suddenly, she saw a shadow. A figure walking up the steps towards the front door. Was it someone coming to answer her cries for help? Or was it *him?* Marcia stepped away.

Quickly, she charged up the stairs and rushed into her bedroom. As she pulled the blankets back, she heard the front door open.

She lay still, hearing the shuffling sounds below her. Footsteps began to get closer. Marcia closed her eyes, and a few seconds later, the bedroom door opened.

'Are you OK?'

She didn't answer. Her head ached on the pillow, but she dared not move.

'Marcia, are you hungry?' Daniel moved closer to the bed.

She listened to his lumbering breaths as he stood beside her, moving closer, feeling his eyes watching her. *Just go away,* she thought. She had to escape.

Her phone contacts had been deleted. No one knew she was here. There were no messages left for her and no missed calls in the time she'd been in hospital. It was like she never existed. But here she was, curled up in a ball in a house she didn't recognise, with a person she didn't want to be with.

And where were the muffled cries coming from?

Again, Daniel spoke. 'Marcia, I think you've had enough rest. It may be good to get up, walk around the house. What do you say?' He reached forward and began rocking her body.

Marcia opened her eyes. 'I'd rather rest if it's OK.'

Daniel pulled the blanket back. 'You need to get up. Come on.' He looked at her dressing gown. 'Where did you get this?'

'Huh.'

'What you're wearing. Have you been up?'

Looking at the gown, she said, 'Only to use the toilet. Is that a problem?'

'Oh, it's not a problem. I just don't want you walking around on your own.'

Marcia sat up. She didn't appreciate the tone Daniel was taking with her. 'Excuse me? I can't walk around my own house? Is that what you're saying?'

Daniel stepped back; his face had turned sour, his eyebrows dropped deep on his face, and the smile disappeared. 'Get up, Marcia.' He walked out of the room, leaving the door open.

When Marcia heard a door close downstairs, she got out of bed. She stared at her phone, wanting to call the police. She could hear the conversation now.

I'm sorry, Mam, it's not a crime for someone to look after you. Has he hit you? Has he threatened you? Oh, wait, huh? He said it's not a good idea to walk around the house on your own? Well, Bingo lady, we got him. We can throw the book at him for this.

Wait there; an officer will be with you soon. Wow, he sounds like a proper bastard, this one.

Marcia tightened the belt around her waist, feeling the warmth of the dressing gown against her skin. Suddenly she had a flashback. Marcia grabbed the bedside unit. Her skin tingled with excitement as she let the memory play out. She was standing in a hallway, possibly of this house. There was a teenage girl with her, perhaps seventeen or eighteen. Her face wasn't clear. Marcia gripped the bedside unit tighter. She was somewhere else. In a room with a brown sofa, deep with fading marks on each end. And red wallpaper, she could see it so clearly—such a bright, dazzling red. Pictures of album covers were hung on the walls. The girl had asked who they were, and Marcia had answered. She remembered the names. Queen, David Bowie. Her mind flatlined, the images disappeared.

'No. Come back,' she whispered. She was bereft, but this was good. It was slowly returning. Her memory was coming back.

'Marcia?'

She heard her name called up the stairs. 'Coming.'

Marcia made her way down the stairs, along the hall, and opened the kitchen door. Daniel had made two chicken salads. A jug of water was placed on a small circular table. Looking around, she tried to familiarise herself. Nothing about the kitchen was recognisable. She eyed the large brown cupboard on the back wall, the silver dishwasher, the white sideboard. She spun around, concentrating, willing herself to remember. Daniel's voice made her jump.

'How are you feeling?'

Before answering, Marcia took a moment to sit on one of the robust-looking chairs, pouring herself a glass of water. 'I had a flashback.'

'Oh my God. Well, that's wonderful. What was it?'

Daniel sounded excited, his mood lifted, his eyes wide and enthusiastic. Watching his face, she saw the gentle smile appear. Marcia held the side of her head. Now it was throbbing. She winced with the pain.

'Wait. We have painkillers.' Daniel opened one of the drawers and removed two tablets from a packet. Then handed them to Marcia. He sat beside her, not wanting to start eating yet. He gave her his full attention. 'So, what did you remember?'

'There was a girl.' She watched as Daniel tensed. It was like he'd heard some awful news. Marcia continued. 'Do we have a daughter?' She watched as his cheeks flushed.

'Of course we don't. I would have said. How can you ask such a question? Your subconscious is getting confused with reality.'

'There are other things too.' Marcia braced herself, fearful of his reaction. She had to push. 'Earlier, I tried to call people. People from my previous life. Every phone number was deleted from my phone.'

'That's weird. Maybe there's a problem with the network. Go on, eat. I think once you've rested more, things will become clearer. You're adapting to this life. A life you don't remember. Everything is new. It's a difficult thing to go through. You're so brave.'

Silence fell as they began to eat. Marcia wanted to mention the muffled cries she had heard earlier.

At this moment, she didn't have the courage.

* * *

Once she'd eaten, Marcia placed her plate and cutlery on the sideboard. 'I want you to show me around?'

Daniel was forking the last piece of chicken into his mouth. He stood, wiping his lips with some kitchen roll. 'OK. Let's show you the place.'

Daniel opened the kitchen door. To his left was a basement. The hatch was closed and locked.

'What's down there?' Marcia asked?

He turned. 'Nothing. We plan on doing it up for extra storage. The floor is uneven and rotting. We haven't got around to fixing it yet. We've had a couple of quotes, but we're waiting for a few more to come in. It's also damp, so breathing the shit in the air isn't good.'

'I'd like to take a look all the same.'

'I said no.' Daniel's voice was raised. He watched Marcia, how she backed away, her eyes closed briefly, and she looked frightened. He reached out and placed a hand on her shoulder. 'I'm sorry, Marcia, but it's just dangerous. Come on; I'll show you the rest of the house.'

She watched as he walked in front of her, sliding his hand along the wall.

Daniel opened the living room door to his right.

As she stepped inside, Marcia's legs became weak. It was almost identical to the flashback she'd had earlier. Although the sofa was black, not brown as in her thoughts, it was the same shape. The wallpaper was blue. In her flashback, it had been a blood-red colour. There were no pictures with album covers, Queen or David Bowie as in her memory, only of her and Daniel, one of their wedding day, another taken on a beach. Marcia moved closer; something wasn't right about them. They looked false, superimposed, and tampered with. She looked around the room. There were no photos of the girl she'd seen in her visions.

Walking towards her, Daniel placed the palm of his

hand against her face, stroking it. 'You're going to get better. I promise.'

As his hand left her cheek, she turned towards the wall. 'Was this ever painted red?'

'No. Not in the five years we've lived here. It's always been blue. Why do you ask?'

She didn't answer. Instead, she pointed to the sofa. 'And this? Did we ever have a brown sofa?'

Looking across the room, Daniel said, 'Always black. It's an Ikea special. Very lush, darling.'

Marcia smiled, watching Daniel's face. 'Tell me about us.'

Daniel walked across the room and sat on the sofa. 'We're happy. More content than most couples I know. We have fun, you know. We share the same interests. We like to go out; there's an Italian restaurant around the corner. You also like Indian food.'

'Where did we meet?' Marcia asked.

'A small pub in Kentish Town. The Queen's Arms. You were with a couple of friends. Two girls. Our eyes met, and I made a move on you. You were putty in my hands.'

Marcia laughed. 'Putty in your hands. Yeah, right, mate. I believe that. Not. Who were the friends?'

Daniels's face dropped as if he'd been punched in the gut. 'I'm not sure. You lost contact.'

Marcia hesitated. 'How?'

His face showed his awkwardness. He looked like a contestant on a quiz show with a barrage of questions outside of his chosen category. The host, smirking, telling him he has to rush him for an answer. The host stares right through him. *We haven't got all day, you imbecile. What is the bloody answer?*

'I think they moved out of the area,' is all Daniel could conjure.

'What about family?' Marcia pushed.

Stretching his body, he leaned his head back, his eyes facing the ceiling. 'Your mother died of cancer a couple of years ago. Your parents divorced. You haven't seen your father since your early teens. He may have moved to Spain. I'm not sure.'

Marcia sat, staring at the wall. 'Wow. OK, this is deep.' She moved across the room, and stood by a large brown cabinet. She picked up a photo of her and Daniel walking along a beach barefoot, the sun glistening on the lens. Something didn't look right. 'Who took this photo?'

'Christ. I don't know. I think we asked someone. Yes, a family, the mother took the photo. I remember you were too shy to ask.'

She turned. 'Do we have a daughter?'

Daniel stirred on the sofa, tucking his right leg under him. 'Marcia. Where is this going? You're getting confused. I've already told you. No. We don't have a daughter.'

Picking up another photo, she held it close to her face. She could feel her heart race; her head began to throb, loud in her ears. It was a picture of her and Daniel, taken years ago. They were sat at a restaurant, a waiter pouring wine, a teddy bear resting on the table.

Marcia tensed, too frightened to confront her husband. Taking a deep breath, she turned. 'I must have other friends, Daniel. I saw names on my phone, but the numbers were missing. All of them.' Marcia moved towards the living room door. 'I'm going to check again.'

'Sit down,' Daniel ordered.

His tone stunned her. 'Excuse me?' Marcia stood in the middle of the living room.

'I said, sit down.'

With shocked eyes, she turned towards the man sitting

on the sofa. 'How dare you order me around. I'm going to check my phone. What is the problem?'

Jumping up off the sofa, he grabbed her wrists, holding them tight. 'Sit down. I'm not going to ask again.'

'Get off me. You're hurting me, Daniel.' In despair, she tried ripping her hands from his grip, wanting to escape.

His voice raised to a yell, his face turned beetroot red, and he looked like he'd explode. 'Sit on the sofa and do as you're told.'

Marcia struggled to move her arms. He was strong, and his thumb and forefingers crushed against her bones. 'Get off me!' She screamed out, hoping someone would hear her. 'I said, get the fuck off of me.'

'You're not going anywhere. Sit the fuck down and control yourself.'

As Marcia struggled to free her arms, she kneed Daniel hard in the groin. He bent over, moaning in agony. She backed away. There wasn't much time. She had to get her phone from the bedroom, lock herself in the bathroom and call for help.

She watched as he winced, his face screwed tightly; the agony was evident on his face. Turning towards the door, Marcia ran. She could hear the slow footsteps following her.

She reached the stairs in the hallway. Daniel was behind her. 'Leave me alone. Who are you?' She climbed up the stairs, her head throbbing, her eyes blurry and her body trembling with adrenaline. At the top of the stairs, confusion adorned her brain. She couldn't remember where the spare room was. Daniel's footsteps were close. Confused, she looked at the empty rooms. She stepped left, then turned, moving to the right. She found it. Pressing her body against the doorframe of the spare room, she gasped for breath. She was tired and weak, but she needed to make the

call. Grabbing her phone from the bedside unit, she heard
Daniel's steps behind her. Marcia raced to the en-suite bathroom, closed the door, and turned. There was no lock. 'Help
me,' she cried out.

A shadow was visible under the door, still and waiting.
Marcia moved her ear to the wood, listening hard and
praying that Daniel would leave her alone. Perhaps he didn't
know there wasn't a lock. Perhaps he would leave her here.
Her body was shaking, her hands pressed against the door,
and then she felt the weight as his body barged against it.
There was a loud, crunching sound, she fell back, and
suddenly, Daniel was standing in front of her. Marcia
dropped to her knees.

He moved over to where she knelt. 'You really shouldn't
make this so fucking difficult.'

With a pounding head, Marcia woke, her right arm pained as if she'd been injected. The last thing she remembered was Daniel standing in the doorway.

She tried to sit up, but her body wouldn't do what her mind asked. 'Daniel. Why are you doing this?' She bowed her head forward; thick rope held her to the bed. Her arms were strapped to her sides. Marcia tried to move her legs, but they too were held tight. She felt contained like she was trapped in a coffin underground. 'Let me go, you bastard.' She listened for a noise, anything to detect where he was in the house. Marcia looked around the room, the same room she had slept in earlier today. She turned her head, seeing the bedside unit. Her phone was gone. 'Help. Someone help me.' She tried to move her hands; the pain in her right arm was almost unbearable.

It felt like he'd jabbed her with something to knock her out.

Slamming her head back on the pillow, she began crying. The last few weeks had been so tough; she had no memory of her life before that night, the intruder had taken so much from her, but she was strong; she knew that much. She'd fight. This man had waltzed into the hospital, told her he loved her, taken her to this house, and tied her up. *Who the hell was he?* She tried in vain to wriggle free of the ropes and get away from him.

A door closed below her. Holding her breath, she waited. A few seconds later, she heard the front door slam. She concluded that it meant he'd gone out. How long did she have? What were his plans? Marcia couldn't be here to find out. She had to escape; it was her only chance to survive.

She tried desperately to free her body. 'Come on.' Marcia moved her fingers and thumb. The rope was strong, and there was no possible way to split it. She had to find a way to slacken the rope. She bent her fingers towards her wrists; her hands arched inwards and ran her thumbs over the rope, feeling the dry, uncomfortable texture.

She jolted. Marcia had a breakthrough. A large knot now dug into the wrist of her right hand, and she grabbed it with her middle and forefinger. Managing to push her middle finger through the hole, followed by her forefinger, she spread them and loosened the rope slightly, finding the end of a loose knot. Taking a deep breath, she pinched the end and began to pull with her fingers and thumb. The rope slackened.

Marcia kept working at it until her right hand was free. Pulling her arm away, she undid the rope on her left side. 'Yes, you beauty. Yes.' She sat up, then reached the rope around her legs, feeling the knots underneath her thighs and undoing them too. She unravelled the rope like a bandage wrapped around a Mummy in a tomb.

Getting out of bed, she searched for the phone, first in the bedside drawers, under the bed, the wardrobe and in the en-suite bathroom. She breathed a sigh of relief, seeing the phone on the floor beside the toilet. It had fallen when Daniel shoved the door. Marcia reached down, keeping quiet, her body in pain and looked at the blank screen. The battery had died. She checked over the room, searching for a charger. Nothing. Placing the phone in her dressing gown pocket, she crept towards the bedroom door.

Marcia eased it open, wary that Daniel could be standing on the other side. She half expected to be smashed over the head with a large object at any minute. She peered along the upstairs hallway. The main bedroom door was closed, as were the rooms behind her. There was no time to check for a charger. She would make her way down the stairs, out onto the street, and get help.

Tiptoeing along the hallway, Marcia stood at the top of the stairs. She looked down towards the ground floor, the house seemed empty. She remembered the sound she had heard – a door closing, the front door being slammed shut.

Had Daniel gone out? If so, for how long?

If he found she'd escaped, he'd most certainly tie her up again, more than before. He may even kill her. Who knows what this man was capable of?

As Marcia stood on the top step, she debated what to do. She was terrified; her head pounded. Her eyes were blurry from tiredness, her lips dry and itchy. Probably the effects of whatever drug he'd used to sedate her.

Taking a deep breath, she began gently creeping down the stairs. She stopped. A shiver powered through her body. *There it is again—a muffled cry.* Marcia turned, wanting to go back upstairs. She listened hard, another silent yelp. She turned around towards the front door. 'Who's there? If someone is in the house, please knock once.' Marcia continued walking, one step at a time. She kept her voice low. 'Is someone in the house?' Agitated, she reached her hand forward at the bottom of the stairs and turned the front door handle. Then she pulled. Nothing happened. Panicking, she forced the handle one way and the other. It was stuck. The door had been chub-locked. Thumping her hands against the glass, Marcia shouted, 'Can someone help me? Please. I'm being held here against my will. Help me, someone.'

Muffled cries.

Marcia spun a hundred and eighty degrees. The noise was coming from behind her. She tiptoed along the hallway —another flashback.

The black sofa.

The red wall.

A daughter.

Marcia stopped. She pushed her head into her hands and began working her forefinger and thumb into the corner of her eyes. A stress relief. She hesitated, wondering if she could get out through the kitchen, into the garden, and call over the fence. Maybe a neighbour would hear her.

Muffled cries.

Marcia turned towards the basement.

Someone was down there.

* * *

Marcia tried the door at the back of the kitchen leading to the garden. Again, it was locked. Backing away, she stood by the door in the downstairs hallway, eyeing the basement to her right.

The cries had stopped. She needed to get the hatch open and help whoever was down there. She looked towards the lock; it seemed weak and fragile. Stepping onto the hatch, fearful of falling through, she leaned down and pulled the lock with her fingers. Marcia needed a tool, a hammer to smash it. But the noise would draw attention, and if Daniel were still in the house, he'd most certainly hear her. Turning, she glanced towards the front door. If it opened, she'd have to hide in the kitchen, under the table. She had to make certain Daniel was out before making any more noise. What if she was wrong? He could be upstairs or in the living room. In sheer desperation, she called his name. 'Daniel. I need help. I beg you, please. I need you.' She listened for an answer, a movement to clarify he was inside the house. Nothing came. It was her signal to move.

Marcia walked back into the kitchen, searching every-where for a toolbox, something, anything to smash the lock. The only thing she found was cutlery in a drawer. She removed a large, robust knife and a small torch positioned at the back.

Stepping out into the hallway and moving to the living room, she pressed her ear against the door and listened. Confident the room was empty, she pushed the handle down and opened the door. Before trying to open the base-ment, she had to be convinced. Daniel had dismissed her flashbacks, denied the memories her mind produced and fobbed off any of her questions. Marcia had to be certain. Now, while he was out of the house was the only time she'd have.

She looked at the black sofa—the blue wall. Were her flashbacks real? Or was her brain playing tricks? Fictitious memories casing real emotions.

Racing back to the kitchen, she pulled out drawers, throwing them onto the floor. The bottom one contained paperwork. Marcia sifted through it, purchases they'd made while living here. The table they'd eaten at earlier. A lawn-mower, tools including a drill, a screwdriver set, a couple of wrenches, a set of chairs. Suddenly she saw a receipt from Ikea.

A black sofa.

Marcia looked at a calendar hanging on the wall. It showed April 2022.

The receipt confirmed the sofa was bought three months ago.

Stepping back, clasping her head, she recalled what Daniel had said. They'd lived here for five years. The sofa had always been black; the wall in the living room had always been painted blue. No daughter. But that sofa *hadn't* always been there; it had only been there for a few months. And their daughter, she envisioned her. The memories felt so real.

Who the hell was this man?

Why was he so adamant that her visions were fake?

The contacts and photos in her phone had been removed. Had Daniel deleted them all? Was it a ploy to keep her here? She had to get out. But the muffled cries from the basement. Who was it? Marcia had to help them. She'd hesitated long enough, a sense of suspicion and dread had stemmed her actions.

The basement needed to be opened.

Moving back out of the kitchen, she stared at the front door, willing her legs to move. To keep going.

But first, she needed to check something else. She walked towards the blue wall of the living room, clutching the sharp knife. Marcia crouched, turning the knife on its side, and started to scrape the paint. It began to flake, dropping onto the floor. As the paint came away, Marcia gasped. She could feel her throat tense and her heart pound—a sick feeling developed in her stomach, churning, working its way through her body.

Red began to show underneath the part of the wall where she'd scratched. The knife dropped to the floor and bounced by her feet. She felt dizzy, knowing she had to get out of the house. What was this place? Who was the man who'd taken her here? She pushed her hands to the wall, staring at the red underneath.

Marcia moved backwards out of the living room, glaring at the black sofa. Daniel was a stranger who couldn't be trusted. A threat. Lying to her and holding her captive. That much was obvious. He'd taken her out of hospital, deleted all her photos and phone contacts, and fibbed when she'd remembered the layout of the house.

Marcia's legs went weak. Her brain was digesting everything that had happened. He'd pretended to be her husband, brought her here, denied she had a daughter, and tied her to the bed.

Moving to the cabinet, Marcia searched for the picture of her and Daniel at a restaurant with the teddy bear on the table.

It was gone.

Suddenly, she was beginning to remember things. Her mind was piecing the memories together. This place was home; Marcia knew that much. So what? Has he killed her real husband? Her daughter?

Marcia thought she was going to faint; her stomach was sore, her head ached, her skin felt on fire. She needed to escape this brute.

He was going to kill her.

* * *

Marcia moved out of the hallway. She'd smash a window in the kitchen and climb through the frame. She could get help; a neighbour would call the police, then she'd be free.

But first, she had to go into the basement. Someone was down there.

Crouching by the hatch, she began picking at the lock with the pointed end of the knife. Marcia kept staring at the front door, petrified that Daniel would come back at any moment. Her heart pushed against her chest as she dug at the wood.

Over the next half hour, Marcia scraped, dug, and pulled at the lock. She had to get the hatch open. She visualised seeing a shadow at the front door and hearing a key in the lock, the door opening, and Daniel charging towards her. She made loud, whimpering sounds as the knife began to go deeper into the wood; fear replaced adrenaline. Her body ached. She came off her knees for a minute and stood, her eyes drawn to the front door.

After a couple of minutes, when the numbness left her hands, and the blood began to circulate, she continued digging at the wood. The lock began to move, becoming looser. She was almost there.

Suddenly the lock came away. Marcia stood for a moment and pushed out a loud sigh. Her hair was wet with sweat, and her hands bloody.

Throwing the lock on the floor, she glared at the front door once more, and opened the hatch.

Marcia shone the torch down the steep wooden steps. She'd never felt so petrified. What if Daniel came back, closed the hatch and pushed something heavy against the door until he could add a new lock? What if there were dead bodies down there? She felt sick with anticipation.

As she moved down the steps, the loud creaks caused her concern. 'Hello? Is someone down here? Hello?'

Now the whimpering sounds were close. Marcia shone the torch ahead, moderately lighting the basement. Stepping forward and whispering into the darkness, the torch peered over a figure towards the back of the room.

A girl with long black hair was sat strapped to a chair. Duct tape had been placed over her mouth.

Marcia saw the girl's wild eyes, the tears streaming down her face. She looked malnourished, cold, and scared. As Marcia moved closer, she saw her pale skin. She looked at Marcia, such sadness in her eyes.

It was the girl in her flashbacks. Although Marcia couldn't remember her, she knew who it was.

Marcia's daughter.

She tried to digest what was happening. Daniel had kidnapped her daughter. Now, he had kidnapped her.

Marcia moved to the girl and placed her arms around her. She felt her shiver, her body trembling, her skin so very cold. 'What has he done to you?' Marcia asked. 'You're safe now. I won't let anything happen to you. We need to go before he comes back.'

Removing the duct tape from around the girl's mouth, Marcia heard the cries for help; then, grabbing the knife from her dressing gown pocket, she cut the ropes which held her to the chair. Marcia lifted her to her feet, watching the small, frail body trying to balance.

The girl was crying uncontrollably.

'Please. You have to be quiet,' Marcia whispered. Marcia held her tight, both of them sobbing, then stood back and looked at her. She watched as the girl's fearful expression melted into a smile.

As a car pulled onto the drive, Marcia spun around.

The girl stepped forward, wrestling the knife from her hand, and stuck it in Marcia's throat.

Marcia dropped to the ground, trying in desperation to pull the knife out.

A couple of minutes later, she lay still in a pool of her own blood.

* * *

Daniel opened the front door. The house was quiet. He'd have to come clean with his wife and tell her the awful truth. She couldn't remember anything before the accident. It was just as well.

He had so much to explain. But Daniel had to make it a little less unsettling. Marcia was still so fragile.

His daughter was a psychopath. She'd tried to kill Marcia and him on many occasions. He'd deleted the photos and messages from her phone, trying desperately to keep it from her that they had a daughter.

While Marcia was in hospital, Daniel had deleted her contacts. He couldn't risk her speaking to someone and finding out the truth.

But the questions, Marcia was getting better, her memory was returning. He worried the shock about their psychotic daughter would drive her over the edge. Daniel saw a happier Marcia, not remembering anything; it was so much better that way.

They'd struggled over her; Marcia never wanted her locked down there, rotting in the basement. Daniel got so angry with his wife. Recently, they'd argued nonstop. He didn't want to go back there.

Life was great for the short time Marcia had come out of hospital.

But it was time Marcia knew about the past.

Their daughter. The person who'd escaped from the basement and hit Marcia over the head. He'd explain why she needed to keep away from the basement and why he had to forcefully tie her to the bed, delete phone contacts and hide photographs.

They'd tried. God knows they'd tried to help their daughter. But a mental institution or hospital wasn't the place for her. Marcia wouldn't hear of it. They'd kept her condition a secret; it was easier that way. Their inquisitive friends would have a field day with their questions. It's why they distanced themselves from people.

But in the end, the basement was the only place they could keep her.

It was safer for everyone, pretending she wasn't there.

In Daniel's mind, only for the food and drinks trips to the basement, she didn't exist.

As he moved towards the kitchen, he saw the basement hatch was open.

'Oh no. Please. Please.' Daniel heard footsteps coming behind him.

The End

THE CALLER

2

Cleo James walked across the parking lot, peering towards the high, bricked wall at the end of the drive, the steep ramp leading to the car park on her left and the empty car park bays.

It was dark, the lights from the offices above had long been turned out, and she was geared up for tonight's show.

She hadn't always wanted to be a podcast presenter. At junior school, she'd dreamed of becoming the next Julie Andrews, her and her mother's favourite actress. They often had musical marathons on the weekend—the Sound of Music, followed by Grease, then either Mamma Mia or Dirty Dancing. She lived for those weekends.

She was an only child. Her father died a couple of weeks after her twelfth birthday, and after witnessing her mother have a meltdown, she spent as much time with her as possible. She'd moved out of the family home a year ago but still visited her mother most weekends.

Cleo rented the ground floor of a maisonette in Chalk Farm, North West London, and attended a local drama class, quickly dropping out due to the stress of learning the lines, dealing with the embarrassment of getting them wrong, and the other students' jealousy when landing the lead part in a Macbeth production at the end of term.

After Cleo dropped out of acting classes, she worked in a local shop selling designer clothes but found it tedious and often watched the clock, willing her life away.

While listening to a horror podcast, Cleo had the idea to create her own show.

At first, it was slow, the sponsorship was non-existent, and the podcast ranking was pitiful, but after throwing herself into it, endless marketing, and getting social media influencers on her show, it took off. She made a comfortable living from it now and looked forward to the broadcast every night.

Cleo walked to the small room she rented, paid by direct debit once a month to a lady she'd never met. She placed the key in the door, opened it, turned on the lights, tapped the four-digit code into the alarm pad, shut the door, and walked to her desk.

It was freezing tonight, and Cleo could see her breath spill into the small space.

Moving to the rickety old heater on her right side, she turned it on, watching the glowing red light and noticing the familiar smell as it struggled to pump warm air.

Finding a jumper in the store cupboard, Cleo pushed her body into it; then, once she'd made tea, she sat by her desk towards the back of the room, facing the front door, and turned on the laptop.

As the screen loaded, she thought about tonight's topic. Urban legends. Something that fascinated her. The show usually started with her talking about a specific topic. She'd read up on it, research Wikipedia and various social media platforms, make notes, and take it from there. Often she'd bring on guests via a link; people could type live messages which appeared on the screen or phone in to participate in the show. Anyone who rang would get straight through.

It worried Cleo at first; a late-night podcast could attract a flood of weird calls and windups, but so far, the listeners were courteous, and she was appreciative of the interaction.

Tapping in her password, she sipped her tea, and waited for the main screen to load. After a few seconds, she hovered the mouse over the link and clicked. A message prompted her to check her Mic and instructed her through several tests for her headphone set. Once the tests were complete, she placed the headphones over her ears and pulled the chair closer to the desk.

This was the time she got anxious. The show ranked well, top ten in a few categories in the UK. She had thousands of social media followers and had attracted sponsorship from a couple of leading brands, dropping their ads in throughout the show.

She had become a success.

Cleo looked around the room. The desk was old and rickety, the legs unbalanced, and it creaked when she moved forward. The walls had pictures of her favourite musicals and a couple of recent awards she'd won, exhibited in black frames and proudly displayed.

A picture of her parents hung above the door so she could see it from the desk. A water dispenser sat to her left, plumbed in, with a fridge and the free-standing plug-in radiator. It's all she needed. The rent was cheap, and the place was quiet, so she wasn't interrupted.

Checking her watch, she realised it was almost 9pm. She aimed for the show to last a couple of hours, but sometimes she'd chat until the early hours if the calls rolled.

Pulling the mic closer to her lips, she braced herself.

Once she was connected to Youtube, Cleo was ready to roll.

She watched herself on the screen, fixing her short, spiky blonde hair, then added a touch of lipstick to her thin lips. Her green eyes looked dull and tired, and she wished she'd added mascara. There wasn't enough time now.

Cleo loved the punk look, and in her younger years, she'd tried to copy Cindy Lauper.

Taking a deep breath, she braced herself. Then she began.

'I'm Cleo James, and welcome to another episode of Tales Of Madness. I'm your host for the next however many hours, and tonight, we discuss urban legends. That's right, folks, the stories we heard as a child that kept you awake at night. You probably heard the one about the lonely highway and the truck? Basically, a woman is driving down a long, open road late at night. She stops to fill up her car. As she pulls out of the petrol station, a truck comes behind her, flashing its lights and sounding its horn. She slams her foot on the pedal and desperately tries to shake off the truck driver, eventually pulling into her driveway and sounding the car horn to alert her husband. The truck driver gets out, races towards her and opens the rear door of her vehicle. A man is hiding in the back seat of her car with a knife. He'd got into her vehicle while she'd paid for the petrol.

Cleo looked at the comments coming in.

PaulandZac. Wow. Thank's Cleo. You gave me proper goose-bumps. I haven't heard that one. Keep up the great work.

Sean101. Oh, love that one. Superb.

Nightmary. Proper chiller that one.

Cleo read them out live on air. 'Thanks, guys, keep the comments coming in. If you'd like to get involved, the number's at the bottom of the screen. You'll get straight through when you call. I'd love to hear your stories.

Another great urban legend is the ghostly hitchhiker. A man is driving along a lonely road; I know, I know, lots of lonely roads. He picks up a hitchhiker, and she gets into the back of his car. As he's driving, he notices how pale and cold she looks, so he offers his red coat, which is hanging over the seat. She places it around her shoulders.

About ten minutes along the road, she shouts for him to stop. He hits the brakes; she thanks him for the lift, confirming that she lives in the house up the hill.

Anyway, he likes her and returns the following morning to the house. An old lady answers, and he asks to see Mamie, the name she'd given him the night before. The old woman begins to cry and says that Mamie died years ago in a hit and run. He's confused and insists he saw Mamie, stating that he'd picked her up and given her a lift to this house. The old woman closes the front door and joins him on the drive. She leads him across the field to a cemetery and points to a gravestone.

The inscription reads, *In loving memory of Mamie,* and the dates she lived and died.

Draped over the gravestone was the red coat he'd given to her in the car.'

She watched as the shocked face emojis and yellow thumbs-up pictures appeared on the screen.

'Of all the urban legends, I think Mamie has always been my favourite. But there are so many; every town and city has their own stories and things that supposedly happened many years ago. Recently, there's been Slender Man, a fictional, supernatural character that originated as a creepy-pasta internet meme created by Eric Knudsen. Stories of the Slender Man commonly feature him stalking, abducting or traumatising people, particularly children. Other recent creepypastas include the Russian Sleep Experiment, The Rake, and Jeff, The Killer.'

Cleo saw the green phone symbol on her screen and pressed the answer button.

'Hello. Welcome to Tales Of Madness. You're through to Cleo James.'

'Oh wow, hi there.'

'Hi. Welcome to the show. What would you like to say?' Cleo felt a buzz of excitement. She loved people calling in but sometimes had to coax the listeners to pick up the phone. She had a feeling tonight would be a huge success.

'I'm Gilbert. My wife and I have just put the kids to bed. We look forward to your show every night; It's the highlight of our day.'

'That's most kind of you,' Cleo answered. 'Where are you calling from?'

'I was brought up in North London, but we now live in Surrey.'

'Oh, lovely. Beautiful part of the UK. What would you like to say?'

'The Babysitter. Remember that one?'

'Oh my goodness,' Cleo answered enthusiastically. 'Go on, tell our listeners for anyone who doesn't know the story.'

Gilbert cleared his throat. 'OK, so, a teenager gets a job as a babysitter. She has to look after two young children. When the parents go out for the night, she lets them watch telly for a while. The story is sometimes tweaked, but the concept is the same. Anyway, when they're tired, she tucks them into bed. She comes downstairs and sits on the sofa. A few minutes pass, and the phone rings. She reaches to the side and picks it up. Then she hears a voice. Have you checked the children? Shaking it off as a prank, she puts the phone down. Then it rings again, the same voice, the same question. After a few times, she's really spooked and calls the police. They trace the number, and the person is calling from the house where she's babysitting.'

'Oh my goodness. I have goosebumps. It's such a great story, right,' Cleo states. 'Didn't they make a film of this? When a stranger calls?'

'That's right. Terrific movie. I know what we'll be watching after the show. Keep up the great work. The show is awesome.'

'Thank you. I appreciate the call. I'm going to a break, and I'll be back after this.' Pressing a music track, she removed her headphones, and stretched. The last story had freaked her out a little. She'd remembered it, often hearing it as a child. The story had always frightened her. Someone calling, a sinister voice on the line, telling them to check on the children, knowing the person can see her, then finding out they're in the house. She shivered. Although she loved the podcast, her room underneath the office building was lonely; she often heard things, taps on the wall, strange noises coming from outside. Sometimes it got to her.

Cleo jolted. A shadow walked past the window. Gripping the edge of the desk, she stood. The road was a dead-end, the room where she recorded the show was at the end of a ramp. No one should be down here at this time of night.

Making her way to the window, she pushed her face to the glass. All she saw was darkness. Cleo moved to the front door and opened it. She looked along the ramp. The office to her right side was deserted. Through the windows, the rooms were black.

Moving out of the room, Cleo walked towards the wall on her left. A tall brick structure. Turning, she glanced up the car park ramp.

No one was there. So what was the shadow she'd seen?

Cleo moved back into the room, closed and locked the door then sat by the desk. She looked at the screen; there was just under a minute before the song finished. Placing her headphones on, she prepared for the next part of the show.

'Welcome back to Tales Of Madness; I'm your host, Cleo James, and tonight, we're talking urban legends, creepypastas, whatever you want to call them; let's hear your favourites. The number is at the bottom of the screen; dial-up and get straight through.' She looked at the screen of her laptop. 'OK, let's see. A message here from *Ifeelya Balls. Great show as always.* Oh shit. You guys. Come on, don't you get tired of catching me?' She laughed and felt her face flush— another message.

Mark R. The last caller was great. Love the babysitter story. I remember the urban legend so well. Keep up the great work. Oh, please say hi to my wife, Clare.

'Well, Mark and Clare, glad you're enjoying the show. Another one from Tess Tickle. She says,' Cleo paused, smirking, 'Oh, I don't believe you lot. Got me again. I'm going to have to put a filter in place.' Again, Cleo laughed at being caught live on air.

The call button appeared on her screen. Cleo hovered the mouse over it and clicked. The person had withheld the number. 'Welcome to Tales Of Madness. What would you like to say?' There was a pause; Cleo waited. 'Hello caller, you're through to Tales Of—'

'I know where I've called.' His voice was deep with a certain menace about it.

'OK, talk to me. Do you have a favourite urban legend?'

'Isn't it possible that urban legends could actually happen?'

'Explain yourself, caller?'

'What I'm saying is these tales, the stories you hear that make you look over your shoulder, the fear they drum up inside, the only relief is that you believe they never happened. That they are just stories passed down through generations to tell around campfires or share at sleepovers. Something to add the scare factor to a weekend in a log cabin, the element of menace, to goad the adrenaline and make a situation more intense, more frightening.'

'What's your point? Sorry, I'm not with you, caller.'

'We call them urban legends. Fictitious stories that supposedly happened in a town where you live, a house you've visited, the local schoolyard, a nearby abandoned building, or a lonely highway. My point being is they *could* happen. The stories you hear. The words 'urban legend' instantly lead you to believe they're fake stories. You mentioned the lady driving along a deserted road, the truck driver flashing his lights for her to pull over, and finding someone in the back of her car. The babysitter, the kids upstairs, her alone in the house, the call coming from inside. It could happen, Cleo. It could happen.'

'OK, I'm with you. Boy, you're intense. So what would you like to tell us?' Cleo felt awkward. She didn't often get callers like this. She wanted him to make his point and move on. 'Do you have an urban legend of your own you'd like to share?'

'Not as such, but they're fascinating stories. Can you imagine being the main character, the lead role? Take the babysitter tale, for instance. You get a job, maybe to make ends meet, or a little spending money so you can buy the latest clothes, treat yourself to a nice outfit, take in a film or two, or go to the theatre and afford a meal afterwards. So you answer an advert in the paper or local shop window, a young couple who want a bit of time together at the weekend. They have young kids; yes, they are devoted, spend time with them, teach them right from wrong, guide them; nothing is a chore. But they want time away from all that. I'm getting sidetracked. Imagine you make the call, Cleo. You apply for the babysitting job. You sit for the children. You have an open fridge, all the shows you desire on the telly, or you read a book. Whatever you want. Then the phone rings. The person asks you to check on the children. You hang up. He calls again and again. Then, bang, the twist, he's in the house. Imagine I said to you, a woman is about to be tied up in a house, held against her will, and may die! But she doesn't know it yet. The psychopath is hiding. The woman he's about to murder is his wife.'

'Look, please get to the point. I'm not sure where this is going.' Pulling the chair closer to the desk, Cleo peered towards the window. She felt uncomfortable.

'The clock is ticking. He's about to kill his wife. The psychopath is watching, hidden, and waiting for someone to come and rescue her.'

'Where is he hiding? Is this an urban legend?' She darted her eyes around the room.

'Let's look at the babysitter story and make our own angle on it, shall we? Like the caller, I'm concealed. I'm planning on killing my wife, and she doesn't know it yet. Her trust camouflages my wicked concept.

I watch her in the kitchen. She's cooking—the flames from the hob flicker, the pan filled with vegetables. The casserole simmers. She adds a little garlic and ginger. She loves to experiment with food. I stand behind her, she knows I'm there, but her trust conceals me.

Later, she moves to the living room, grabs the remote

control, and flicks through the channels, searching for
something to watch. She looks over to where I'm sitting.

We talk about our friends, work, current affairs, and get
ready to watch an episode from the latest boxset we've seen
reviewed on social media.

I'm sitting in the living room.

I'm her biggest threat.

But she has no idea.

How about that for your next story?'

'I'm sorry. I have to end this call. It's all becoming a
little too weird.' Leaning forward, Cleo looked at the
comments on the screen. Listeners were telling her to
hang up. Others were commenting on how weird he
sounded.

Moving the mouse over the screen, Cleo disconnected
the call.

'Let's go to another break.' Cleo listened as the spon-
sored ads played. A local car showroom explaining why
they're different, the latest deals and how they add that
personal touch—a local family-run florist with a rundown
of prices and how they deliver within a five-mile radius. The
ad break finished with Cleo's pre-recorded voice advertising
a crime podcast. She sat at the desk, the conversation ran
through her head from moments ago. The caller had
sounded threatening, and Cleo felt vulnerable, exposed.
She thought about the shadow she'd seen earlier, passing by
the window.

Was he out there?

Watching the comments appear on the screen, she
began to talk. 'Welcome back to Tales Of Madness. I'm your
host, Cleo—'

The green call button appeared on the screen. Again the
phone number was withheld.

'Hi, caller. Welcome to the show. What would you like to say?'

'Have you heard the one about the podcast presenter who tries to save the caller's wife but fails?'

Cleo knew it was him. The same person who'd called a few minutes ago. His voice was slow, controlled, and sinister. 'You need help. I suggest you speak to a professional. Why would you say something like that?'

'We're discussing urban legends. I'm giving you an idea for a new one. Don't you like it, Cleo? The caller rings the podcast host on urban legend night. She discusses stories, including one about a babysitter. I love that story. There's such tension and pressure on the girl. The babysitter knows that the antagonist may kill her. She has a dilemma. Run and save herself or risk her life and save the children. She knows she could die. My wife doesn't suspect a thing. I'm in the house, and I'm going to kill my wife. Only the podcast presenter can save her now.'

Banging her fist on the mouse, she ended the call. 'We're going to another break.' Removing her headphones, Cleo leaned back on her swivel chair, and took a deep breath. Her heart was racing, and her cheeks felt hot. She placed her head in her hands and remained in that position for a few moments. She wanted to go home and didn't feel safe. Since doing the podcast, she hadn't dealt with anyone so morbid or sick. Something in the way he spoke, the threats, didn't sit right. He sounded believable, like he really was going to murder his wife. She wanted to end the podcast, go home and call it a night.

She could call the police, but he rang from a withheld number.

A shiver raced through her body. Watching the window at the front of the room; her mind was playing tricks. She thought someone was standing outside, watching her. She gripped the edge of the desk, her heart racing, then looked away to the walls, the floor, anywhere but the bleakness outside.

Cleo watched as a string of comments came through. They moved so fast that she didn't have time to read them all.

Standing, she moved into the back kitchen and poured herself a glass of water. Could she leave? Pack up for the night? It would be a waste as the comments and support had gone off the scale. There were so many listeners it would be a shame to stop.

Placing her hands on the sideboard, she tried to compose herself. *Come on; you can do this. It's just a crank call. He probably gets off on ringing people and upsetting them. Jerk.* The track she played was almost finished. Did she continue, or go home? She hesitated for a second, then sat back at the desk and placed her headphones on.

'Welcome back to Tales Of Madness. I'm your host, Cleo James, and tonight, we're talking urban legends. The number is at the bottom of the screen, and if you call now, you'll get straight through. As always, I'm live on Youtube and various other platforms.'

The green button appeared on the screen. 'Hello, caller. Welcome to the show. You're live on air. What would you like to say?'

'Have you checked?'

Cleo recognised the voice. 'Checked what?'

'Oh, come on. You're playing dumb here. The babysitter story, remember? Have you checked?'

'OK, I'm going to ask that you don't call again. I don't appreciate what you're doing here, and I have no time for prank calls.'

'Have you checked my wife?'

'I'm certain your wife, if you even have one, wouldn't appreciate you talking like this. It's not funny. Go and find your kicks elsewhere. I don't want you to call again. Is that understood?' Cleo heard a door close. The caller sounded like he was outside. His breathing became stronger, his voice a little more distant.

'I think you should check my wife.'

'Don't call again. Please, go and get help, talk to someone, but don't call my show anymore.'

'I'm going to send you a picture from a burner phone. Give me a second.'

The wind rattled in her ears, the shuffling sound as the caller moved his phone around. 'I told you I'm hanging up.' Her phone pinged—a WhatsApp message came through.

'Look at the picture.'

'Goodbye,' Cleo shouted. 'Wow. I'm so sorry, guys. What an arsehole. I don't usually swear, but wow, this guy is getting up my goat. OK, we're talking urban—' Cleo glanced at her phone. She zoomed in. A caption underneath read, *"Check my wife."* Cleo thought she was going to pass out. A woman lay in a storeroom or cupboard. Her hands and feet were bound with rope, and a gag was placed around her mouth. Her eyes looked fearful, as if she were screaming, scared for her life. Another message came through. It began with the letters "BS." Possibly a take on the babysitter story. She read the comment.

I'll kill my wife in one hour. If I hear a police siren, I'll kill her instantly. Then I'll come for you. The clock starts now.

* * *

Cleo's body began shaking uncontrollably. She felt nauseous and ended the show with an apology to her listeners. She watched the sad emojis appear on the screen as she clicked the end button and removed her headphones. She sat on the swivel chair at the desk, petrified.

The room was so isolated. She glanced towards the window. Again, she gripped the side of the desk as a shadow seemed to move across the glass. Cleo dug her nails into the wood, too frightened to stand. She waited; her skin tingled as she listened to her own sharp breaths.

Her eyes were drawn to the picture of her parents above the front door. Pleasant memories flooded her mind. She looked to the front door, needing to leave this room, get to her car, and drive. She'd be safe then.

Here, Cleo was vulnerable and exposed. Glancing back to the blank laptop screen, she closed the lid.

Cleo pushed the chair back and stood. Suddenly she heard a tapping noise. Spinning around, she looked wildly between the kitchen out the back, the bleak window, and the front door. *Was there someone tapping from outside? Could the caller be here, standing in the parking lot?*

Edging slowly across the room, Cleo pressed her face to the glass. Outside looked desolate. No one ever came down here. Why would they? She must have imagined that shadow across the window. Her room was situated at the end of a side road. The staff from the offices above had long gone home. The car park was empty. It's why she loved this place—the solitude.

She was able to do the show with no interruptions.

Cleo moved away from the window. She glanced at her watch—almost 11pm. Visions played in her mind of the woman tied up in the cupboard. Could it be a prank? She was discussing urban legends after all. But the way that the caller announced he was going to kill his wife, and the picture, sent to her phone, of a woman bound and gagged. She looked terrified. It had to be real. Who would do something so sick?

Picking up her phone, her hands trembling, she opened the picture again and wondered how the caller had her phone number. Then it dawned on her. She was included in her street WhatsApp group. A couple of neighbours started it to inform each other of suspicious activity.

Another tap on the door. Cleo was certain this time. Someone was outside.

Pressing her ear to the wood, she listened. Cleo stood still, waiting, urging whoever was on the other side to leave her alone. She stepped back, looking at the door. It was flimsy and would be so easy to open, even though it was locked from the inside.

She jumped as her phone rang from the desk. Cleo composed herself, brushing a hand through her short, blonde hair, then moved to the desk.

She looked at the screen, the number withheld. 'Hello?' she said.

'Here's the first clue. I'll leave the front door open. You have until midnight to save my wife. Call the police, and I'll kill her. If you manage to save her, I promise I'll let you live.'

'Why are you doing this?' Cleo screamed.

The phone went dead.

A message came through a few seconds later with the street name.

He lived on her road.

* * *

Leaning against the desk, Cleo tried to compose herself. The picture was lodged in her mind. The woman tied up, the look of dread on her face, her eyes so fearful.

Pulling on her coat, she grabbed the laptop, tucked it under her arm and made to leave. She switched off the lights, tapped the code for the alarm, and opened the door.

She screamed. A man was standing there. He wore a thick jacket, ripped jeans, and steel toe capped boots. He looked around sixty but could have been much older.

'Do you have any change?'

Cleo felt her body trembling. Was it him? She'd seen shadows earlier; there'd been a tapping noise on the door. Had he been watching her all the time? Reaching her trembling hand into her bag, she opened her purse, and found a five-pound note. She willed herself to run, get help or move back into the room and slam the door. Her eyes moved from the bag to his face, peering into it, trying desperately to hide her fear.

He reached out, took the money, thanked her, and started walking slowly up the ramp.

Once he'd gone, Cleo leant against the door and cried. She couldn't remember the last time she'd been reduced to tears. The caller was wicked and had ruined her night. The frustration spilt from her body. But the harrowing experience was only just starting. She composed herself, breathing deeply, swallowing the chilly air and pushing breaths out. Turning, she looked along the side street, the ramp to her left leading to the car park. She took one more deep breath in, and then ran towards her car.

Cleo watched the empty spaces as she opened the door of her Ford Puma. She sat in the driver's seat, locked the doors, and pulled out of the car park.

As she drove along the side street and pulled out to the

main road, the caller's voice played in her mind. How could someone be so evil? How could he do this to his wife? How could he put Cleo through such an ordeal? She'd never get the image out of her mind. The woman, bound and gagged, would haunt her forever.

She contemplated ringing the police, but the caller had warned her. *Call the police, and I'll kill her.* His words. As soon as sirens rang out, he'd do it. Then he'd come for her.

As Cleo drove, her mind seemed to evacuate her body, it was as if she was looking at herself from above. She lost concentration and became numb, dazed, and unaware of her surroundings. She drove, the silent roads swallowed by her vehicle; her eyes were heavy, staring ahead, processing nothing of what was in front.

She swerved as a young woman stepped onto the road. Cleo hit the brakes, checking the rear-view mirror to ensure she was still alive. The woman shouted something as she stood on the crossing.

Glancing at the clock on the dashboard, Cleo estimated she'd be there in around thirty minutes; what then? What terrifying fate awaited her?

She looked at her image in the mirror, the tired, pale complexion, the dark marks under her eyes, testament to how exhausted she felt.

How had it come to this? How did she get involved in such a sick, twisted game? From the picture and tone of the caller's voice, she had no doubt he'd kill his wife if she didn't get there in time. He said he'd leave the door open. So what? She enters the house, unties her, while he waits, hidden, and kills them both? That's how she saw it play out. That's the only way she envisioned it ending. He seemed obsessed with fucking urban legends. Wanting to invent his own story, which would be told for generations. With him at the centre of it.

What a psycho.

Cleo had to stop it from happening.

But how?'

Moving the gearstick, she pressed the accelerator. Again the image of the woman tied up and lying in the cupboard, so desperate to escape, exploded in her mind.

There was no choice; she had to be brave. She had to save this anguished woman. Go into the house, no matter what fate awaited her, and find a way to get them both out safely.

* * *

She was over halfway home when the phone rang. Cleo hesitated, hovering her finger over the answer button. She had no choice.

'Hello?'

'Tick, tick. Time is running out. If you don't get to her within the next twenty minutes, I'll kill her. That's an absolute promise.'

'Why are you doing this?' she shouted. Cleo approached a roundabout and turned left down a narrow side street. She stopped behind a taxi parked in the middle of the road; the hazard lights blinked at her. Hitting the horn on the steering wheel, she watched as the driver began to pull away.

'Because you like your stories. So why not be part of one?'

'You sick bastard. How can you do this?'

'Did you see the picture? She's petrified, right? See, I've often thought about killing her. Recently it's been tough. Life has been somewhat of a struggle. You know how it is.'

Cleo thought she could hear the sound of an engine, like the caller was on the move. Suddenly headlights came on behind her—full beams blasted like a sudden explosion, reducing her visibility. The vehicle came closer. She watched through the rear-view mirror. As Cleo reached the end of the road, she turned right. The vehicle behind went left. She pushed out a heavy sigh. 'So get a divorce or work it out. Please don't do anything to her; I'm begging you.'

'For too long now, she's been unbearable to live with. You should walk a mile in my boots. See it for yourself. I won't put up with it. She knows how she irritates me, the things she says and does. I won't stand for it. I've contemplated doing this for so long. Your show tonight was the ideal opportunity. Now, I'm getting what I want, and so are you.'

'What you want?' Cleo asked.

'That's right. The recognition. My story. Something people will talk about for years to come. A story everyone will remember. The podcast presenter trying her best to save the distraught woman from the perilous murderer.'

'How are you getting satisfaction from this? It's sick. You're fucking sick.'

'Oh, you're just like my wife. Funny, she says that too. Now you're involved in your own wicked, twisted story. You don't have long left. The door is open. Be there on time and get her out. Then it ends.'

The phone went dead.

Cleo ran the conversation through her mind. He was serious. No doubt about it. She had to do as he said, then it would be over. But would it? Surely he'd be there? He'd kill her the moment she entered the property.

The caller lived on her street, the sick neighbour from hell. But who was he? She thought about the people who lived beside her. There was Mrs Norris on her left side, living alone. A widow and in her nineties. She's out of the question. Guy and Michael to her right. Young men, both hard working. Not them either then. The caller's voice was much older. Cleo thought about the other neighbours. She knew most of them only by sight, the occasional nod as they passed on the street or the courteous smile in the park.

Cleo pulled off the main road; steering left onto her street. Jabbing the brakes, she slowed the car, watching as she drove past the first houses on either side, looking for an open front door.

The streetlights were off and the blackened houses made it difficult to see.

Cleo needed to pull over.

Finding a parking space, she jerked the steering wheel and pulled her Ford Puma to the curb. She yanked the handbrake up and turned off the engine. She waited, assessing the predicament she'd been forced into. This was so dangerous. Cleo feared for both her own life and that of the woman tied up in the house. She checked her watch. There was about ten minutes to find her. That was it. Ten minutes to untie her and get her out of the house.

Undoing her seatbelt, she pushed the driver's door open and stood, glancing along the empty road.

The caller could be anywhere.

As she walked, she glared at the bleak windows on either side of the road, watching for a sign.

It was late, curtains were closed, blinds were pulled down, and Cleo assumed most of her neighbours would be asleep.

Moving along the pavement, she wondered if the caller could see her, if he was watching from the darkness. She felt defenceless, weak. What could she do if he grabbed her and tied her up too, holding her in the cupboard with his wife, like a collection of frantic women?

Cleo peered to her right side; large, semi-detached houses, all with closed front doors. She envisaged walking to the end of the road, finding out it was all a wind-up. A crew of people racing over to her with cameras, laughter ringing out through the cold night air and someone informing her of the amazing prank they'd pulled. She'd be angry, but the rage would turn to relief.

Cleo spun sharply, sure that someone was behind her. Had she heard footsteps? The road was deserted. She moved forward again, aware of her footsteps, trying desperately to silence them and shake the feeling of exposure.

Can he see her?

Is he hiding?

Waiting for the right moment?

Looking at the parked cars, she wondered if they were empty, then imagined a door opening and the caller springing out. She'd charge to the nearest house and smash a window or scream for someone to help.

Cleo contemplated going back, getting in her car and locking the doors, ignoring tonight and the wickedness she'd been drawn into. But it wasn't an option. She was the only person who could help.

As she took a few more steps, a coldness ripped through her body. A security light blinked above an opened front door.

She stopped, her heart felt like it had moved to her throat. Cleo stepped back and hid behind the bushes on the front lawn. She stared at the house. The lights were off, the door wide open. It had to be the place.

Taking a deep breath to compose herself, Cleo crept to the front gate. Her eyes flicked from window to open doorway, trying to see if anything moved, a shadow, a figure, anything to suggest that someone was there.

Reaching the front door, she gently tapped the wood, instantly regretting the announcement. 'Hello. Is anyone here?' She realised her stupidity in letting him know she was in the house. Too late now. 'Hello?' Cleo stepped further inside, moving along the hallway. She shouted now. 'Hello?!'

A man appeared from the kitchen at the back of the house. 'Who are you? What's going on?' he asked. His voice sounded genuinely shocked.

She watched as his silhouette moved towards her. 'I'm sorry. You left the front door open. I thought I heard a cry for help,' she lied. 'I'm so sorry if I startled you.'

He flicked a switch which brought the lights on. 'I'm going out. Nightshift, but I appreciate the concern.'

'I really am sorry,' Cleo offered again. She turned, thinking he'd grab her and drag her to the cupboard the wife was being held in. *He sounded different from the caller though. His voice was higher. But then people can change their voice,* she thought.

As Cleo reached the pavement unharmed, she swiftly looked either side of the house, a reassuring glance behind and then broke into a jog. There were only minutes left. Her eyes darted left and right, glancing at the front doors she passed, unsure if she'd missed any. There wasn't time to check. Again, the image of that poor woman held in a cupboard pounded through her mind, the caller's rough, sickening voice. She hated him for putting them through this.

Cleo was tired, her legs ached, and her skin was numb with the cold, but she forced herself to keep going, to push through it.

As she raced along the deserted street, the houses

morphed into each other; a line of similarity, all the lights were off, all blackened.

Finally, she could see the end of the road. Had she missed it? She stopped, worried the house was behind her. She'd have to go back and recheck each property, but there wasn't enough time. She panicked. It was too late. The caller was going to kill his wife, and there was nothing Cleo could do. Had all this been for nothing? Had he drawn her into this wicked act knowing she'd fail? What good is an urban legend if no one dies? A useless, uninteresting story that will evaporate and vanish into thin air.

Cleo stopped to take a breather, her head was heavy, and her chest was sore. She looked across the road—a semi-detached house with the lights off. A spotlight on the wall that looked strategically placed pointed down at the open front door.

It had to be the house. But was she too late? Was the woman already dead?

She braced herself, pushing her body to keep going. The adrenalin had swallowed her energy, and she longed to lie down on the road. At this moment, she'd never felt so frightened.

Cleo crossed the road, reached the gate and looked through the blackened windows. Glancing up, she gasped. Was that a figure watching her from one of the rooms? It was too dark to be certain. Pressing her hand on the front door, she braced herself. Cleo stood in the downstairs hallway. She envisioned an arm grabbing her, a punch to the side of the head, and her slumping over the caller's shoulder. She had to fight the terror inside. She had to do this.

The house was pitch black and motionless. As Cleo moved, she swept her left hand along the wall. 'Is anyone here?' Her voice sounded pathetic and weak. 'I'm here to help you. If anyone is here, can you knock once?' Cleo stood and listened.

No knock.

No sound.

Touching a door handle on her left, she pushed it downwards. The door groaned as it opened. Cleo felt for a light switch, found it and flicked it on. A large figure stood in front of her. He was tall, menacing-looking and towered over Cleo. He appeared strong; his large shoulders and chest bulged through his jumper. His eyes were like small slits in his skin, and his head was shaved tight.

Cleo screamed as dread twisted in her stomach and anxiety pulsed through her body. She turned the light back off. It was him. An arm grabbed her wrist as she backed away. 'Leave me alone. What the fuck is wrong with you?'

Suddenly a different light came on. Cleo struggled to see. The caller was wearing a head torch; the fierce glow pointed into her eyes. He pulled her towards him with great force and slapped her face with the back of his hand. Then he threw her to the ground.

She lay on her side and brought her knees towards her stomach. 'Why? Why are you doing this?'

'I thought you liked games?' His voice was deep and harsh. 'You get so excited, telling your stories, urging people to call in and talk about their experiences. I've listened to the show many times. I have wanted to speak to you. I've planned this so you can take the lead role, tell your story, how you tried to save my wife and failed.'

Trying to turn over, Cleo felt a heavy boot come down on her chest. She must have passed this house so many times. Had this man been watching from the rooms upstairs? If so, for how long? How could she not realise what this creep was planning? 'I'm here. You don't need to do this. I made it on time.'

He lifted an arm and looked at his watch. 'I'm sorry, you're past the deadline. I told you what would happen.'

'Let her go. I'm here. I did everything you told me.'

The caller leaned down, grabbed her under the arms, and lifted her up.

Cleo knew that she had seconds before he'd hit her again, or worse. She had to do something. As he moved forward, she turned, guided by the light and grabbed a heavy vase from the table. Swinging it as hard as she could with one hand, she caught him square on the nose.

Cleo reached behind and turned on the overhead light.

He was shouting in agony. It looked as if his nose had exploded. Blood gushed from his nostrils, and he dropped onto his knees.

Cleo ran into the hallway. As she headed for the front door, she heard muffled cries for help. It was coming from upstairs.

Even though she knew the danger, the adrenalin kicked in again. Her phone was in the car, parked at the top of the road. She had no other choice.

Cleo turned on the stairs. She felt the wall for a socket and switched on the lights, then took two stairs at a time to the first floor. 'Where are you? I'm going to help you. Please tell me where you are?'

A chilling groan came from one of the rooms further down the hallway. She looked back, expecting to see a shadow, but there was no one on the stairs. It would be a matter of seconds before the caller came after her. She had to be quick.

Cleo pushed the first door on her right, guided by the

hallway light. Moving into the room, she closed the door, leaning her body against it. 'Hello? I'm here to help you.'

The desperate groans were close. Cleo reached her hands to the wall on either side and hit the switch. Rushing to a large cupboard on the other side of the room, she pulled the double doors open.

Cleo gasped as she saw a woman lying on the floor, tied with rope. 'Are you OK? Oh my goodness. Here, let me help you.' Undoing the knot, Cleo removed the rope around the woman's wrists and then pulled the gag from her mouth. 'Please keep quiet. He's downstairs. We have to get out.' Once the rope had been removed from her ankles, she cradled the woman and helped her to her feet.

She was disorientated. Her face smudged with mascara. She struggled to balance, and her legs were unsteady. The woman began crying hysterically. Cleo pleaded with her to stop.

Once she'd controlled herself, the woman whispered, 'Thank you so much. How did you know I was here?' Her long brown hair was wet, her eyes were bruised, and her nightdress was ripped at the sides.

Cleo turned towards the door. 'I haven't got time to explain. Quick, let's go.'

As they moved towards the bedroom door, they could hear footsteps coming towards them. Cleo closed the door and pressed her body against it. 'Do you have a phone?'

'No. It's in the kitchen. He just flipped. One minute we were downstairs. I was cooking. He came behind me and accused me of going through his phone. He started shouting at me, saying I was no good, that I didn't trust him. Then he slapped me hard in the face. He dragged me up the stairs and tied me up. I don't know what is wrong with him?'

Cleo felt the force of the door moving against her body. 'I can't hold him. Quick, throw something at the window?'

'What? Throw what?'

Cleo's body began to slide along the floor. 'Anything. Quick, smash the window and scream. Do it!'

The woman searched on the floor and moved to the bed. She grabbed a lamp, unplugged it and began to smash the glass. A few seconds later, it shattered. 'Help. Someone help us. Help us, for God's sake.' Her screams were deafening.

The door stopped moving, and Cleo could hear his footsteps as the caller raced along the landing and down the stairs. A moment later, the front door slammed shut.

'He's gone. I think we're safe,' Cleo said. She watched as the woman fell onto the bed, weeping again hysterically.

They heard a voice calling from the street. 'Is everything OK?'

Cleo stood, her eyes blurry from adrenalin; the voice lifting her panic as she moved to the window. A young guy she recognised stood on the pavement outside the house. He was staring up at the window. 'Can you call the police? There's a domestic situation up here. We need your help.'

The man dug into his jacket pocket and dialled 999.

Once the police arrived and made sure the house was safe, they took statements from both women. The lady Cleo had freed was Sara Longmate, and although she was distressed, she managed to answer their questions. She told them everything.

Cleo waited with her; all of them sat around the kitchen table. Sara was struggling to explain the events which had taken place and work through why they had happened.

As the police made arrangements for Sara to be brought to hospital, they thanked Cleo for her heroics. She gave them her phone number and asked Sara to call if she needed any more help.

Cleo was entangled in the story, and she felt it was her duty.

'I can't thank you enough,' Sara said as Cleo left. 'He would have killed me if you hadn't intervened.'

Cleo hugged her at the door. One of the policewomen asked her if she had someone to stay with, but she wouldn't let the caller win, determined to get her car and go home. Again, she asked Cleo to go with them but she refused.

After a policewoman dropped Cleo to her car, she sat in the driver's seat of her Ford Puma, stunned by the evening's events. She went over it all in her mind. Her, arriving at the small room she'd rented, the podcast discussing urban legends. The caller ringing in and making threats, insisting she take part in his twisted game—the picture he'd sent her on WhatsApp, the hunt for the house, the rescue.

Christ, the guy was an absolute lunatic, she thought.

Her phone was still on the dashboard. Making a grab for it, she suddenly thought again about the stories they had been discussing on her show. Before the story of the babysitter, she'd told another one. A woman alone at night, sat in her car. But the woman in the story hadn't been alone. There had been someone in the back. Gripping the steering wheel with both hands, she tried to relieve the tension. Slowly, she looked in the rear-view mirror. Was there someone lying on the back seat, maybe on the floor? She braced, her body tense, laboured. Turning to the side and pushing her left hand into the passenger seat, she leant over.

Cleo pushed out a sigh, her lips vibrating. The car was empty. Cleo laughed. *Get a grip. Come on. You're better than this. Don't let him win. The police will catch him, they are out there hunting right now.*

She jumped as her phone rang from the dashboard. A withheld number. Taking a deep breath, she started the engine, picked up the phone and held it to her ear. 'Hello?' Her voice sounded so feeble.

'Tut, tut. How is this story ever going to be remembered now?'

Cleo looked out of the car window and onto the street. 'You sick bastard. You lost, not me. You.' Cleo pulled onto the road, watching for another vehicle or a shadow in the bleakness. 'Why are you doing this?'

He continued to speak. 'Your discussion on urban legends. I needed to pick the right person—someone in the spotlight. Someone who'd appreciate my plan, my way of thinking. It had to be the right person.'

Cleo continued to watch the road. She felt more bolshy and confident, like she'd triumphed over him. 'But I beat you. Now, no one will talk about your stupid game. No one will ever remember you.'

There was a pause for a few seconds. 'Take the woman on the lonely highway—the stopover at the petrol station. The trucker, flashing his lights and sounding his horn. She pulls onto the drive, sees him open the truck door, step down, and charge towards her. Only to help her. A great twist. He unveils the psycho in the back of her car.'

'What is wrong with you? I've had enough of listening to your riddles.' Cleo was about to hang up. Reaching the end of the road, she pulled into a space a few doors from her house.

'I want people to remember. I want you to recall this night. To talk about it in years to come on your podcast.'

Cleo turned off the car engine and opened the driver's door. She looked up and down the road, fearful he'd jump out. 'Believe me, no one will remember. You're just a sick individual who tried to play a game to frighten me. To try and invent a story that backfired. I found the house. All that planning. Your sick game. It was all for nothing.' Cleo started laughing down the phone. 'It won't be long until the police catch you.' As she walked along the road and stood outside her house, she could still hear the caller talking.

'I know you'll tell this story, Cleo.'

The words didn't register. Cleo pushed the gate and walked up the front path. She froze; her body felt paralysed with apprehension.

Her front door was open.

She'd turned the lights out before leaving this evening. Now, the hallway light was on. As she walked along the drive, the kitchen was visible at the back of the house. Standing at the door, she glanced upstairs, then behind her. 'What is going on?' Cleo shouted. The only comfort was Cleo's certainty that the caller was on the move and not in the house. The wind pushed through the phone and she could still hear a car engine.

Stepping inside the house, she slammed the front door, feeling safer.

'You failed to realise two things.' His voice on the phone sounded more sinister. Calm and in control.

Racing up the stairs, she intended to lock the bedroom door, call the police and wait. Listening to his voice meant he couldn't jump out on her. At the top of the stairs, Cleo peered along the hallway, wondering if the caller was waiting. Barging against the bedroom door, she opened it, slammed it shut and locked it. 'What did I fail to realise?'

'That there was more than one open front door. And that the woman you saved was my lover. Not my wife.'

In the moonlight coming in from the window, Cleo saw a figure in her bed, lying under blood-soaked blankets.

Reaching her trembling hand forward, she ripped the covers away.

Cleo's screams echoed through the house.

The End

ROOM 9

3

F rank Tully stood behind the desk of The Oak Hotel, comprehending the long winter months ahead, hopeful for prosperity.

It was Friday morning, the first week in September. They'd had a busy spring and a somewhat crazy summer. Usually, the hotel would be more occupied with couples taking advantage of lower prices due to the new school term.

The Oak was situated in the centre of St Ives in Cornwall – a beautiful picturesque town in England, famous for its surfing and art scene. With an array of shops, bars, restaurants, and incredible beaches, it was a major tourist hotspot. Although the rush had backed off somewhat, Frank and his wife, Carrie, kept afloat with locals drifting in for a drink and a bite to eat in the restaurant, people attending work conferences, and those who chose a naughty weekend away.

Frank stared at the clock. 9.15am. The double doors opened further down the hall. A chambermaid wheeled a trolley towards the front desk, its wheels recklessly twisting on the patterned carpet.

'Kayleigh, there are wine stains on the carpet in room nine. Bloody typical. I knew when I saw them arrive that they'd be riffraff. You can tell, you know. Their first question. Oh, is the bar open late? That, my dear, is the immediate sign you're in trouble. Carrie left at 11pm. I managed the bar for another three hours. I was sure it was going to be an all-nighter, you know, listening to the shit talk. Oh, I love you. I love you too. This is what we needed. A break, an escape from the norm. Recharge. You know what I'm saying, Kayleigh? As if a night away at The Oak will repair their marriage. What she was doing with that ugly bastard is beyond me. Hideous mug on him. He looked like he'd had a head swop with a wild boar. Talk about punching above his bloody weight.' Frank watched Kayleigh nod. Her cheeks were flushed, her long, damp hair tied up, and her lips twisted, indicating her annoyance.

'I'll get on it now.'

'Thank you, Kayleigh. You're a star. I don't like ugly people. You can't trust them. You get what I'm saying, Kayleigh?'

Again, she nodded without speaking.

Frank ran his fingers along the maple worktop, feeling the rough splinters, the knots deep in the wood. The tv played behind him, hung on the wall, a breakfast programme on low, and a member of parliament was being interviewed.

Frank stared at the high ceilings, the thick white walls opposite, pictures of celebrity guests who'd stayed at The Oak were proudly displayed. A couple of him and Carrie, news articles set in frames of their arrival, cutting a ribbon and a handful of people in the background wishing them well in their new venture.

Frank watched as she wheeled the trolley to the store

cupboard, removed the key from her trousers and opened the door. As she bent over to grab the cloths and detergent to clean the carpet, Frank watched her. He imagined what it would be like to bring her into one of the rooms, rip her blouse off, and throw her onto the bed. He fantasised about reaching behind her back, brushing against the soft, tan skin, inhaling the smell of her body as he unclipped her bra and began to kiss her pert breasts. Then, he'd lift her skirt, teasing himself and make love to her while she whispered in his ear what a wonderful lover he was. They'd do it again and again until collapsing in a sweat induced heap.

He'd often thought about the staff, Kayleigh being his latest infatuation. Frank thought about her so much. While in bed with Carrie, he imagined Kayleigh's long, brown hair brushing his shoulders as she sat on him, moving her body slowly and teasing him.

'Frank.'

'Huh?'

'I asked for a coffee!'

'Oh, Carrie. When did you get here?' Frank looked out to the car park. His wife's Volkswagen Polo sat in the second director's space. 'You know you have to earn that spot.'

'Can you just make a bloody coffee?'

He watched Kayleigh as she moved past the desk. She smiled, greeting Carrie, then walked through the double doors to deal with the alcohol spillage in room nine.

'Frank?'

'Huh?' He turned to look at his wife with her stylish blonde hair, chic red suit, and piercing blue eyes. Carrie always looked glamorous. Frank felt inferior to her. He hadn't shaved for days; his hair was long with no particular style, and the bags under his dull green eyes were noticeable from insufficient sleep.

'I asked for a coffee,' Carrie pointed out. 'I don't know what's with you sometimes. You drift off, unaware of your surroundings, gormless and totally perplexed. What is it you think about? Where do you go, Frank? You know, one of these days, someone will come in, rob us blind, and you'll stand there like a dummy in a shop window, oblivious to everything. What time did you go to bed?'

Frank thought for a moment. 'After that alcoholic couple left. I locked up, made a sandwich and then slept on the sofa.' Frank turned and pointed to the office out the back. A blanket and pillow rested on the black leather.

'Do I have to ask again? Coffee. Now.'

Stepping forward, Frank placed his arms around Carrie's waist, kissing her cheek.

She smiled, staring into his eyes. The smell of coffee on his breath was strong. 'I do love you, Frank, but you do my head in sometimes.'

Smirking, he walked to the office. He grabbed two cups from the sideboard and then scooped a spoon of coffee into each cup. Once the kettle had boiled, he added hot water and walked out to the front desk. 'OK. There you go.' Frank placed the cups on the counter.

'How are we looking?' Carrie took a sip and removed her coat.

Frank tapped a couple of keys on the laptop and looked at the monitor. 'Most of the rooms are vacant upstairs. Still five rooms unoccupied down here. The alcoholics left room nine an hour ago. No calls this morning so far. It's not too bad, Hunny bunch.' The phone rang. 'Oh, let's hope we can fill another room. Hello, The Oak bar and hotel.' Frank pressed the speaker function. It was more comfortable.

'Hi. Do you have any rooms?'

Frank smiled and put a thumbs up to his wife. 'Oh, let's

see. It's hectic at the moment, but I think we can squeeze you in somewhere. How does the basement sound? I'm kidding. How many of you and how many nights?'

'Er, two and one night.'

'Sounds great. Yes, we can put you into room nine.' Frank hoped the wine stains didn't cause a nasty odour.

The man's voice remained calm. 'Great. We'll see you a little later.'

'Thanks. I didn't catch your name.'

The phone went dead.

Frank turned to his wife. 'Another room filled. See, there's nothing to worry about.'

Frank had taken over The Oak at short notice. Frank's father passed away after a battle with leukaemia, and the hotel had been willed to Frank. Although he and his father hadn't spoken for years, he saw them as being close.

His childhood was pretty average; he'd had the odd falling out with his parents in his early twenties, but nothing too serious. When his mother died from cancer, he moved in with his father to help run the hotel for a little while. But Frank dreamed of living in a bustling city, a penthouse in central London or Paris.

His father didn't want him going due to his ongoing health issues. Frank was an only child, and his father saw Frank's motive as selfish, but there was no way to persuade him to stay.

After the move to London and a job he hated, the stuffy office, the heat and noise around him, two failed relationships, and his father's death, Frank moved back to Cornwall and into The Oak. He met Carrie, who he'd known from school. She was on a hen weekend, and they hit it off.

After a short relationship and a small marriage ceremony, they decided to run the hotel together. Carrie worked as a childminder, but The Oak was an opportunity she couldn't turn down. She'd always loved the building with its old-style brick, thatched roof, and prime location. St Ives was her happy place, and she hated the thought of ever leaving.

The Oak in St Ives was perfect for her. She'd grown up here, and although she'd left school over thirty years ago, many of her old friends were still around.

Later that evening, Carrie was working in the bar. Frank had filled the shelves with crisps, nuts and other bar snacks. He'd changed a couple of barrels and was now filling the fridge with bottles of alcohol. It was Friday night, the bar was busy, and people drifted in on their way to a club or plush restaurant. Although they served food, the area was small and didn't seat many. They'd applied for an extension and were waiting to hear from the council. They offered bar food, but people preferred fine dining, space and the luxury of an a la carte menu.

The bell sounded. Frank looked from the bar to the front desk. A couple stood in the foyer. They were well dressed, and the man acted impatiently. The woman who stood with him wore a short skirt and cream coloured jacket.

Frank looked to Carrie. 'They must be the ones who phoned earlier. Room nine. I'll go.' He walked to the front desk and moved behind the counter. 'Welcome. How may I help?'

The guy was tall, handsome and wore a black jacket, white shirt and dark blue jeans. His hair was black, gelled back, and his blue eyes gleamed under the light.

'I called earlier. Two of us for one night,' the man said.

'Yes, indeed you did. Would you like to eat with us tonight? It's nothing plush, but we can whip up bar snacks. Burgers, chips, pizza.'

'We're fine,' he abruptly instructed. 'We'd just like to go to the room if that's OK.'

'Of course. No problem at all. The bar is open late if you'd like to come for a drink. Well, I say late. Until the last person keels over. I don't think I've had an all-nighter for some time,' Frank confirmed.

'Just the room. Thank you,' the guy announced.

Frank looked towards the woman. She hung back and had a fearful look on her face. She was pale and her long blonde hair extended past her shoulders. Her lips were fake but not unsightly, and her large green eyes looked fearful. Frank noticed how beautiful she was. A Marilyn Monroe caricature with a charming innocence about her. It was as if she didn't know she was so stunning—the shy, introverted type.

'OK, the room is ready.' Frank pointed down the hall. 'Go through the large double doors; room nine is near the end of the corridor on your right' Frank reached for the key in one of the drawers by his foot. 'Tap it against the security box. When it goes green, push the door. Simple. Enjoy your stay. Oh, if you need anything, there's a phone by the double bed. Just press zero, and we'll be happy to help.' Frank asked for a credit card, but the man declared he'd pay cash, announcing he didn't like credit cards for fear of losing them.

'Would you like breakfast in bed? A newspaper perhaps or an early morning call?' Frank asked.

'We're good. Thank you.' The guy grabbed the handle of his black suitcase, the wheels squeaking as it moved, and strolled along the hall towards the double doors. The woman followed close behind. She looked awkward in her high heels and strived to keep up with her partner.

Frank's eyes were drawn to her long, muscled legs, and he struggled to control his arousal.

* * *

'I'm off. I'll see you in the morning.' Carrie kissed Frank on the cheek and moved from behind the bar.

Frank watched the man sat on his own at a table down the back. He had half a glass of beer left and was reading a large newspaper. There was no phone or electronic device on his table, and it looked as if technology frightened him.

'I doubt he'll stay for long,' Carrie insisted. 'I'll see you tomorrow. It was a good night. The bar has been busy all evening. The takings should be great. Love you.'

'Yeah, there's the winter to worry about, though. It's always a long, cold one here in Cornwall.'

'Oh, Frank, don't be such a pessimist. We've been steady for months. Take the good times with the bad. Greed is the death of pure souls.'

Blowing his wife a kiss, he asked, 'What the hell are you on about? That makes no sense.'

'I'm just saying. We should be pleased with the way it's going. Rather than wanting more and more.' Carrie turned at the door. 'Night, Frank.'

'Night.' He watched as her Volkswagen Polo pulled out of the director's space, and a moment later, she was gone.

* * *

Sitting behind the bar, Frank watched as the old boy supped his drink, wanting him to spill the contents back and go to his room. He tried to stare and make him feel awkward. The old boy never looked up.

Frank waited, now getting impatient. Finally, the man lifted the glass with his right hand and gulped the rest of the drink. He folded the newspaper under his jacket and held it there. Then he stood and walked towards the bar

Please go to your room. Don't order another. Go away, for Christ's sake. Piss off, already, Frank thought.

'Thanks. Good night,' the old boy said.

'Thanks, mate. See you tomorrow. Sleep well.'

He lifted an arm to acknowledge the kind gesture from Frank and disappeared along the corridor.

This is it. It's time, Frank thought. He moved out of the bar and stood in the foyer, looking towards the double doors leading to the rooms. The hallway was empty, as was the front desk. It would be extremely unusual for someone to come in at this time of night. All the same, Frank moved to the front door and turned the sign over. "No vacancies" displayed towards the street.

Frank left the front door unlocked and tapped the alarm code into a pad, an aide to warn him if Carrie came in. The hotel and bar was advertised as open twenty-four hours. One of the reasons Frank stayed overnight. People could check in any time they liked. Especially if there were rooms unoccupied. Carrie would be enraged if she knew. Frank wondered how he'd explain the sign if she turned up. He'd say he made a mistake, that he'd cleaned the windows, and it flipped over.

But there was a reason Frank Tully turned the sign in the window, averting people from coming into the hotel at night.

* * *

Frank stood in the foyer, again checking along the hallway. Then he moved towards the double doors and down to the rooms. He edged past each one, listening at the doors, making sure there was silence.

He walked to the end of the hallway, past ten rooms, and opened the storeroom on his right. Stepping inside, Frank turned the key behind him, and locked the door.

He felt the rush of excitement, the elation as he moved towards the steps and began to climb. At the top of the stairs, he ducked into the eaves, a secluded area between both floors, the musty smell working into his lungs, avoiding the hefty cobwebs, the nails in the floor and crawled on his hands and knees until he reached the first room.

Frank did this every night. He loved to watch the guests. He'd seen so much over the past year and had gotten to know the guests intimately. He'd made small holes in the ceiling before reopening the hotel. Peepholes, or his gateway to ecstasy as he liked to call them. He'd watched. Often for hours. Captivated. He saw couples making love, the passion intense and demonstrations for him to take away and play out with Carrie. It made their lovemaking sessions so much more thrilling. He'd watched gay couples, lesbians, threesomes, onesomes, all on show at his hotel. If Carrie ever found out, she'd kill him. She'd most certainly leave him and report him for his perverse traits.

But she'd never find out.

How could she?

This was Frank's hotel. He ran it at night.

So why shouldn't he enjoy all it had to offer.

Placing his eye to the ceiling of the first room, he balanced on the old wooden beams and lay flat on his stomach.

A woman had come out of the shower. Her hair was held

with a towel, and she wore the hotel's dressing gown. He could see The Oak Hotel's emblem on her right breast. She moved across the room and sat on the bed. The telly was on, and she began flicking channels with the remote control. In her hand, she held a small glass. It looked like she'd filled it with a gin and tonic from the minibar.

Frank watched as she opened her phone and read a message. Then she began laughing to herself.

She'd been here for the last three nights. Frank had watched her as she checked in, dressed impeccably, and he recalled her sweet perfume. The last couple of nights, she'd gone to bed early. Frank had missed her with the late nights in the bar.

Now, he imagined opening her bedroom door, moving towards her and kissing her passionately while opening her dressing gown.

She got up, moved towards the door and turned off the lights.

Shit. I don't believe this. Turn the lights back on. Frank lay on his stomach, pissed off that she'd gone to bed so early.

He lay still for over a minute, then pressed against the beams and pushed himself upwards. On his hands and knees, Frank began to crawl gently along the void. He often feared he'd drop through, landing on a bed or the floor and having to explain his actions. He was catching a rat or sorting the air conditioning units. *Yeah, that would wash in September,* he thought.

As he edged across the void, his body low and his eyes watching below, he saw darkness in the next room. Frank waited. He'd learned that sometimes the silent rooms often produced the most excitement. He recalled a couple in their fifties had checked in for a week. The first few nights, nothing exciting had happened. But then, he waited, watching through the darkness. After about twenty minutes, the lights came on. She was dressed in a catsuit and had a whip in one hand. She threw the blankets back and began to thrash her husband. He woke, frightened out of his wits. He asked what on earth she was doing, and she replied that she'd always wanted to try it. He got out of bed and left the hotel. Frank had laughed so much to himself that he thought he'd been heard.

Now, he waited, listening to the heavy snores; he pushed off the floor and crawled to the other side of the eaves.

Room Nine. The couple who had checked in late, refused food, breakfast in bed and a newspaper. The lights were on.

The guy was lying on the blankets in his underwear. Frank hoped this room had the potential to liven up. He scanned the room from above, looking for the woman. Frank remembered her shyness, and how she hid behind her partner at the main desk.

He watched as the guy closed his eyes, appearing to sleep.

Suddenly he heard a door open. For a second, Frank thought someone was beside him in the void. It was impossible. He'd locked the door.

Then he realised the sound was coming from below, in room nine. He watched as the woman came out of the bathroom and stood, looking out over the gardens. The spotlights gave a sense of calmness. Again, she wore one of the complimentary dressing gowns. She was in her bare feet, just staring out of the window.

The guy was still lying on the bed, eyes closed and his body still. Frank thought they were an odd couple. In the time they'd arrived at the hotel, they'd never even looked at one another, no communication, no intimacy. Like they were strangers.

Maybe she's an escort, Frank thought.

He waited, becoming impatient. The woman continued staring out of the window. No movement, no words.

The guy lay still, eyes shut, motionless.

About to push his body off the floor, ready to give up and move to another room, Frank saw the guy open his eyes. He looked across the room and saw his partner.

Frank lay back down, keeping as silent as possible. He fought the buzz in his groin, fantasising what they'd do to one another. *That's better. Go on. Go to her. Pick her up and bring her to the bed.*

The guy got up off the bed. He looked towards the door, then back to his partner.

Frank watched as he grabbed the belt from his dressing gown on the floor.

Oh, kinky. Now we're talking. It's going to be a good night after all.

The guy began pulling it as if checking for its strength and then sneaked towards the window. He seemed to creep, like he didn't want her to notice him.

That's it, mate. You two like your games. What's the time, Mr Wolf? So what? She turns around at the last second, and you lift her and strap her arms to the bed? I like it, Frank thought.

The guy reached his partner. She remained still, looking out of the window. Suddenly, he lifted the belt and placed his hands over her head.

'No. What are you doing?' she squealed.

Frank watched in horror. It looked like her head was about to explode. She tried in vain to talk, to scream, but the guy lifted her off the floor and pulled the belt tighter around her neck.

Frank shuffled. He kicked something.

The guy moved backwards, all the time pulling on the belt. Then he looked up.

Scrambling to his hands and knees, Frank tried to stem the sound of horror coming from his mouth. He was petrified, certain he'd been seen.

Below, the guy dropped the woman on the floor. Her still, lifeless body lay there. He knelt over her, placing his hands on her neck and squeezed hard.

Frank vomited. He was never so frightened, gasping for breath and struggling to move. His eyes were glued to the dead woman in room nine.

Standing up, the guy casually walked across the floor and got into bed, barely glancing at the woman on the floor.

Then the lights went out.

Crawling back along the void, Frank moved down the stairs. He wanted to call the police. But they'd ask too many questions.

What were you doing up there, Sir? Why crawl around in the eaves and watch the guests? Kinky bastard, are you? You'll pay for this, young man. Wait until Carrie finds out. Sicko.

She'd leave him for sure. He'd lose the hotel, maybe serve some prison time.

In the supply cupboard, he bent over and vomited for a second time, worried the noise would draw attention as he wretched.

Frank wiped his mouth and went to the door. He pressed his ear against it, listening, worried the guy from room nine was on the other side.

Grabbing the keys from his jeans pocket, he counted

backwards from three and unlocked the door. He looked out, leaning forward and stared along the hallway. No sign of him. Had he left? Killed his partner and walked off, leaving her on the floor. If so, it wouldn't be long until someone found her.

Frank walked along the hallway, past the first couple of rooms. Standing outside the door of number nine, he contemplated what to do, frantically trying to work out a plan. This man had killed his partner in his hotel.

It was Frank's problem now. He had to deal with it.

Suddenly he heard something. A noise further along the hallway. Frank turned and charged to the end of the corridor, back to the door leading to the eaves. He grabbed the keys with his fumbling hands, trying to push them into the lock. He dropped them on the floor, and then pressed his body against the locked door, trying in desperation to hide.

Frank faced the door, his hands and feet positioned like he was performing a star jump, stuck in mid-air, slammed against the door, a squashed cartoon character.

He listened as the footsteps approached. Any second now, whoever was out here would see him. Frank desperately tried to stem the vomit which threatened to project from his mouth once more. *No. Please don't. Not now. Please.*

A door opened along the corridor. Frank waited, holding his breath, his heart punching hard in his chest.

A door closed.

Gradually moving, he peeled himself away from the door, looking towards room nine, watching, anticipating what would happen next. Surely the guy was going to leave? But what if he didn't? What if he slept by the corpse all night, huddled into her?

Frank had to distance himself. Taking a deep breath, he

quickly strolled along the corridor, his head down and as silently as possible.

As he passed room nine on his left, he thought he heard the door move. Frank stopped, held his breath, hesitated, and then ran, looking back to ensure no one was there.

In the foyer, Frank moved around the desk and into the back office, locking the door. He sat on a rickety stool and watched the monitor. Cameras covered the hallway and foyer so he could see if the guy left the room.

Frank was still awake at gone 3am, too fearful of sleeping. He'd been staring at the monitor for hours, only breaking to use the toilet next door. In the time he'd been in the office, no one had come in or out of the lobby.

He was tired, and sick with worry that the guy from room nine had seen him. Frank was certain he'd looked up after killing his partner. If he had, if he'd heard Frank, he could be next.

He stood, leaning over the table, trying to think what to do. Should he go down there, knock on the door and see what the hell had happened? No. He wasn't brave enough, and besides, Frank was the only person who worked the night shift. He had no backup. The first people to arrive were Gus, (the chef), and the chambermaids at 7am. Four hours away.

Frank always stayed at the hotel overnight and dealt with any problems. But this was a problem. A huge, fuck up of a problem that he didn't know how to deal with.

He thought about going home, but he'd wake Carrie, and she'd be mad at him for leaving. Plus, his hands were tied. The guy in room nine may blackmail Frank to keep him silent about the murder. If he did, if Frank went to report what he'd seen, room nine guy could spill Frank's sordid secret. Carrie would find out about his grotesque hobby. Then what? She'd go up to the void, crawl through the eaves and see what a perverted bastard she'd married. Frank had to stay and face it himself. He had to take charge and—

His eyes darted back to the monitor. The double doors had opened, and a man walked along the hallway towards the front desk. It was the man from room nine. *Shit.* Frank checked the door to the office, making sure it was locked. He moved to the back wall and placed his hand over his mouth. On the monitor, he saw the guy walk to the desk and pause. He looked at the camera, wearing a dressing gown, his hair slicked back, then he smiled as if he'd been picked out at a football match. He mouthed something. Frank moved towards the monitor so that he was just inches from the screen. The guy was still talking into the camera.

He tried to make out the words he was saying.

I saw you. I saw you.

Was that it? Was that the sentence spilling from his mouth? Frank was uncertain. Suddenly, he felt claustrophobic, like the walls were locking together, pushing inwards and about to crush him like a vice.

Sliding his body down the wall, Frank collapsed on the floor. He placed his head in his hands, driving his fists hard into the carpet. He wanted to stay there for the rest of the night, but he raised his head again to watch the screen.

The man from room nine backed up a little. He gave one last smile at the camera, then he walked back through the double doors. Frank dropped his head back into his hands in relief.

* * *

Frank jumped; he opened his eyes and focused on his surroundings. He was sitting in the office, leaning against the wall and facing the locked door. He was cold and felt wrecked.

Looking to the security camera, he checked the foyer, the double doors leading to the rooms, then towards the front door. No one was visible on the screen. His wristwatch showed the time, 4.08am. He'd slept there on the floor for over an hour.

Moving to the computer, he rewound the live recording. He watched as the guy had moved towards the front desk, staring at the camera and mouthing something.

I saw you. I saw you.

Frank was sure that's what he was saying. Gripping the stool, he stood and walked towards the door, making certain it was locked. Frank pulled the handle and then began pacing back and forth in the office. He felt like a caged animal. How the hell would he get out of this situation? If Frank went to the police, he'd have to tell them how he saw the murder happen. Frank cursed himself for all of the nights he'd spent in the void above the rooms, watching. What kind of a man was he? Why did he do it?

Sitting back on the stool, he slapped his closed fist against his head. If this got out, he'd be ruined. Carrie would most certainly leave him. His hotel would be shut down. He may even be arrested.

Turning to the monitor again, he peered at the empty hallway.

He drifted off to sleep, waking every few minutes. His head ached from needing proper rest. He couldn't stop going over and over what had happened – he'd watched the guy in room nine murder his partner, then he looked up towards the ceiling.

He knows Frank saw everything.

* * *

In the early morning, The Oak seemed like such a tranquil, welcoming place, nestled in the bustling town of St Ives. All was quiet on the monitor, the camera recording nothing but emptiness.

Frank was locked in the back office, hiding.

The double doors leading to the rooms were closed.

At some point in the night, Frank had moved to the small, two-seater sofa against the back wall. He'd given in to the exhaustion, his body unable to cope any longer.

Something made him wake with a start and he jumped up in his seat, glancing at his watch. It was just after 7am. He peered towards the monitor and saw Kayleigh at the front desk, disabling the alarm. She'd asked Frank why he'd kept it on at night; his only answer was for security. She couldn't get to grips with the alarm going off every time a guest came in; Frank never explained.

Getting off the sofa, he moved to the mirror, relieved that someone was here with him. He felt safer now. He looked like death, a corpse which had been removed from a cemetery. Gaunt, pale and lifeless. He didn't recognise his reflection.

Taking a deep breath and trying to force his face to appear normal, Frank made his way to the front desk. 'Hi, Kayleigh. How are you this morning?' He felt more confident now; the terror began to ebb from his body at the sight of a familiar face and the morning light.

She gave him an enquiring look. 'Are you OK, Mr Tully?

You don't look well.'

'Me? No, I'm fine. Thanks for your concern. I'm good. Just a bit of a headache, you know. It will pass.'

'Shall I call Mrs Tully?' Kayleigh asked.

'No need to bother her. She'll be here shortly anyway.'

'Where shall I start?'

At the ordinary sight of Kayleigh in her work clothes, Frank had momentarily forgotten that there was still a body in room nine. He couldn't risk Kayleigh going in, finding it. It was too early for Frank to think, uncertain how to act. Or did the guy get rid of it? Also, he was sure the guy was still in the room. 'Eh, one second. Let's see.' Frank clicked the laptop pad and pretended to go to the diary. He pointed slowly down the screen. 'OK, the bar. Why not start there.'

Kayleigh looked across the foyer. The lights were out, and the door was closed. 'What about breakfast? Anyone sorting that out?'

Food had slipped Frank's mind. Any minute now, people may wander in and ask to eat. *Shit.* A surge of pressure pushed through his body. 'I'll start with some bacon, eggs, sausages, toast, that sort of thing. Would you mind helping to lay the tables before you start with the cleaning? Also, if you could place the cereal out on the side table and fill the juice machines. Sorry, Kayleigh, I'm usually on top of all this, but I'm not well.'

'It's fine. Pass me the key, and I'll start.'

Frank watched as Kayleigh made her way over to the bar and unlocked the door. She turned on the lights and moved to the small kitchen behind the bar area.

Frank stood watching the double doors leading to the rooms, hoping the guy from room nine had left while Frank had been asleep. Somehow, he doubted it. He heard the sound of jazz drifting from the bar area and Kayleigh moving around the room. Frank was grateful for her help. As he walked around the desk, the double doors opened. Frank stood as if paused; his heart raced, and his stomach tightened.

'Excuse me?'

Frank moved his eyes, then turned his body, mustering the strength to face the voice. 'Hi.' Frank blew a sharp breath from his lips. It was a guest who was staying upstairs. 'Good morning. How may I help?'

'What time is breakfast served?'

Frank looked at his watch. 'About ten minutes. We've just started, so you can come in and sit down if you like. What are you having?'

'Cereal will do us. We need to be somewhere. Maybe a pot of coffee too.'

'Absolutely. We're ready when you are.'

The guy thanked Frank and moved back through the double doors. Frank watched them close. Visions flashed in his mind, the woman moving out of the bathroom, standing by the window, the guy getting out of bed, removing the belt from his dressing gown and placing it around her neck. Pulling it tight.

His body jolted with terror. He recalled the man looking towards the ceiling, right at him. Later, the same man coming to the front desk and mouthing to the camera.

Frank wanted to run, to get out of here and never return. He'd taken such a stupid risk, watching the guests. He knew it was wrong, but like a magnet, he was drawn to the void above the rooms and felt he couldn't stop. The excitement was too much. The adrenaline was overbearing and so bloody powerful.

Frank needed to keep busy. If the man had any sense, he would have made a sharp exit in the brief time Frank had slept anyway. Or that's what Frank hoped with every fibre of his body. He could rewind the camera footage and check when he had time. But then, what about the body? It would only be a matter of time before one of the staff found her. How would Frank act? Could he be convincingly surprised? Or would his demeanour give away his sordid secret?

For now, he would concentrate on breakfast. Frank went across the foyer and into the back kitchen behind the bar area. He reached into the fridge, removing four packets of bacon, poured a generous amount of oil into three large pans and began to cook. The smell made him nauseous. He listened to the soothing sound of jazz from the radio and tried to relax, first tensing, then dropping his body.

He jumped as someone came behind him.

'Mr Tully. Someone has arrived. He wants the full works. An English breakfast,' Kayleigh instructed.

'Is he on his own?' Frank inquired.

'Yes.' Kayleigh left the kitchen.

Instead of cracking on with the sausages, Frank put his head around the door to the bar. He looked to where the man was sitting and felt the tension drop from his body like a broken lift. It was the old guy who'd been up drinking late in the bar. Moving back to the kitchen, he cracked some eggs into another pan, turned the sausages and bacon and popped bread into the toaster.

As he cooked, he listened to couples coming into the bar area and Kayleigh instructing them to the seats. She joined him in the kitchen to make coffee and tea.

Grateful for her help, Frank thanked her, again explaining about his headache. Kayleigh had applied for the job a few months ago, Frank conducting the interview. He'd already made up his mind before she'd sat down. Now, he realised he'd be lost without her.

Frank turned every few seconds, watching for the man in room nine. He was sure he hadn't come into the bar.

Normally, Frank would greet the guests, ask them about their plans for the day ahead, where they intended to go and recommend a few local attractions. He'd tell them about the history of The Oak and how he and Carrie had met. His wife would often join him if it was busy and add a little sarcasm to the conversation. Guests liked to know the history of the place, and he'd enjoyed acting like a tour guide.

But Frank wasn't in the mood this morning.

He needed breakfast to be over and the guy in room nine out.

Once breakfast had finished and the last guest had left, Frank returned behind the main desk. A few minutes later, he watched his wife's Volkswagen Polo pull into the parking space. He felt the world spin around him. Hiding what he'd seen and acting like nothing was wrong was going to be impossible. All Frank could see was visions of the beautiful woman lying on the floor. In his mind, she was already starting to decompose, the smell beginning to fill room nine. Placing his left hand on the desk, he tried to steady himself.

The front door opened, and Carrie's smile beamed towards him.

'Morning. How was your night?' she asked.

Bang. The question he'd been dreading. How was it, Frank? How was it?

Oh, you know, got to love spying on the guests; there's such a selection. Such an array of personalities to observe and admire. It's so satisfying, Carrie. Oh, before I forget, the couple in room nine. He killed his partner last night. She's dead on the floor. We might need to deal with that first. Can you imagine? Someone checking in and finding her? It might dissuade them from staying. It could even affect our Trip Advisor rating.

'Frank. Are you listening? Do you hear anything I say? How was last night?'

'Fine. All good. No problems. The last of the guests left the bar at around elevenish. I slept in the office after that.'

'Well, you look like shit,' his wife confirmed.

'Thanks.' Frank could feel his stomach turn, like he'd vomit again. He needed to get home, to sleep and forget about what he'd seen. He needed to act normal. 'Oh, Kayleigh helped with the breakfast this morning. She's great.'

'Why didn't she start on the rooms?' Carrie asked.

'Well, I needed her to help me. Gus isn't well. We had rather a rush on about seven-thirty, so I told her to leave the rooms until later.'

Carrie stared at her husband. 'Leave the rooms? I don't get it. It's the weekend, Frank.

What if there's an influx of guests and the rooms aren't clean?'

'I just needed help. It's no big deal.'

'It is if guests can't check in. Always be ready for the cavalry, Frank. You know that. Honestly, I'll have to go and start myself.'

'No. I'll do it.' The panic was almost paralysing. Frank watched as Carrie seemed to stare through him. Had she suspected something? He needed to remain calm, take a breath and sort this out. 'You wait here. I'll go and help Kayleigh. I owe her after her assistance earlier.'

The double doors opened. Frank turned. He saw a man wheeling a suitcase along the hallway.

Carrie smiled. 'Hi. Are you checking out?'

The guy nodded and remained expressionless. He walked in their direction.

It was him.

The man from room nine.

Staring, Frank became aware of his body trembling and tried to curb it. Attempting to turn one way, and another, the ground under his feet resembled quicksand with his shoes stuck. He felt hot, clammy, as if a spotlight was shining into his eyes.

Letting go of the suitcase, the guy moved close to where Carrie stood. Frank couldn't look at him; he was petrified. He glanced at the black suitcase, its wheels robust. The same one he wheeled yesterday. But it looked bulkier. Frank wondered if the dead body was inside. He imagined her twisted, like a contortionist, or worse still, cut into tiny pieces. He felt his stomach spinning.

Carrie tapped the keypad of the laptop.

He needed an excuse to leave; the awkwardness was too taxing.

'Frank, can you go to the back office and get a discount card?' Carrie glanced at the man in front of her. 'If ever you return, you get twenty per cent off your bill.'

No. Don't invite him back. Are you mad? What are you doing?

'Frank?'

'Huh?'

'The discount card. Go and get it.'

As he walked around the desk, Frank knew his legs were clumsy, and his body trembled with anxiety. Opening the door, he heard his wife total the bill. He listened as the man handed over cash, and a few seconds later, the printer began to churn out his receipt.

Grabbing a card, he listened to his wife making conversation. Joining her, he passed the discount card across without looking at his face.

'Did you and your partner enjoy yourselves?' Carrie asked.

'Yes, thank you.'

'Oh, where is she?'

Frank did everything to avoid passing out. His mind pleaded for Carrie to let him go, knowing she'd be inquisitive. It was the one question he didn't want her to ask. How would room nine guy answer this one?

Holding his breath, he could feel the colour drain from his face. He looked, braving it out and aware of the man's gaze.

He stared back, his lips forming into a curt smirk. 'She left us last night.'

The subtle hint, Frank thought. *The bastard is being smart. She left us. A play on words. Oh, you're good.*

'I hope she's OK? Leaving early, I mean?'

Frank listened to his wife, the endless questions, needing to know about the guests. *Keep quiet and let him leave, for Christ's sake. Shut up.* Frank willed her to close her mouth.

'She's fine. Her mother isn't well, so she had to go early. We'll be back, though.'

Frank watched him; the way he said the last sentence sounded a tad menacing.

Suddenly the guy looked at Frank, then to Carrie. 'I heard something last night. It seemed to come from above our room, in the ceiling?'

Feeling faint, Frank tried to keep a blank expression. He was worried he'd make a weird sound if he tried to say anything, or worse, shout for him to leave them alone.

Carrie continued. 'Oh? What did you hear?'

The guy looked at Frank. He kept silent for more time than was tolerable. Any second, Carrie would ask what was going on, suspicions filtering into her mind.

Frank wanted the ground to open and swallow him whole, never letting him out.

Finally, he broke the gaze with Frank. 'Rats, or maybe squirrels. One or the other. It usually is. But you can be sure they'll pay. Pests always lose in the end.'

Frank felt a convulsion power through his body.

Carrie handed over the receipt. 'Thank you for letting us know. We'll see to it. Make sure to come back soon.'

'Oh, I will. You can be sure of that.' The guy pushed the front door, dragging the suitcase behind him.

Looking at his wife, Frank expected her to say something about the odd behaviour or threat. But she hadn't seemed to noticed anything out of the ordinary.

Frank was just glad to see him leave.

'OK, we have to make a start on the rooms,' Carrie ordered. 'Gus has called in sick, its put us behind, so we'll give Kayleigh a hand.'

'I'll start at the end,' Frank announced. He grabbed the key from the drawer, needing to deal with room nine himself. He was unsure if the body was still there. What if she was lying on the floor? Frank had to go in and see.

'I'll come with you,' Carrie said.

He felt an ache develop in his chest. 'What? No, it's alright. Deal with the others.'

'I said I'm coming. Let's do it together. It will be fun.'

Frank followed Carrie along the hall, through the double doors and down to the back of the hotel. He tried desperately to rid the image of the woman lying on the floor from his mind, praying she wasn't still there.

As they passed room nine, he felt a tightness in his stomach. He inhaled, trying to smell any evidence, certain a body would begin to push foul odours into the air. He smelt nothing.

They entered room ten directly opposite. The bed had been made, and the minibar was untouched. After twenty minutes, they moved to the room next door.

As they entered room eight, Frank saw Kayleigh working her way towards them. She pushed a trolley loaded with cleaning aids, smiling at Frank.

'Not gone home yet, Mr Tully?'

'I've been roped into helping. Gus has let us down again.'

Kayleigh grinned, preferring not to say anything derogatory about the chef.

Room eight had been left much the same as room ten. A young couple had stayed. Again, the beds were made; they'd cleared their rubbish, hung the dressing gowns on the bathroom door and placed the used bath towels in a pile on the floor.

Frank was about to tell Carrie that he'd start in room nine when he heard a door open. His body tensed. Kayleigh was entering a room opposite. He watched as Carrie grabbed the bedsheets from the store cupboard. She ripped the old ones back, asking Frank to help her. As he moved towards her a scream rang out through the walls.

Frank grabbed his wife's arm. There was fear on her face. 'I have to tell you something,' he said hurriedly. 'Last night—'

Ignoring her husband, she dashed to the bedroom door.

'Carrie,' Frank shouted. 'Wait!'

Kayleigh was standing at the open door of room nine. Her phone was in her hand, and she was staring down at it.

'What's happened?' Carrie asked.

Frank appeared in the hallway, his face white.

'Oh my goodness. I'm sorry if I alarmed you,' Kayleigh laughed, a huge smile appearing on her face. 'My daughter is pregnant. They've been trying for so long. She was told she could never have children. But it's happening. It's finally happening.' She began to cry.

'My God. You scared the life out of me. I thought something had happened. Go on. Go and ring her. This is delightful news.' Carrie turned, seeing Frank standing behind her. 'It's great, isn't it?'

'It sure is. Completely wonderful news. I couldn't be happier. Truly wonderful.' He felt his body unwind.

Moving to Kayleigh, Frank used the excuse of a hug to peer into the room.

Room nine was empty.

* * *

Frank informed a still-grinning Kayleigh to continue with the rooms upstairs after she got off the phone to her daughter. He and Carrie would tackle room nine. First, they made the bed. They stripped the blanket and sheets away, replacing them with fresh ones. Then Frank brushed the hoover over the carpet while Carrie replaced the wet towels and topped up the toiletries.

Watching the window, visions of the blonde woman late last night flickered through his mind; stepping from the bathroom, the towel fixed around her head, wrapped in the complimentary dressing gown. The man rising, moving behind her. His hands holding the belt, then around her throat, her lying on the floor. He'd wheeled her out in the suitcase, bold as you like and under their noses.

As Frank pushed the hoover over the carpet, he bent forward, taking a closer look. There were no hairs, or bloodstains. Nothing to remotely show she was here last night. But Frank saw her. He had watched from the void above.

Her partner had strangled her to death.

'Frank?'

He turned, switching off the hoover. 'Yeah?'

'You'll wear out that section of carpet. It's clean. What's wrong with you today?'

'Sorry.' He picked up the hoover to take it back to the store cupboard.

In the hallway, Kayleigh was still on the phone, her eyes tearful as she kept repeating how *amazing* the news was.

'Erh, the rooms upstairs?' Frank insisted.

'Oh, yes. Sorry, Mr Tully.' Hurriedly saying goodbye to her daughter, she put the phone back in her apron pocket.

Hearing a bell, Frank edged past her and walked to the reception area. He stopped dead in his tracks, completely numb. The hairs rose on his arms, and he felt unsteady.

The guy from room nine was standing by the front desk, his icy blue eyes scanning the place. Another woman was stood next to him.

This can't be happening. It's not real. Get a grip, Frank. He slowly moved behind the counter, averting his eyes from the people in front of him.

The guy wore a smart suit. A black jacket and trousers with a white shirt. The woman he was standing with wore a knee-length skirt, cream coloured blouse and high heels. She had black hair, tied into a ponytail, and her face wore a blank, serious expression. Her dark brown eyes seemed uninterested in her surroundings. Like she was programmed to seem dull and disengaged with life.

Frank looked at the man. He gripped the same black suitcase, and the wheels spun awkwardly as he dragged it to the desk.

'I'd like a room, just for the night. Room nine if it's possible?'

Frank stuttered as he spoke. 'Er, I'm sorry. I think we're pretty booked up tonight.'

The guy stared straight through Frank. 'I'd like room nine again.' He gripped the handle of the suitcase, and Frank felt his stomach somersault.

Carrie came through the double doors. 'Hello. A room, is it?'

The guy slowly turned, and Carrie smiled.

'Oh, it's you. Back again so soon?'

Frank eyed his wife as if to tell her to keep quiet. 'I was informing the gentleman that we're pretty booked up. I think all the rooms are taken.'

Carrie moved around the desk and tapped the laptop pad. A moment later, the screen came on. She hovered her finger over the mouse. 'No. Room nine is free.' She looked up. 'It's all yours.'

Frank watched in horror as the couple took the key, walked along the hall and out through the double doors.

* * *

Frank stood in the back office, his hands leaning on the edge of the sofa, fighting a panic attack, breathing hard and struggling to get it together.

He wanted to go home and felt beyond tired. It wasn't safe. He couldn't leave the hotel with the psycho back in room nine.

His emotions were stretched, he'd hardly slept, and he felt physically wrecked.

The guy from room nine was audacious, fearless, and he was goading Frank. He wanted to call the police, tell them about last night, tell them everything that had happened in room nine. But the consequences outweighed his possibilities. Frank could lose everything. He knew it was selfish, but his predicament needed to remain hidden.

There was no doubt that, if he went to the police, the guy from room nine would blackmail Frank into taking back his statement. If Frank refused, he'd tell everyone how he watched the guests, and they would both go down. The police would only have to check the ceiling space and find his sordid set-up. Carrie would leave him, or she'd kick him out, and Frank's face would be all over the news.

Hotel pervert found guilty.

Eaves and leaves. Frank Tully kicked out by irate wife.

The Joke Hotel. Owner gets his kicks from snooping on guests at The Oak Hotel, St Ives.

Rank Frank is sank.

Frank wanks as he lies on the dank planks.

He stood to lose everything.

The guy was so brazen though, what was his game? He knew Frank had seen him, and now he was taking the piss as he knew too well that Frank couldn't say anything. He'd already murdered someone last night. Now the bastard was back with another woman.

Could Frank get to her, warn her that the guy she was sharing a room with was dangerous?

Frank's head was spinning. He was tired, confused, and he needed to sleep.

But he had to know what the hell was going on with the man in room nine.

* * *

Frank spent the day behind the counter, answering the phone and catching up on paperwork. Adrenalin kept him going and fighting the fatigue, but occasionally he power napped in the back office, grabbing a half hour when he could.

Later that evening, Carrie came out of the bar. 'Frank, Go home. I'll work the night shift. It's not a problem. You look like shit. Go on. Go home.'

His body felt fragile and sluggish. How he'd love to jump into bed, to pull the sheets up and listen to the radio, for his head to sink into the soft pillow and not wake until at least midday.

He inhaled, trying to wake himself up. 'I'm good. Go on. I'll see you in the morning. I'll sleep in the office when the guests have left the bar. Hopefully, it won't be too late.'

'Well, at least go into one of the empty rooms. You need rest, darling.'

'I'm fine. Go home,' Frank insisted.

Carried leant across the counter and kissed her husband on the cheek.

He watched her Volkswagen Polo pull out of the car park.

* * *

Thankfully the bar was quiet that night. Frank watched the last couple leave at 11.35pm. He switched the lights off and locked the door, fuelled by the earlier power naps.

The guy in room nine never left his room.

Now, Frank was going to check him out.

Moving down through the double doors, he stopped outside room nine. The floorboards were solid, so no one would hear him outside.

Frank placed his ear to the door. He could hear voices. A woman was shouting from the bathroom. Frank stepped away from the door and crept to the storeroom. He pulled the keys from his jeans pocket, opened the door and locked it behind him.

Then he climbed the steps up to the ceiling area. Usually, Frank felt aroused, his body drenched in excitement, but he only felt dread now.

Frank crawled along the eaves, breathing silently, keeping low until he'd reached room nine. The sounds of sex coming from another room did nothing for him tonight.

The bedside light was on, and he saw the guy lying on the bed, much the same way as he had last night. The woman he'd come in with was lying next to him.

Frank watched as they lay there silently. She held a mobile phone in front of her face, tapping the screen as if messaging someone. He was flicking channels on the telly with the remote control.

Lying on his chest, his arms out in front of him, Frank tried to get comfortable. He watched, trying to imagine what the deal was. This lunatic had come into his hotel with a woman last night. He'd walked up behind her, strangled her and obviously dumped her body in the suitcase, casually wheeling her out past the front desk. Frank felt annoyed; the frustration was ebbing inside of him. How dare this bastard abuse their hotel. It felt like he was laughing at him and Carrie. Frank had to do something.

He watched; his eyes began to feel heavy; any minute now, Frank would fall asleep. But he couldn't. What if he snored? He slapped his face to try and force the tiredness away. Then he pinched the skin of his hands. Roughly twenty minutes later, when Frank was about to give up, the woman got out of bed. She yawned, then headed into the bathroom and locked the door.

Frank pushed his body upwards, stretching, then lay back down. *Shit, had he been heard?*

Suddenly the guy looked up, directly where Frank was lying.

Frank watched as a smirk developed on his face. The guy lay on the bed and placed his arms behind his head.

Shit. Bloody shit, Frank thought. He needed to go, to get down from the ceiling void. He'd head to the office behind the main desk, lock the door and ignore the activities in room nine.

As he pushed himself up, the bathroom door opened. Frank saw the woman come out and stand by the window.

'It's so warm in here. I fancy a drink,' she confirmed. 'Can you pour me something from the minibar? Maybe a gin and tonic.' She wore the same skirt as earlier, but the high heels were gone.

Frank darted his eyes towards the man. He was getting out of bed. He watched in terror as the guy tiptoed towards where the woman stood.

No, no, no. Please. Turn around from the window. He can't. He can't do this again. Please turn around.

Frank watched as the man reached her. He lifted his arms, then he grabbed her around the throat and strangled her.

A minute later, her body slumped to the floor.

The guy looked up to the ceiling and smiled.

* * *

Lying on a ceiling beam, his body in complete shock, Frank was disorientated. His head ached as he closed his eyes. The woman at the window, strangled, lying on the floor of room nine. He'd seen her earlier at reception. She looked calm, removed from any emotion, unaware of the sick, twisted mind of the man she entered the hotel with.

Frank opened his eyes. He watched the guy walk back to the bed, then he peered up, looking where Frank lay.

Suddenly he left the room.

Shit. He's coming for me next, Frank thought. His heart raced, now beating hard. Pushing off the ground, he crawled backwards along the eaves, reaching the stairs. There was only one way out. He waited, listening for footsteps. Where had he gone? Was he waiting outside, ready to murder Frank too?

He placed his left foot on the stairs and crept to the bottom. He stood at the door and listened. Could he hear footsteps? Was the guy waiting on the other side of the door? Frank needed to get out of here. He needed to get to the office, lock the door and observe the security camera. Here, he could do nothing. There was no way of telling where the guy from room nine had gone.

Suddenly, he heard a tap on the door. Frank felt ill. He thought his legs would give way. He wanted to tell him to go, to leave him alone. As he opened his mouth, he struggled to muster the words, his lips quivered, and his throat was so dry.

Another tap on the door caused Frank to step back. He remained silent, gulping breaths to stem the panic which threatened to rise through his now weak, sleep-deprived body.

Remaining in the same spot, he waited to see how it played out. More taps, Frank tried to keep as quiet as possible. His eyes closed for a moment, hoping he'd wake from this terrifying nightmare.

Now there were heavy footsteps, becoming faint. A door closed. Whoever was outside the storeroom had gone.

He waited, hesitant to open the door. Too frightened to move in his own hotel.

Grabbing the keys, he gently unlocked the door, aware the slightest thud could expose him.

He stepped out into the hall, glaring along the corridor, then closed the door behind him and locked it. He began walking, watching the rooms to his left. The doors were closed. He reached room nine, about to explode with angst. As he passed the room, he was certain the door handle moved. Frank stopped, staring down at it. Did it? Did it move?

Frank waited briefly, then quickly crept to the double doors, watching behind him.

He pushed through the doors and into the foyer, making his way around the desk and into the back office. Frank locked the door, sat down and looked over to the security camera.

He wasn't going to get any sleep tonight either.

* * *

Frank was beyond exhausted. His whole body ached for sleep. He spent the night in the back office with the door locked and watching the security camera. He felt physically sick and worried he'd pass out. Frank wanted to close the hotel, lock up, go home and never return.

He and Carrie had run the place for almost two years. In that time, they'd never had a problem. The guests were always polite, always obedient to their rules, and in the bar at night, Frank couldn't recall a time when he'd had to ask drinkers to leave.

Now, his world had been turned upside down. The guy staying in room nine was a maniac—a psychopath of the highest order. How the hell was he going to deal with it? He needed to ban him from their establishment, but how could he do that without confronting him?

It was obvious the man had done this before. How many people had he murdered in how many hotel rooms? How many other women were there?

Frank was also annoyed at himself. If only he hadn't seen the events unfold in room nine at all. If only he'd had a night off from watching, of just kept going past their room, watching the other residents, getting his kicks, and then moving back to the office, he'd be none the wiser. Now, Frank was a part of it. He was a piece of the twisted story.

* * *

He glanced at his watch. Almost 7am. Kayleigh would arrive shortly. Guests would start to filter into the bar area for breakfast.

Frank watched the security camera, glued to the screen. The hotel's front door opened, and Kayleigh walked into the lobby. Again, she disabled the alarm. Gus, the chef, followed her. Thankfully it looked like he was feeling better.

Frank pushed out a heavy sigh, the cloud temporarily lifted from his head. He was safe for the moment. But it wouldn't last. There had to be a way to stop the bastard in room nine and get him out of here. Otherwise, what the heck had he planned next? To use The Oak as his evil lair? His sordid killing room here in St Ives?

Frank *had* to do something.

He moved to the office door and opened it, half

expecting the guy to be stood there, arms reaching for his neck. 'Morning Kayleigh,' he muttered.

'Morning. How did you sleep?' she asked with a smile.

'Oh, like a log. The last couple left the bar at about 11.30pm, so I had an early one,' Frank lied. He nodded to the chef. 'Morning, Gus. You feeling better, mate?'

Gus smiled. 'Yeah, I'm good. So what's been happening while I've been away?'

Frank took a deep breath. 'Nothing exciting.'

* * *

Carrie came in a short while afterwards. She looked at Frank; the shock was evident on her face. 'My God. You look like death. What's going on, Frank?'

He wanted to tell her, to break down and sob in her arms. The last two nights had been unbearable. He'd been petrified. He hadn't slept, and his nerves were shattered. He wanted to hold Carrie and cry into her shoulders. 'Nothing. I'm going to go home this morning. I'm struggling to sleep in the back office. I need my bed.'

'Well go. It's too much for you here every night. Maybe we should get more staff. That way we could spend more time together at home. We're able to cope. Go on; I'll see you later.'

As Frank bent forward and kissed his wife on the cheek, the double doors opened. He peered along the foyer and saw the man from room nine, walking towards him. Again, he wheeled the suitcase, and again he was alone.

Carrie smiled at him. 'Hello. Are you checking out?'

He nodded.

'Is it just you?' Carrie asked.

Frank felt like his body would catch fire; heat seemed to

penetrate through his skin. He couldn't look the man in the eyes. He turned his body away as the guy walked to the desk.

'My partner left early. She went out the back way. She had an emergency that needed attending to, but she'll be back.'

Yeah. I'm sure she will. I'd like to see how. I have to say something. I can't let this psycho just leave. What will he think of me if I don't say anything? Grab the suitcase, make up an excuse that you need to look in it. Go on, do it. Do it. As Frank turned, he watched Carrie pass him the receipt.

'Thanks so much. We hope to see you again shortly.' Carried moved around the desk and opened the office door.

The guy moved out onto the street, pulling the heavy looking suitcase behind him.

* * *

For the next few days, Frank was plagued with visions of the women who'd been strangled in room nine of The Oak Hotel. Their faces were the last thing he saw before he slept, and the first images when he woke.

He watched his back at home. When he drove, he looked for anything suspicious, and at work, Frank continuously stared at the front door. He felt nervous anytime the phone rang, and he kept the office door locked behind the desk while on the night shift, choosing to watch telly rather than spend time in the ceiling void watching the guests.

It was a new start. Frank couldn't do it anymore.

Six days had passed since the guy from room nine had walked out for the second time, pulling the suitcase onto the street and casually walking away.

It was Friday morning; Frank had finally slept through the night. The visions of the dead women had evaporated, and the guy from room nine was beginning to become a distant memory. He could almost believe that it never happened, that it was some awful, sordid nightmare.

Feeling almost good, Frank moved out of the office and greeted Kayleigh as she walked in. Gus arrived while they were talking, and the three of them started to prepare the bar for breakfast. Most of the rooms were occupied. Things were returning to normal.

As they served breakfast, Frank saw Carrie getting out of her Volkswagen Polo. She looked tired. Running the hotel was strenuous. They needed to spend time together, and the two of them sleeping separately was beginning to take a toll on their relationship.

Frank was going to take Carrie away. He'd ask Kayleigh if she could manage a weekend on her own, maybe he could get a temp in. It would give them a much needed break.

He turned, seeing Carrie's beaming smile as she stood in the foyer.

'Hey, handsome. How was last night?'

'Oh, the usual. A food fight in the bar, followed by a punch up and then a mass orgy in the hall. Nothing I couldn't handle.'

'So, you went to bed early and fell asleep watching telly?' Carrie laughed.

'You could say that,' Frank answered.

Usually, the guests left after breakfast. Carrie moved across the foyer and behind the desk, firing up the laptop, ready to greet them as they settled their bills. She watched as Frank came out of the bar, seeing how washed up he appeared. The night shift was taking a toll on his health, and she wanted to help.

'Frank, I thought you were going home. You look so

tired. I think we need to get help. Maybe someone else can do a few shifts during the week.'

He smiled. 'Maybe. It's trusting someone, though. They need to deal with fire alarms, trouble with the guests. I'm a light sleeper, so I hear everything. Right, I need to go and get the BMW sorted. It's booked in for an MOT. I thought I'd get it serviced too. Then I'll sleep. Are you OK here?'

She smirked. 'What's going to happen?'

He kissed her cheek and walked out to the car.

* * *

Frank went home and slept for most of the morning into the early afternoon, feeling much more alive. Once he'd dropped the car at the garage, he treated himself to a late lunch. He sat at the back of the cafe, scrolling the latest posts on Instagram and watching as families spilt in and out through the front doors. He went for a pie and chips, smothered in gravy, a pot of coffee followed by a cream tea, scones with jam and clotted cream.

He sat, thinking how lucky he and Carrie were. Although they spent a lot of time apart, they were fortunate to have such a lucrative business.

They'd worried after the summer holidays, but it didn't look like the cold winter months were slowing them down too much.

His phone rang, it was the garage calling to say the BMW was ready.

Settling the bill and leaving a decent tip, he grabbed the car and drove back to the hotel.

When he arrived back, Carrie had gone home. Kayleigh said she had complained of a headache and had ordered her to rest.

'What? And she listened to you?'

Kayleigh laughed.

'How is it looking? Are we busy?' Frank asked. He couldn't be bothered searching on the laptop. He needed to get dinner sorted, the tables prepared, and the drinks fridge stacked. He'd also need to change a couple of barrels.

'It's been steady. A few arrived earlier. I think most of the rooms are booked out. Carrie and I haven't stopped.'

'Are you OK to help with dinner? I wouldn't ask, but we're going to struggle with Carrie going home. I'll sort you out with the wages.'

'Yeah. Sure you will.' Kayleigh answered sarcastically.

'I will.' Frank watched as Kayleigh walked into the bar and began to lay the table. He answered a couple of phone calls. The first was a man asking about a specific date and if he could have champagne and flowers delivered to their room before they arrived. They were celebrating a wedding anniversary. The second was an elderly lady who asked if they allowed dogs.

As Frank ended the call, he glanced towards the double doors towards the back of the hotel. His world began to spin. Frank placed his hands on the edge of the desk, feeling like he'd collapse to the floor any second. The guy who'd murdered two women in room nine was standing on the other side of the doors, staring straight at Frank through the glass. He was grinning, goading Frank, making sure he could be seen.

Frank stood, trying to stabilise his body. He wanted to call the police, explain what this psychopath was doing in his hotel. How he'd brazenly walk in with a woman, murder her and bring the body out in a suitcase, as bold as you like. But the man knew Frank's sordid little secret. He knew what he did at night when the residents were locked up safely in their rooms. His hands were tied.

He had to do something. This was his hotel. He couldn't let it continue.

Frank moved around the desk and walked towards the double doors along the hallway.

The guy stepped back, moved into room nine and locked the door.

Standing outside, Frank braced himself, then tapped on the door with his left knuckles. He waited, then knocked again. 'I know you're in there. Open the door; we need to talk.' Frank knocked louder. 'I said, open the fucking door.' He waited, then pressed his ear to the wood. There was no sound coming from inside. 'This can't go on. It can't keep happening. I need you to leave. Do you hear me?' No answer. He considered getting the key from reception and forcing his way inside. But Frank was scared. He didn't know what he'd find. Backing away from the door, cursing to himself, he walked along the hall to the bar.

Frank helped with dinner; it was busy, and he needed to keep occupied while considering his next move. People were talking to him, but nothing registered. It felt like he watched himself from above, unattached from his body and unable to control the reins. He called Carrie to make sure she was feeling better. Her voice comforted him.

Once he and Kayleigh had served the last dish, he instructed her to go home, thanking her for the help. He kept an eye on the clock. It was almost 10pm, and the bar was half full. He had an awful feeling that tonight would be a late one.

At 11.50pm, Frank watched as a couple finished their last sip of wine from their second bottle. They thanked him on their way out.

This was it. Shut the bar and do what you have to do.

Turning the sign on the front door, Frank moved to the back office. Taking his phone from his jeans pocket, his hands trembling, Frank wiped the lens with a cloth. Swiping the camera app and activating the video recorder, he carried out a dummy run. He moved the phone around the office for a few seconds, ensuring the light was off and no beeping sound could be heard to alert anyone he was recording. Then he watched it back and deleted the footage.

He was good to go.

Frank walked along the corridor and pushed the double doors. As he passed room nine, he kept his eyes shut, his body was tense, and he prayed the door remained closed.

At the end of the hall, he removed the keys from his jeans, his hand shaking as he pushed it into the lock, turned it anti-clockwise and gently opened the door. Once inside, he shut it, leaning against it for a few seconds to prepare for what he had planned. Frank locked the door, turned and started climbing the ladder to the roof area. Then he crouched, balancing on his hands and knees and crawled across to room nine.

He was going to record tonight's events. It was the only way Frank could get one up on the guy in room nine. The only way he could take control, threaten him to stop. If he had everything recorded, the guy could never report Frank for his sordid secret. He'd scrub the void area to within an inch of its life, leaving behind no evidence and denying everything. If he were asked by the police how he'd made the recording, he'd say there was a complaint of rats scurrying around in the void, and Frank needed the recording for pest control. And that he'd heard a commotion below, recording the murder. He had it covered.

Frank would hold all the cards.

This was it.

He had to put an end to it.

He peered from the void into the room below. His heart pumped so hard he could almost hear it, and he imagined falling through the ceiling onto the bed. He needed to keep focused, take charge and record what room nine guy was doing.

Frank waited; ten minutes passed, twenty. The sidelight was on, and the guy was lying on top of the bed. Suddenly the bathroom door opened.

Frank grabbed the camera and started to record.

A woman walked out of the bathroom. She wore a dressing gown. Frank watched as she turned towards the guy in the bed. Opening the dressing gown, she dropped it to the floor, standing naked and slowly walked towards him.

Frank's mouth was jammed open in shock. He dropped the phone beside him, making a thud on the ceiling.

The guy looked up as he stood and moved towards the woman, and then he removed his clothes.

The woman was Carrie.

Frank watched as the couple made love on the bed. He felt revulsion. He'd never despised or hated someone more. He wanted to pummel the guy to within an inch of his life. But Carrie. He'd never expected this. How long had the affair been happening? How the hell did these two get together?

She was lying on the bed, with him on top. The guy knew Frank was watching and was putting on a show.

When they finished, he got off her and lay beside her on the bed.

Frank could hear them talking.

'Aren't you worried your husband will find out?'

'How?' Carrie laughed. 'He's asleep in the back office.

Anyway, it makes it more exciting.' She kissed his neck, his cheeks and finally his lips. Then she left the room.

Frank crawled back along the floor, sobbing. He'd never been so humiliated in his life. This would end everything. There was no coming back. Frank was going to leave her. He'd sort out the hotel, split the money and run.

He climbed down into the store cupboard and vomited on the floor, then sauntered back to the office.

* * *

Frank spent the night awake, watching the security monitor. He was in a daze, staring, mystified at what had happened. The hours dragged as he sat on the sofa, watching the walls, the door, unable to feel emotion. His world had caved in, turned upside down and spat him out. He hated the guy for what he'd done. But he hated Carrie just as much.

In the morning, when Kayleigh arrived, he walked to the front desk and gave her orders for what needed doing. He didn't bother ringing Carrie. He couldn't face hearing her voice. At this moment, he despised her.

He stood behind the desk as the guests filtered out, taking their card details as they settled their bills.

The guy from room nine pushed through the double doors and walked towards the desk. As Frank saw him, he signed to Kayleigh to take his cash while he moved to the back office and locked the door. He couldn't face him. The bastard had used his hotel for his sick perversion and then seduced his wife. Frank didn't have the guts to talk to him.

He watched him leave on the monitor, and then Frank dropped onto the sofa, crying.

* * *

Frank had another shock later that morning. The guy entered the hotel with another woman. She was much the same as the other two he'd brought here. Tall, well dressed and completely stunning. He noticed her long, blonde hair reaching her buttocks. She was breathtaking. Too stressed and emotional for an argument, frightened of what the guy would do if Frank confronted him, he moved to the back office and phoned Kayleigh, asking her to come to the front desk and check them in. Frank had to think, to get everything straight in his head. He told her he'd explain later.

Frank left the hotel, got into his BMW and sped out of the car park.

He needed to get away.

The pressure was becoming too much.

* * *

Frank returned to The Oak Hotel while dinner was being served.

Kayleigh saw him while in the bar and moved towards him. Her face was bright red, and her skin was glistening with sweat.

'Frank. What's going on?'

'Nothing. I'm sorry. I just needed fresh air. I have a migraine, and I'm struggling.' He moved along the foyer and out through the double doors towards the back of the hotel.

* * *

It was late; Kayleigh and Gus had managed the bar by themselves. The final guests had left. Frank had been missing all night and Carrie hadn't been in all day.

Kayleigh removed her phone from her handbag and

rang him for the third time. Again, she heard his voice asking to leave a message. She didn't leave one. She glanced at her watch. It was gone midnight, and she was peeved that Frank had left her to it. She'd called Carrie earlier in the evening, asking her to come over, but again, she couldn't get through.

Pushing her arm through her handbag, she fixed her headscarf and walked out the front door.

* * *

The guy in room nine lay on the bed. He stood, moving like a predator across the room towards the window. Turning, he peered at the bathroom door, clutching the belt from his dressing gown. Waiting patiently, excited, the buzz clawing its way through his body, he tapped on the bathroom door. 'How long are you going to be?' he asked.

The bathroom door burst open.

'What the fuck?' he shouted.

Frank saw the shock on the guy's face, hearing the gasp. He drove a knife straight into his chest, then pulled it out and stabbed him a second time.

The knife dropped to the floor.

So did the guy in room nine.

* * *

Earlier that morning, Frank had left the hotel, telling Kayleigh he had a migraine and needed fresh air. Frank was distraught. Not only had the guy murdered two women in The Oak Hotel, in *his* hotel, but he also seduced his wife and made love to her while he knew Frank was watching.

Frank had tried to record the guy in room nine and his

next murder to hold as evidence if he attempted to black-mail Frank. He'd lose everything if it got out that he watched the guests at night.

If the guy in room nine threatened to tell Frank's sordid secret, Frank would have protection via the recording. That way they could both keep quiet.

But it had gone so drastically wrong.

Knowing Carrie was at home after telling Kayleigh she was unwell, he pulled up at the drive, saw her Volkswagen Polo and went into the house. He wasn't going to tell her what he'd seen, her and room nine guy together. When he brought her tea in bed, he acted as normal as possible, adding a few of his sleeping tablets to knock her out. Frank could do what he needed to do without Carrie catching him.

He left when she'd gone into a deep sleep, Carrie missing all of Kayleigh's phone calls.

The plan was set in motion.

Later that evening, when Frank returned to the hotel, he saw the woman from room nine going to the bar to buy a sandwich. Frank called her aside and explained that he suspected the guy of bringing women to the room and hurting them in sordid sex games.

After the shocking revelation, she walked out without returning to the room.

In the car park, Frank smashed the guy's car window with a brick and instructed Kayleigh to knock on the bedroom door to let him know his alarm was sounding. Frank then slipped into room nine and locked himself in the bathroom.

When the guy returned to the room, Frank could hear him shouting, furious at what had happened to his car.

Lying on the bed, the guy sipped a beer from the minibar and fell asleep.

Frank had waited in the bathroom for hours.

Finally, the guy woke, moving across the floor towards the window and tapped on the door.

The bathroom door burst open, and Frank stabbed him.

* * *

The following morning, Frank woke early and walked to the foyer; finally, he felt fully rested.

'Morning, hun. Wow, I have a throbbing headache?' Carrie was standing behind the counter.

Keeping silent, Frank walked to the desk.

'Are you OK? What's going on?' she asked.

'You keep asking me the same question. I'll show you exactly what's going on, shall I?' He removed his phone from his jeans pocket and opened the video clip. He pressed play and watched Carrie's jaw almost hit the floor. It was a short clip of her and the guy in room nine. Frank had filmed them in a clinch before dropping the phone. It was all the evidence he needed.

She tore her head away; a look of pure shock on her face. 'Frank, I'm so sorry. It was only the once. Please. You have to believe me.'

'I need to deal with some shit. When I come back, I expect you gone.'

She watched as Frank left the hotel through the front doors, pulling the bulky suitcase behind him.

The End

SEANCE

4

Chelsy Tucker stood at the window of her one-bedroom flat in Islington, North London, looking over Angel tube station. The traffic on the road was pretty much a standstill. Pedestrians weaved around each other on the pavement, and a light drizzle of rain sprayed against her window as she stared below.

Reaching into her pocket, she removed her mobile phone and tapped Daisy's name. They'd been friends since school and were now at Uni together.

Daisy studied law and dreamed of working for a top London firm, while Chelsey elected a fashion course and had already begun working on her clothing brand. She sold garments she'd designed on her social media platforms and already had enquiries from local high street shops.

Chelsey listened to the ring tone, loud in her ears, waiting with unease and apprehensive for this evening. They'd booked a Seance for Annette's birthday. A girl they'd bonded with at Uni. It was something they'd spoken about for ages. Having all lost loved ones, they'd wondered if it was possible to contact the dead. It was time to find out.

Daisy answered, her voice vibrant and energetic. 'Hey. All set for tonight?'

Chelsey was nervous. She'd never dabbled with the occult. She was fearful of how it would go but reluctant to admit it. 'Oh, God. I don't know.' They laughed, the nervous energy evident as it dawned on them what they were about to do. 'I am worried, you know?' Chelsy added.

'Yeah, me too. But it will be fun. See it as an adventure. It will be one tick off the long bucket list we've accumulated.' Daisy was trying to lighten the mood; she could hear in her friend's voice she wanted to back out. 'What time does it start?'

'8pm. Why don't you call here on the way? I've got a bottle of wine. Come over about six-six thirty. I think I'll need a drink.'

Daisy laughed. 'You're on. See you later.'

The phone went dead.

Next, Chelsy rang Annette. She asked her to call at the flat too, but Annette said that she wouldn't get away from work until around seven, so they agreed to meet there.

After the call, Chelsy glanced at her watch. It was just gone 5pm. Dread began to fester deep in her stomach and she wondered again if she could back out. But it was too late to cancel, and besides, Daisy was right. It probably *would* be fun. It was something they'd wanted to do for so long. The medium came highly recommended by Darren Fletcher, another of their Uni friends who Daisy had the hots for.

Darren found her through a friend of a friend; he'd gone to the séance with an ex-girlfriend and said Miriam Yau was amazing. She'd contacted an uncle of Darren's who'd died many years ago and said things only he could know. Apparently, she was worth every penny—his words.

Chelsy opened the laptop, her body tingling with nerves

and excitement, and tapped Miriam Yau's name into the search bar. She scrolled down the page, finding her website, which she clicked into. The headline read, "Why wait? Don't let death be the end. Use me as a portal and communicate with your loved ones."

Chelsy read the quote a second time. A shiver darted through her body. It was strong, hard-hitting, and a claim she was curious to discover for herself.

She closed the laptop, not wanting to spoil the evening. She'd been guilty of it many times before, reading reviews, articles and star ratings for restaurants, bars, and theatre shows, only to be met with major disappointment.

She'd go in blind and enjoy the experience.

* * *

After taking a shower, Chelsy dressed in a pair of faded black jeans and a light jumper. Although a fashion designer, she wanted the look uncomplicated tonight. Sitting at the dressing table in her bedroom, she straightened her long, brown hair, then added a touch of lipstick, blusher and pencil to highlight her deep green eyes.

Chelsy gazed out of the window; the rain had eased off, and it began to get dark.

* * *

The doorbell rang at 6.25pm. Chelsy looked through the spy hole of the front door and opened it. The smell of her friend's perfume made her cough. Daisy held a bottle of red wine and a large bag of Doritos. She wore a long blue dress with flat shoes, and her fiery red hair draped over her shoulders.

'Hey. You look great,' Chelsy said.

'So do you.' Daisy followed Chelsy into the living room. 'Oh, I'm nervous. I don't know what to expect.'

'Me too.' Chelsy turned, seeing the excitement on her friend's face. 'She's supposed to be good. If anything, it's a night out.' Chelsy took the wine, then grabbed two glasses from the kitchen unit above the sink and began to pour. Placing the drinks down on the table, she grabbed a plate for the crisps. 'So, how was your shift?' Daisy worked in a local cafe during half term to bring a bit of extra money in.

'Oh, boring. I don't know how much more I can take. The owner's a bit of a creep. He's always leering, you know.'

'Really? Well, complain about him. Threaten to put it on social media if he doesn't stop.'

'I would, but I have no proof. He's just weird,' Daisy said. 'And anyway, It's only for another few days. We'll be back in Nottingham soon.' She looked around, noticing how clean the flat looked. The kitchen was large with a window that looked out over Islington High Street. The walls were a bright white and spotless. Fashion pictures hung, showing the latest designs and trends which Chelsy had created. The living room was spacious, with a long, brown corner sofa. A flat-screen telly hung on the wall, and an artificial fire added warmth. Daisy was envious. They came to London every half term when Uni finished. Chelsy's parents had died when she was young, hence, the flat they'd left her in their will and why she'd often mentioned wanting to talk with a medium. Daisy had wanted to stay here, but a one-bedroom apartment made it impossible. Her parents had moved to Spain a few years ago so whenever in London, she stayed at a hostel in Islington, a couple of miles from Chelsy's flat.

They sipped their wine, talking about the last week at

Uni. The lectures, their future plans and their latest love interests.

'How're things progressing with Darren?' Chelsy asked.

Daisy curled her feet under her bottom on the sofa. 'Oh, they're not. I don't know. It's like there's always a brick wall that's hard to break down.'

'Keep smashing it.' Chelsy insisted. They laughed, sipping more wine and eating crisps. Chelsy looked at the clock. 'Right. You ready?' She saw the tense expression on her friend's face.

'Yeah. Let's do this.'

* * *

They took a taxi which brought them the scenic route. The guy was rude and uninterested in conversation. Chelsy watched as the fare moved like a petrol pump display, the numbers jumping like bare feet on hot coals.

They arrived on a quiet side street in Swiss Cottage. Chelsy and Daisy got out without thanking the driver or leaving a tip. He sped off as the back door closed, the wheels spinning like a hamster on speed.

Grabbing her phone from her jeans pocket, Chelsy opened the notes app and found the address. 'I think it's across there.' She pointed to a large, semi-detached house at the end of the street. It looked dark and unoccupied. The lights were off, and the front window was boarded up.

'This can't be the place,' Daisy insisted. 'It's like a squat.'

They stood outside, hesitant of approaching the front door.

'I'm sure this is it.' Chelsy looked to the top window. She gasped as she spotted a figure there. A woman with long, dirty-looking hair, and a pale complexion stood, motionless, peering down at them.

Chelsy looked away, turning to face the other side of the road. 'Let's go. I don't feel good about this.' She turned back. The woman was gone.

'Let's give it a go. If we don't feel comfortable, we can always leave.'

The front door opened after Daisy knocked confidently on it three times. She walked forward, followed by a reluctant Chelsy.

'You've come for a reading?' the lady asked. Her hair was lengthy, greasy-looking; her face a ghostly pale complexion with heavy bags under her dark brown eyes. She grinned, revealing her blackened teeth, one of them pushed outwards, almost hanging on her bottom lip. She was short and bony looking, giving a deathly appearance.

'That's right.' Chelsy introduced them both.

'Come this way.' The woman turned and started walking through the house.

As the girls were making to follow her, another taxi pulled up.

Annette jumped out of the back, an enthusiastic look on her face, the passion evident. 'Hey, you two. Sorry if I'm late,' she called over while paying the driver. She walked to Chelsy and Daisy, still standing on the doorstep, hugging them both a little too tight. She wore a knee-length black skirt, ankle boots and a white blouse. Her black hair was tied back, and she wore minimal make-up. Her skin was clear, lightly tanned, and her deep brown eyes were full of anticipation.

'Wow, calm down.' Chelsy laughed. 'I can feel the energy coming off you.'

'Thanks for this. I've been looking forward to it for ages,' Annette insisted. 'Right. Let's go.'

The three women stepped over the threshold and closed the front door.

* * *

The hallway was dark, but a dim light shone in the kitchen towards the back of the house. They were whispering, feeling like they were walking through a fright night experience.

'Where did that woman go?' Annette asked.

'This is ridiculous. I can't see anything.' Daisy pressed her left hand to the wall and used it to guide her way along the house. Annette and Chelsy bundled close behind.

The smell was musty and damp. The air felt toxic, as if full of disease. The floorboards underneath their feet bowed as they stepped on them and seemed to groan at their presence.

'Hello?' Daisy asked. Her patience was wearing thin and it was evident in her tone.

As they reached the living room door, they jumped at the sight of the old lady standing there.

'This way.' The old lady moved to a circular table. A small sidelight hanging on the wall provided just enough light for them to see. She sat, beckoning for her guests to join her. 'Don't be frightened, children. That's it. Take a seat and make yourselves comfortable.' She watched the apprehensive faces join her.

They took their seats, facing the old lady.

Chelsy felt vulnerable with her back to the door. 'I'd like to turn the table —'

'Hush. Please don't interrupt the spirits. They are sensitive and don't like change,' the old lady snapped.

Daisy wanted to make light and come back with a sarcastic answer. *Well, death kind of put pays to that.* She chose to keep her thoughts to herself.

'I'd like to start by welcoming you all to this session.'

Chelsy watched as the old lady grinned. Her mouth was hollow, her face set with heavy wrinkles, and she watched the tooth almost pointing at her. Her eyes were small, directing slightly towards each other, and her long hair almost flicked sweat at them when she turned her head. She looked like she hadn't washed for weeks. It wasn't how Chelsy had imagined her after seeing the modern looking website.

The old lady pulled her seat closer to the table and asked everyone to hold hands. 'We need to form a circle. It helps to communicate. The ring is everlasting, a sign of infinity that never ends. A bit like the souls who have departed, they never leave us.'

Daisy looked to Chelsy, wanting to laugh. The evening was weirder than she could have ever imagined.

The old lady continued. 'I want us to close our eyes—all of us. Now, please can you concentrate on someone who has passed. Someone you were close to while they were here. Please, keep your eyes shut tight, relax, let your thoughts take their own path and think of that person. It could be a friend, a relation, a school teacher—anyone you'd like to communicate with. I am the channel, the radio that will tune in to the correct frequency. Like a knob being turned.'

Daisy burst out laughing.

The old lady opened her eyes, staring directly through her and tutted. Daisy blushed; her red face was visible from the wall light which shone towards them.

'I see a woman. She's in pain.'

Again, Daisy smirked.

Chelsy was beginning to get pissed off with her friend. She let go of the circle and gently nudged her in the ribs.

'Sorry,' Daisy whispered.

They held hands again, sealing the circle.

'The woman is in pain. She's old, she's lying on the kitchen floor, and she's reaching forward. She wants to talk. I can see her so clearly. She's wearing a white nightdress, arms outstretched, her hands clasping at the air. Her fingers are long, bony; she's got arthritis. Oh, I can see her face. Her eyes, there's blood dripping from the sockets.'

Daisy jumped. She wasn't smirking anymore. The last sentence was so poignant. She opened her eyes and looked directly at the old lady. 'There's blood dripping from her eyes? Is that what you said?' She pushed back on the chair, holding the edge of the table. 'I know who it is.'

The old lady continued as if Daisy hadn't spoken. 'She wants to talk. She's so desperate to reach out. It's why her arms are extended. She's begging to be heard. Oh my goodness, her eyes.'

Daisy was uncomfortable. She squeezed Chelsy's hand so tightly. She began to gasp for air and stood for a moment. Once she'd composed herself, she sat back down.

'The old lady continued. 'There was an accident—a horrendous injury. I hear loud voices, deafening. A man is shouting at her. He's pushing her up against the kitchen worktop. She's trying desperately to get away from him.'

Daisy began crying.

The old lady stopped talking.

'It's my Grandmother. She died after an intruder broke into the house. I—'

'Please don't interrupt her. They can go as easily as they

come. We must give them priority over everything this evening. Let them speak. She's fighting with this man. He's tall, heavyset, with thick grey hair. He has a moustache. I can hear a little girl's voice. Giggling. She's telling him it looks like a moth. She's pulling it, trying to take it off.' The old lady's voice elevated in tone. 'Granddad, it looks silly.'

Daisy pushed her body forward; tears began to fill her eyes. 'It's me. It's what I used to say.'

'She's in the kitchen. This man is still leaning against her, pressing her body into the worktop. He turns, then moves to the cupboard behind him. He's grabbing a glass. She's so frightened; her body is tense, her face so desperate. She wants to get away, but she's petrified of this man. He's got the glass in his hand. Now, he's smashing it against the edge of the worktop. He moves to her; his bulky frame is too hard for her to get around. *No. Don't. You can't. I beg you. Don't do this. We can work it out. I swear, we can work—* He's rammed the glass into her face. It's destroyed. She's lying on the kitchen floor as blood streams from her eyes. Her poor eyes.' The old lady became silent.

Sobbing, Daisy announced, 'It was my grandmother. How do you do that? How can you know these things? But you're wrong. The story is incorrect. It was a burglary that went wrong. She woke in the early hours and was killed. The intruder pushed a glass in her face, but it wasn't my grandfather. He was kind.' Daisy raised her voice to a scream. 'He was kind, do you hear me?'

'I think it's time for a break,' the old lady insisted. 'Let's take five. We can make another circle shortly.'

* * *

Furiously pushing her chair back, Daisy stood. Chelsy and Annette followed her out of the living room, along the hallway and out of the house.

Chelsy reached her arm forward, placing it on Daisy's shoulder. She was shaking, and Chelsy sensed the agitation. 'Are you OK?'

Drying her tears with the sleeve of her top, Daisy said, 'It wasn't my granddad. He was kind. He'd never have glassed her. There was a burglary that went wrong. She came down the stairs, surprising the intruder. She was stabbed in the face.'

Chelsy looked at Annette. They didn't say anything, but both women knew what the other was thinking. Chelsy wanted to ask if Daisy believed her grandmother had come through during the seance to tell her what really happened. Realising Daisy was too upset to answer such a question, Chelsy chose to keep it to herself.

The three women stood on the front doorstep, their bodies shaking with a combination of cold, emotion and excitement.

'It's so weird, isn't it?' Annette stated. 'Christ, she's good.'

Turning, Daisy said, 'She's got the story wrong. She can't be that good.'

Annette didn't bother to answer; instead, she asked what the plan was afterwards.

'I say we hit a bar and then maybe a club. It's your birthday. Come on, let's make the best of this while we're here,' Chelsy insisted.' Let's not take it too seriously. It's meant to be a bit of fun.'

Daisy smiled and nodded. Her face was smudged with mascara, and her nose was wet.

The old lady appeared behind them, causing the women to jump. 'It's time,' she stated.

Daisy was unsure whether to go back inside, but she didn't want to spoil it for the others.

Chelsy walked in first, followed by Annette and, finally, Daisy.

The old lady stood at the table. 'Please, take a seat.'

'We don't want to face the wall,' Chelsy insisted. 'We don't feel comfortable, and my friend is a little freaked out.'

'It's not advised,' the old lady said, her voice sounding somewhat sinister.

'Then we leave.'

Annette and Daisy joined the table.

'Very well. As you wish. But you have been warned.'

Chelsy didn't bother replying. They moved around to the other side of the table. The old lady sat opposite them, now facing the wall.

Once they were all seated, they were asked to form a circle again. The friends held hands, clasping each other tightly; their discomfort was obvious. Daisy had freaked out with the earlier revelations, and they were all feeling dubious about continuing.

The old lady closed her eyes, ordering the others to do the same. Throwing her head back, she began muttering under her breath. 'I see a woman. She's asleep. Her bed is large, a four-poster. She's tossing and turning. I hear her calling out, asking for it to leave, but it won't go.'

Opening her eyes, Chelsy wondered if the old lady was describing her mother. She kept quiet, not wanting to give anything away.

'This thing, this monster, visits her when she sleeps. So many times, she wakes, petrified. I see a man coming into the room. He's short, tubby, and he's balding. He sits on the bed. He's saying something to her. What's he saying? I'm trying to make it out. Madge, it's only a nightmare. Or, it's a nightmare. He's telling her reality is much more frightening. He says it to her often. To comfort her. They laugh together.'

Braking the circle, Chelsy said, 'It's my parents. They died in a car crash when I was young. It's them.' Tears formed in her eyes.

Annette and Daisy placed an arm each around their friend.

'My mum suffered from night terrors. Christ, it was awful. My father would always come into the room. He'd sit on the edge of the bed and place his hand on her face. He'd say that — reality was much more frightening. It would ease her tension. Often, she'd sleep during the day. Mum had the most horrendous migraines. My father would always hear her calling out. She had the same reoccurring dream. I'd hear her late into the night, shouting, often screaming for this thing, this hideous creature, to leave her alone.' Chelsy dropped her head. The memory of her parents and how they died was difficult to take.

'Do you want to stop?' Daisy asked.

Chelsy shook her head.

The old lady continued. 'I see a figure. It's maybe nine, ten feet tall. It's slim, grey looking and translucent. It's standing by the bed, watching the woman as she reads.'

Gripping the table, Chelsy said, 'No. You're wrong. It came to her while she slept. It was in her nightmares. It wasn't real,' she whispered. 'Mum told me when I was older. She was able to describe this creature so vividly. She said it would come when she slept.' She looked towards the old lady. 'You are correct about what it looked like though. The figure was tall and slim. It resembled a demon, something from your worst imagination. It tormented her for years. But whenever she woke, my father would be there. It never came while she was awake. How the hell do you know all this?'

The old lady chose not to answer. 'The woman is bouncing in the bed. Moving one way, then the other. She pushes the blankets back, then moves further down, now hiding in the fetal position. Her eyes are closed; she's asleep. The creature is there, but not just in her mind. Not just a part of her nightmares.'

'Stop. I don't want you to continue.'

'I see a car. The woman from the bed is in the passenger seat. The man is driving. As they take a bend, the figure moves out onto the road. They swerve around it, but the car slams into a tree. The figure watches.'

Screaming, Chelsy demanded, 'Stop it, I said. Fucking stop.' She stood and raced out of the living room.

* * *

Daisy went after her friend, finding her standing in the hallway. It was dark, and the only light came from the living room door. Daisy's face looked pale and ghostly in the half-light. 'Do you want to go home?'

Chelsy remained silent for a few seconds. 'It's horrible. The things she knows. My mother suffered for years with night terrors. I remember hearing her so many times. They died in a car crash.'

Holding her hand, Daisy said, 'I remember.'

'So what is she saying? Was this thing real? Not only in her nightmares? Is that it? She said it killed my parents. That they saw it before the crash. It's fucking ludicrous, Daisy.'

'Chelsy. I don't like the way it's going. She had to have had information about us before we arrived. She could have searched our social media. Then began with the mind games for effect. It's fake. But it's so wrong, the strings she's pulling. The buttons she's pressing. She's out of order.'

Chelsy looked at her friend. 'But what if it's real?'

'Oh, come on. So my grandfather, a good, kind man, murdered my nan, the woman he loved? He stabbed her in the face and blamed an intruder? That the creature from your mum's nightmares, a . . . demon? Was real, and caused the crash which killed your parents? It's bullshit, Chelsy. It's all bullshit.'

Staring at her friend, Chelsy asked, 'Do you think so?'

Daisy saw the fear in her friend's face. 'Yes.' She smiled. 'I think so. Come on. Let's give it another few minutes and go. It's Annette's turn. Remember it's her birthday present. Let's try and enjoy tonight. After this we'll go to a bar and have some real fun.' Taking a deep breath, Daisy walked back into the living room, and Chelsy followed. They sat in the same position, facing the door they'd just come in and again, they held hands.

'Are you both OK?' Annette asked.

The women mustered a smile.

The old lady closed her eyes without saying anything.

Daisy wanted to speak. She wanted to tell the old lady how out of order this was. How she was scaring them, the mind games, the stories, the lies. But it would only spoil the evening. They'd all paid for this. They'd all wanted it.

'I see a woman. She's lying down.'

Daisy braced herself for the next shocking revelation. But how much worse was it going to get?

'She's confined, held in, and unable to move. Earlier, she'd heard voices, but now it's quiet. So still. She tries to move her arms, pressing them outwards, but it's like she's trapped. Where are you, dear? Why can't you move? She's struggling, so frustrated. She wants to turn over, to get out. She screams. Oh my goodness, this woman is so very frightened.'

'Of what? What is she frightened of exactly?' Annette asked.

'She has a purple top. It's her favourite—a ring on her thumb. But half of her forefinger next to it is missing.'

'Stop,' Annette shouted. 'That's my mother. You're describing my mother. She died almost three years ago.' Annette tried to calm herself, getting ready fo what came next.

The old lady continued. 'She's trapped. She wants to get out, but she has no way to escape. She was asleep for so long.'

Breaking the circle, Annette bowed her head. 'She went into a coma for several months. Then she died. I never got to say goodbye.' Tears began to stream down her face.

The old lady resumed. 'She's in a box. She's so desperate to get out. Someone help me, she screams. But no one comes. No one is there to help. Wait. She's somehow managed to free her left hand. She's thumping on the wood. It's a coffin. She's desperately trying to force it open.'

Annette threw her head in her hands.

'Stop it! Just fucking stop this ludicrous act,' Daisy shouted.

Thrusting the chair back and standing, Annette raced to the hallway. Her friends joined her outside as she bent over, gasping for air.

'I'm sorry. It's just too much. How the hell did she know about the thumb ring? The missing finger?' Annette asked.

'Daisy and I spoke. She has to be fucking with us. There are things she knows which seem impossible. But these people can search. They can find anything.'

'But my mother was never on social media. She had no interest. And I've never posted family pictures anywhere. I've never mentioned anything about my mother's finger. I'm sure of it.'

Daisy put her hand on Annette's face, moving her head so she could look her in the eyes. 'It may have been the slightest mention. A conversation. Anything you posted. She'd have picked up on it.'

'Is it true?' Annette asked.

'What, darl?' Chelsy asked.

'Was she buried alive?'

The three women stared at each other, expressionless, standing by the front door.

They had no answer.

* * *

Back inside, the girls sat down for the final time. They were shaken and completely petrified. Whoever or whatever this old lady was, she was good at her job. She'd played the part well and succeeded in frightening them.

Chelsy, Daisy and Annette had wanted to do this for so long. They'd been excited about it for weeks. Now, they were all regretting it. But together they had decided to see it out until the end. They couldn't leave it like this.

Again, the old lady asked them to form a circle. 'We need to say goodbye. We need to thank the spirits for their inter-action.' She closed her eyes, asking the girls to do the same. Complete silence fell over the room. Suddenly the sidelight flickered. A buzz resonated over the room, and the light went out.

Annette shouted, 'What's happening?'

'She's done it,' Daisy hissed. 'She has a remote control or something. This is bullshit. I've had enough.'

'I said, we need to say goodbye. We need to do it properly or—'

'Or what?' Daisy screamed.

Something moved in the darkness. They could hear the living room door open. Just slightly, but it moved. Daisy grabbed her phone and put on the torch, shining it across the room. A deep groan resounded like a bull breathing hard in your ear. Suddenly, a dark shadow seemed to form at the door. It appeared to slowly move through the air and then settle. They all stared, watching it, the mist-like shape, the tall silhouette. It watched them, facing towards the table.

'What's happening?' Chelsy yelled. She stood, moving around the table as the figure seemed to evaporate. The sound of footsteps echoed through the hallway. Something was running, the noise, loud and bouncing off the walls— then faint laughter. After a moment, it went quiet.

Visibly shaken, Chelsy charged through the living room door and out of the house.

The other two women followed her.

The old lady sat at the table. She whispered, 'You haven't said goodbye.'

* * *

Chelsy, Daisy and Annette sat in the back of a black taxi, asking to be dropped off at the nearest bar. When the light had gone out, and they'd seen the shadow forming at the living room door, it was all too much.

They could hear the old lady calling, talking to herself as they'd left the house.

They'd paid online before the event and had no reason to stay in the house longer than needed.

'Bloody hell. I've never seen anything so fucked up,' Annette said. 'What on earth happened in there?' She looked to her friends, who were still shocked by the evening's events.

'It was horrible,' Daisy added. 'That's the first and last time I ever visit a medium. Christ, she was an absolute freak.'

Looking out the window, Chelsy saw the clouds above were a thick grey and rain whipped against the glass. She turned back to her friends. 'What if it were true?'

Daisy hesitated, digesting tonight's events. 'What? Are you serious?'

Chelsy continued. 'It's just . . . there's no way she could have known about my mum's night terrors. No possible way. She described the figure perfectly. Ever since I was a child, mum had been plagued by the vision. A tall, slim, menacing-looking creature who visited her while she slept. What if the old lady was right? That it wasn't just while she slept?'

'Oh, come on, Chelsy.' Annette faced her friends, sat on the end. 'Really?'

Chelsy turned, again looking out of the taxi window. She watched as they passed shops, the neon lights blinking, the dark, uninviting alleyways, and the pavements embellished with people on a night out. 'She said it was the cause of their death. That before they'd crashed, mum and dad had seen it on the road.'

Daisy's body spasmed as a cold chill ran through her veins. 'How the hell did she know about my nan? She said my grandfather stabbed her in the face with a glass. But it was an intruder. The old lady could see her, lying on the floor, reaching out, blood dripping from her eyes. But what if—?'

The girls were stunned into silence.

Annette cracked the stillness. They could hear the sobs as she began to speak. 'She knew about my mother. She'd died after going into a coma. She said she could see her, clawing at the casket, screaming to get out.' Annette broke down. 'It's too painful to imagine. It can't be true.'

Daisy placed her arm around her. 'Look. It's not true. None of it is. You hear me? The doctors, nurses, they'd have known if she was alive. Your mother was dead before they buried her.'

'But what if—?'

'She was dead,' Daisy insisted.

'Here.' Chelsy shouted. 'Drop us here.'

The driver pulled over to the kerb, outside a swanky bar in Belsize Farm, North London.

Chelsy got out and handed the driver a twenty-pound note. Daisy and Annette followed. 'Hey, I just want to say thanks for tonight.'

'Thanks for what? Chelsy asked. 'It was horrible.'

Annette tried to hide her fear. 'It was certainly different. And thanks for staying until the end. Let's go and have a good drink. Put it down to an awful experience.' She placed her arms around Chelsy, and Daisy joined them.

The bar was rammed, and a DJ stood in a corner of the stage towards the far side, playing the latest dance tracks. It was loud, and the women had to shout to hear each other.

They sat as far away from the speakers as possible, and

once settled, Daisy went to the bar to order a jug of Pimm's. She returned ten minutes later.

They sat, listening to the music and soaking up the atmosphere.

When they'd finished the jug of Pimm's, they moved onto the dance floor.

They were relieved to see the DJ finish at 11pm; the loud, emphatic music was replaced with soft jazz. At least they could chat now without straining themselves.

The women returned to their seats, hot and sweaty from dancing. They watched as the hardcore party animals left to move onto another boisterous venue.

Ordering another jug of Pimm's, Chelsy placed it in the centre of the table. She saw the distracted look on Annette's face. 'Are you OK? Are you enjoying your birthday?'

'Oh, Chelsy. It's fab. I'm having a great time. Thank you both so much for this.'

'I'm sorry about earlier,' Chelsy offered.

'There's no need to apologise. Wow, I still can't believe what happened. It's surreal. How does she do it?'

Taking a sip of her drink, Chelsy said, 'It was something else, wasn't it? I wouldn't have booked her, knowing how weird she turned out. Bloody hell. I still feel pretty shaken by it.'

'I don't know how she did it,' Annette added.

'Let's forget about it. We know never to go near her again,' Chelsy said with a smile, but she was thinking about the tall figure that plagued her mother's nightmares for so long. The old lady insisted that Annette's mother was buried alive. That she came out of her coma, banging the lid of the coffin in desperation. And that Daisy's grandmother was stabbed in the eyes with broken glass by her own husband. She pushed the images to the back of her mind.

Daisy was turned away from them, watching an argument at the bar. A man raised his voice, telling the barmaid he gave her a fifty, not a twenty.

'You OK, Daisy?' Chelsy asked.

Daisy turned around. Both her friends gasped in unison.

A trickle of blood was dripping from her eyes.

'Whoa, what the fuck?' Chelsy shouted.

'Your eyes,' Annette screamed. 'What have you done?'

Daisy was oblivious to what was happening.

Chelsy pointed. 'There's blood coming from your eyes. Have you cut yourself?'

Daisy reached into her handbag, removed a small mirror and looked at her face. Quickly, she grabbed a piece of tissue, dabbing at her eye sockets.

Chelsy stood, shakily. 'Come on; I'll take you to the toilets.' She linked her friend's arm and steered her to the ladies' room. Once inside, she grabbed more tissue from the cubicle, placing it under the warm tap and patting it on Daisy's face. 'What happened? Have you scratched them?'

'No. I don't think so. Unless it's a reaction to the Pimm's or something? But it's never happened before.'

Chelsy kept wiping the blood until it stopped. She looked at Daisy. 'Are you OK? Do you want to go home?'

'No. Don't be silly. It's a little blood. I'm fine.'

They left the toilet. Again, Chelsy linked arms with her friend and guided her to the table.

'Are you alright?' Annette asked.

Daisy nodded. 'What a weird fucking night.'

* * *

They chatted for the next hour while downing tequila shots. The alcohol had loosened them up and made them less apprehensive. It had been a night they'd never forget, but at least now, in a London bar, the soft music playing, the atmosphere and each other's company, it would end on a high note.

Chelsy stood and walked to a couple who sat beside them. 'Hey, would you mind taking our picture?'

The guy stood and took her phone. 'No problem.'

She moved beside her friends, the three of them smiling towards the phone. He took four photos and handed the phone back.

'Thanks so much.' Chelsy looked at the pictures. The three of them smiling, their faces flushed from the alcohol, a couple directly behind them, chatting at another table. The guy was leaning forward, holding his partner's hand. Then Chelsy saw it. She dropped the phone, and her mouth emitted a nervous cry.

'What on earth's the matter?' Annette laughed. 'We're not that hideous, surely?'

Chelsy rubbed her face; her eyes were wild and confused. She pointed to a picture on her phone. 'Do you see that?'

Grabbing the phone, Annette asked, 'What?' She looked at the last picture—the three of them staring at the camera, smiling, the couple behind. In the left corner of the photo, a tall, slim figure was standing, watching them. It looked like a deep shadow, a transparent image from a horror book or a chilling website. But it was real. It was there. Annette spun around. The couple were still behind them, but the tall figure was gone. 'What in the name of God is happening?'

'I want to go home,' Chelsy said. 'The night is getting weirder. I've had enough.'

Daisy asked to see the picture. She didn't need confirmation of what it was. The tall, sinister-looking shape was distinct and so obvious in the corner of the photo. Turning, she looked at where it appeared on the screen. Then she moved across the floor, standing in the same position. An icy chill caused her body to shudder. A deep coldness suddenly ran through her. As she moved away from the spot, she returned to the normal, hot, clammy temperature of a London bar late at night. She looked towards her friends. 'We need to go.'

The three women downed their drinks and left the bar.

* * *

Outside, Chelsy, Daisy and Annette felt the cold night air hit their skin. The streets were still busy. A group of young lads passed them on the pavement, their laughter raucous as they searched for late-night bars and live music.

A couple of London buses swept by, pushing wind in their faces and spraying dirty water from the road.

'I don't understand what's happening tonight?' Daisy stated. Some blood had dried around her eyes, leaving a stale substance on her face resembling a squashed moth. She needed sleep; she was exhausted and wanted to go home.

'I don't know. It's like the old lady summoned something,' Chelsy added.

'Summoned something? Are you for real? Listen to yourselves.' Annette glanced behind her, searching for a taxi. The road was empty.

'Well, how else would you describe it?' Chelsy tried to fight the fear; her body trembled with the chill as it whipped into her face.

'We all saw it. The shadow. For Christ's sake, I stood in the same spot; the temperature dropped like a thousand

fucking degrees,' Daisy yelled, trying to release the tension.
'My eyes. How do you explain the blood?'

Chelsy watched as a taxi moved along the road towards
them. The "For-Hire" sign illuminated. She placed her arm
out, waving frantically.

The driver pulled over and asked where they were going,
and the three women got into the back.

'I'm sorry. It wasn't supposed to happen this way. Bloody
hell, it was meant to be a fun night.' Chelsy stared out the
window. 'I feel so guilty.'

'It's not your fault,' Annette added. 'I'm sure things will
seem different after we've slept. We're tired, emotional.
That's all.' She held Chelsy's hand. 'I mean it. Thank you, it
was an . . . *interesting* night.' She smiled.

Looking out of the taxi window, then back to her friends,
the emotion and despair charged through Chelsy's body,
and the feelings played with the chemicals in her brain.
Suddenly she laughed, releasing everything. She watched as
the taxi driver peered at her through the rear-view mirror.

Soon, the three of them were giggling, feeling somewhat
embarrassed at the night and how seriously they had taken
everything.

'We'll look back with amusement. Honestly, thank you
both,' Annette added.

The taxi driver pulled over to the curb.

Chelsy's flat was the first stop. She leant over and
hugged her friends. 'See you both. I'll call you tomorrow.'
She opened the door and got out, watching the taxi move
along the street and turn left at the end of the road. *What a
weird freaking night,* she thought to herself. She looked up at
her flat on the first floor of her building. The lights were out,
and she felt a shudder of fear. The old lady's voice pushed
through her mind, the things she'd said. How her parents

had crashed after seeing the tall figure that used to haunt her mother's dreams. The same hideous shape in the photograph. She didn't have the courage to take another look at it now. She'd delete the picture tomorrow.

She thought about Daisy's nan. How she'd been glassed in the face. The old lady insisting it was her husband, Daisy's grandfather.

She stopped and turned around. Visions of Daisy's eyes swirled in her mind, all the blood. She peered along the vacant road; the sounds of Chalk Farm seemed so far away, the music replaced by stillness. Laughter by panic.

Climbing the steps, Chelsy reached into her handbag and grabbed the keys, opening the front door. She moved around the bike, which the neighbour below insisted on placing in the front hallway, and climbed the stairs to the first floor.

She opened the door to her apartment, stepped into the darkness and fought the voices in her head, trying to clear the image of Daisy's bloody eyes, everything the old lady had said. She remembered her last comments.

You didn't say goodbye.

What had she meant?

Chelsy stood in the hallway, moving her hand along the wall and turned on the lights. Grabbing her mobile, she called Daisy. It went straight to her voicemail. As did Annette's phone.

Chelsy stood, tempted to look at the photograph on her phone from the bar, the sinister shape which had appeared. She couldn't.

Grabbing a glass from the cupboard, she filled it with water and drank it, trying to stem the headache which had threatened and then downed another glass.

She moved to the window, looking over Angel Station,

thinking back to a few hours ago and how excited she had felt about tonight. So much had happened in the space of a few hours.

She needed sleep. Everything would feel better in the morning.

Chelsy walked into the bedroom and closed the door. After removing her clothes, she pulled back the blanket and got into bed; the feeling of the soft mattress as she leaned against the headboard was a welcome comfort.

Opening Facebook, she thought of something to say about the seance. Chelsy began typing.

Well, that was weird. Tonight, Daisy, Annette and I went to see—.

The bedroom door burst open. Chelsy's hands shook violently, and she dropped the phone onto the bedsheets. Filled with panic, she peered at the bedroom door, breathless and wanting to run. Looking through the dark living room outside, she thought about calling out, asking if someone was there. She'd have seen a hand, someone pushing against it, wouldn't she? Lying still, too afraid to move, Chelsy listened hard for a sound, something to clarify someone was in the flat. She pushed her body against the headboard, glancing at her phone, then picked it up and gently placed it on the bedside unit. She touched the sheets, the tips of her fingers spreading over the soft material and lifted it away from her body. Gently turning, her body facing the door, she felt the sudden chill which swept towards her, then stepped onto the floor and crept to the bedroom door. She wanted to put the lights on in the living room but was too frightened.

Chelsy reached forward and closed the bedroom door. She watched it, leaning against the wood to ensure it was shut. She turned and moved to the bed. For a couple of minutes, Chelsy lay still, horizontal, her head deep in the pillow and her frame buried in the mattress, then she moved her body slowly up against the headboard.

Again, she opened Facebook and began writing.

Well, that was weird. No, Chelsy didn't like how the sentence started. She continued to tap the backspace until the words had disappeared. *Tonight, Daisy, Annette and I had the most peculiar encounter. That's better,* Chelsy thought. She continued tapping the keys on her phone. *We went to see a medium—*

Chelsy's body convulsed. She thought her heart would leap out of her chest. A loud, groaning noise came from the living room. It was the sound they'd heard at the séance, she was sure of it. Like a bull breathing through its large nostrils and into her ear.

Watching the bedroom door, she was certain the handle moved.

Suddenly she screamed. 'Leave me alone. Do you hear me? Go away.'

Frantically, she gripped the end of the mattress tight to alleviate the terror she felt.

The sound stopped. Chelsy watched as the door handle began jumping, flipping up and down. Covering the sides of her head with her hands, she screamed as the door began opening.

Desperately charging forward, she slammed her body against it, then sunk to the floor, trying not to let it into her bedroom.

* * *

Annette and Daisy sat in the back of the taxi, chatting.

Suddenly the driver pulled over to the kerb.

'Oh, this is you,' Annette confirmed.

'Thanks.' Daisy undid her seatbelt and hugged Annette. 'Sorry, it's been such a crazy night. It's something we won't forget in a hurry.' She opened the door and stepped out onto the pavement.

Annette laughed. 'You know it. Thanks again. It was fun.'

Closing the door, Daisy ran towards the hostel where she was staying. A tall, grey building along Islington High Street. She turned around and watched as the taxi pulled away.

* * *

Annette sat in the back, watching the payment meter; the digits seemed to go so fast she couldn't make out the numbers.

Closing her eyes, she listened to the music now coming from the front.

The old lady's voice resounded in her ears. She was so frightening. Annette heard her voice, insisting her mother was alive while in the coffin. That she could hear her, banging on the coffin lid and desperate to get out. Annette felt sick; she'd never been so upset.

For the sake of her friends, she put on a brave face, but inside, she was torn apart. How could the old lady say such wicked things? She was going to put in a complaint about her. Yes, they'd booked a seance. It was supposed to be fun, but the old lady had taken it too far. It was cruel, the things she'd said. Annette was fuming. It wasn't Chelsy's fault, or Daisy's. They'd all wanted to do it.

She watched the taxi driver turning the steering wheel, his head moving to the music. He looked in his own world.

They caught each other's eyes in the rear-view mirror, and he smiled. Annette smiled back.

'Had a good evening?' he asked in a strong London accent.

Annette didn't feel like conversation, but not wanting to appear rude, she answered him. 'Yes, thanks. We visited a medium.' She regretted the words as soon as they spilt from her mouth.

He turned. 'No way. I've often wanted to go to one of those. How was it? Were they good?'

'Well, I'm not sure, to be honest. She was certainly creepy. She told me things that were a little distressing, you know.'

Turning the steering wheel to the left, he pulled into a side street. He seemed in his element now that he had someone to talk to. The excitement on his face was obvious.

'I often wonder how they know,' he continued. 'It's like they're in tune, like they can communicate with those who have passed. A friend of mine went to medium a while back. She told him things she couldn't possibly know. He said it was weird, alright. I've always been curious. But I think the dead are better left that way. If they wanted to communicate, they would.'

Annette smiled. 'Exactly. It was a birthday present, but I think we regret going now if I'm honest.'

The driver turned right at the end of the road, moving towards East London. 'It's your birthday?'

'Yeah, it was a present from the girls we dropped off.'

The driver turned on his seat, facing towards the back. 'Well, happy birth—'

'Look out,' Annette screamed.

The driver spun around, watching as a large truck headed straight towards them. He turned the steering wheel ferociously, trying in desperation to avoid the heavy goods vehicle. The taxi smashed into the metal railings along the road.

Annette could hear the tyres skidding as the truck moved towards them.

The back end of the trailer swung hard, almost turning on its side as the truck smashed into them and crushed them against the railings.

Annette tried in desperation to get out, to release herself, but the back door pressed so hard against her body that she couldn't breathe. She could feel her chest cave in, her airways close as she tried to push air from her mouth. She couldn't inhale, everything was blocked and her body compressed.

The last movement were her fingers, clawing against the roof of the taxi.

* * *

Daisy stood in the lift on her way to the third floor. She glanced at her face in the mirror, looking at the dry blood around her eyes. Nothing like that had ever happened before, and wondered now if she'd imagined it. She wiped her face, thinking how crazy the night had been.

The lift opened, and she stepped out into the hallway. As Daisy walked along the dark corridor, an automatic light came on.

Someone was lying on the floor outside her room—an older lady in a white nightdress, reaching into the air.

Momentarily, Daisy froze, panic gripped her body, then she turned around, looking towards the lift. She needed to get help. Maybe one of the security guards were on duty.

Suddenly the lights went off. Daisy stood in the pitch

black, pawing the wall to try and find the lift and waving her arms to summon the automatic light. Nothing happened. Turning back towards the direction of her room, she called into the darkness. 'Wait there. I'll get someone. Are you OK?'

As Daisy found the lift doors, the lights came back on.

The figure was gone.

'Where are you? Hello? Are you there? Hello?' Groans sounded behind her, as if it were an animal, an old toilet filling, or someone possessed. She screamed, covering her ears with her hands, then charged towards her door.

Daisy fished for the key in her handbag, stabbing it hard into the lock.

The door opened, and she slammed it behind her, dropping to the floor.

Lying there, sobbing, she tried to understand what was happening. To grasp the events of tonight. She needed her bed, to sleep. Everything would be OK in the morning.

Daisy stood, wiping her eyes, then stepped towards her bed. Her hands felt sticky. She looked at the back of her palms.

'No, no, no. Don't do this.' Blood dripped off her hands and onto the floor. Her eyes were sore, and she struggled to see.

Swiftly moving to the bathroom, she turned on the lights and doused water on her face. The more she wiped, the more blood appeared. She grabbed handfuls of tissue, soaking them with water and holding them to her face.

After a few minutes, it stopped.

She glanced at her face, the mess, and then studied her reflection. It looked like she'd suddenly aged fifty years.

Daisy held her hand to the mirror, touching her fingers to the glass, but they went straight through it like the mirror had a deep hole filled with liquid. Only it was red, gooey.

Blood.

Howling with terror, she turned; more groans were coming from the hallway. She backed out of the bathroom, moving towards the end of the flat. She felt weak, light-headed.

The blood was pouring from her eyes again. Her legs were weak, her mind clouded. As the growling noises surrounded her, Daisy staggered to the bathroom, closed the door, and she dropped to the floor.

Five minutes later, she lay in a pool of her own blood.

* * *

Just after 8am, Chelsy woke, still leaning against the bedroom door. Opening her eyes, she glared around her bedroom, recalling the events of last night. The weird old lady who knew so much. The bar. The blood which began pouring from Daisy's eyes and the creepy shadow figure in the picture. Had it tried to get into her bedroom? Chelsy sat, her knees to her chest and took a deep breath.

She wanted to reach for her phone and look at the picture again, but she wasn't courageous enough. Last night was horrible. Maybe the old lady had played with their minds, brought them into some kind of trance. Whatever had happened, Chelsy would never visit a medium again. It was truly terrifying.

Pushing her hands to the floor, she stood, grabbed her phone and dialled Daisy's number.

After the second attempt and already leaving a message on her voicemail, she called Annette.

A man answered on the third ring.

'Hello?'

'Oh, hi. I was looking for Annette.'

'Who's speaking?' the man asked.

'I'm Chelsy. A friend. I wanted to make sure she got home safe.'

'We're trying to locate a next of kin.'

'A next of kin? What are you talking about?' Chelsy asked with concern.

'There's been a terrible accident. I'm afraid I can't say too much until I speak to a family member.'

'Annette's parents have both passed. She has no siblings. I'm her closest friend.'

'Well, I'm afraid I have some tragic news. Annette was in

an accident early this morning. We found a handbag containing her phone and passport lying next to her body, confirming her name. Annette Ryan.'

'Her body?' Chelsy sat on the edge of the bed. She felt numb; her hands began to twitch. 'Is she—?'

There was a pause. The man continued talking. 'I'm afraid she didn't make it. The taxi she rode crashed; it was found turned on its side. It looks like your friend died on impact. I'm so sorry.'

It felt like her head would explode. Her mind raced. Confused, she said, 'No. You're mistaken. It's not true. It's not fucking true.'

'Look, have you got a friend or relative who can join you? Maybe a neighbour who can sit with you?'

'Where is she? Where is Annette?'

'A coroner took her body after the firefighters extracted her from the taxi. I really am so sorry. Please call someone to sit with you. I know it's a shock. I apologise for delivering the message this way. It must be so very tough.'

Chelsy hung up the phone and scoured her social media accounts. Opening Facebook, she put Annette's name into the search bar. A post from a couple of days ago showed her with a glass of wine, sat around the table in a bar in the West End. She was smiling and looked so happy.

Another showed her on a recent shopping trip. There was nothing to indicate she'd died last night and no comments from any friends.

Chelsy went onto Twitter and searched local police reports. As she scrolled, she saw comments about a car crash. A lorry had rammed into a London taxi. The driver of the heavy goods vehicle had survived with minor cuts. The taxi was wedged against the railings, and the driver and passenger had been crushed.

Some sicko had posted a picture of the taxi as they travelled on a night bus.

Tears ran down her face as Chelsy widened the screen. The taxi was completely mangled, like it had been driven off the roof of a tall building.

Chelsy watched the picture, staring at it in disbelief. There were police cars, fire engines, and paramedics on the scene, flashing blue lights illuminating the night sky.

Getting off the bed, she raced to the bathroom, and was violently sick into the toilet. She wiped her mouth with an old towel and splashed cold water onto her face. Pressing her hands against the wall, she pushed her body into it and sobbed.

Once she'd composed herself, she grabbed her phone, again calling Daisy. 'Come on. Answer for Christ's sake. Where are you?' Chelsy didn't bother to leave another message. Instead, she began to type.

It's me. I'm desperately trying to get hold of you. Please call me as soon as you get this. It's an emergency. Chelsy. xxx

Quickly moving back to the bedroom, she grabbed a T-shirt from the drawer, stepped into a fresh pair of jeans and pulled on her boots.

She grabbed a jumper from the back of the chair in the kitchen and began to pace the flat. She needed to go over to Daisy. Something was wrong. She wasn't completely sure if what had happened to Annette was connected to the strange events of last night, but she needed to find out.

Panic drowned her body as Chelsy moved to the front door. She leaned against the wall, pulling at her hair. It was starting to sink in, to filter into her mind.

Annette. The old lady had told her about her mother being buried alive. Was it possible that she'd summoned something during the seance?

Come on, Chelsy, this is fucking ludicrous, she thought. But it would make sense. The police officer said the fire crew had to cut her body out of the car. She had been trapped.

Daisy. The old lady had insisted her grandfather, murdered her grandmother. That they'd had an argument, and he'd smashed a glass, stabbing it in her face.

Last night, when they'd hit the bar, all of them distressed, agitated, blood began to seep from Daisy's eyes.

It was a nightmarish crazy thought, but it was happening. The old lady may have summoned something. As they'd left her house, after seeing a shadow at the living room door, she'd said, *You didn't say goodbye.*

The words went over and over in Chelsy's mind. Resonating, grating on her brain.

You didn't say goodbye.

Chelsy stood at her front door, needing to speak with Daisy. She had to tell her about Annette, but the thought made her feel sick. How could she tell Daisy that their friend, who they'd been with just hours ago, had died so tragically in a freak accident?

Behind her, a chair sliding across the living room floor caused Chelsy to jump. Turning, she listened as groans filled the room. A shadow seemed to develop in the corner, like a cyclone, twisting, moving towards her.

Chelsy froze, her body unable to take the command from her brain to open the door and get out.

Trying to move her hands towards the lock, it felt like she had no control. She closed her eyes, talking aloud. 'Open the door. Lift your right hand in the air and open the door.'

Heavy footsteps started racing towards where she stood. Chelsy yelled, not able to bring her hand to the lock. The sound was on top of her, all around; any second, the figure would grab her, swallow her up.

She pulled the lock down and opened the front door, racing out to the bright hallway. Slamming the front door behind her, she leant on it, crying uncontrollably. She bolted as something pressed against it, loud knocks reverberating around the hallway, coming from inside her flat. She could hear the footsteps moving away, large, awkward thumps resembling a hammer crashing against a wooden floor.

Chelsy closed her eyes again. A voice startled her.

'Are you OK?'

She jumped, focusing on a lady from the floor above. 'Yes, thank you. I have a migraine,' Chelsy lied. 'I'm just popping out to get tablets.'

The lady moved up the stairs. 'If you need me, knock on my door.'

'Thank you. I appreciate it.' A few seconds ago, it sounded like her flat was being smashed to pieces; the neighbour hadn't mentioned the noise. Did Chelsy imagine it? It felt like a hideous nightmare, like she was losing her mind.

Chelsy had to speak with Daisy. She would make sense of everything, and they'd get through it together.

* * *

Chelsy headed down the stairs and out through the front doors onto the street. It was a bright, chilly Sunday morning. Normally, she'd go to the cafe or grab breakfast from a local sandwich bar. She'd lounge around the flat, speaking to friends from Uni on FaceTime or meet up with Daisy and go shopping.

This morning, it felt like her life had turned upside down. Like she'd been chewed up and spat out onto the pavement. She thought about Annette. Chelsy's mind flooded with images of the previous night. The old lady. The Seance. What had happened? What had they summoned? The more Chelsy thought about it, the more realistic it seemed. Seeing Daisy, her eyes bleeding. Annette. The crash leading to her death. Chelsy would talk to Daisy. Then they'd go back to the old lady. They'd have to say goodbye to whatever they'd disturbed.

Feeling safer in the brightness, Chelsy moved around the side of the building towards her car. Pressing the fob, she unlocked the doors of her Fiat 500. As she approached it, she glanced up at her window on the first floor.

A shadow was visible through the glass, watching her. *Get a grip, Chelsy. Get in the car, drive to Daisy and let's sort this out.* She stood, seeing the figure move to the side and out of view. *This is crazy. You're seeing things.*

Opening the car door, she watched her window on the first floor. The shadow had gone. An icy chill drove up her spine as she placed her seatbelt on and closed the door. With the Fiat 500 in gear, she exited the car park.

Ten minutes later, Chelsy pulled up at the hostel where Daisy was staying. She called her again from outside. There was still no answer.

Standing at the door, she waited until someone came out through the main entrance. A few minutes later, a young couple stepped out and onto the street. The guy was in his early twenties; the woman looked around the same age. They were speaking in Italian and held the door for Chelsy as they stepped onto the pavement.

Inside, she walked along the hallway and took the lift to the third floor. It creaked, the mirror was smashed, and it stank of weed. Chelsy wondered how Daisy could stay here. The place was depressing, dank, and the management didn't seem to care about the state of the building. Though anything would be better than her flat at this moment.

The lift stopped, and she stepped out and onto the third floor, praying her friend was sleeping off last night. How was she going to tell her about Annette? How would she react? It was too much. If only they hadn't gone to the seance.

Guided by an automatic light on the wall, Chelsy walked along the dingy hallway, reached Daisy's room, and then knocked on the door. 'Daisy. It's me. Open up.' She waited a few seconds and thumped the door hard with her fist. 'Daisy. You're scaring me. Open up. It's Chelsy.' No answer. Kneeling, she opened the letterbox. Chelsy jumped back. The room stank, like there was a rotting corpse inside. The smell hit her immediately. Drenched with fear, she stared through the darkness. 'Daisy. Are you in there?' She winced as the odour began filling her lungs. Chelsy called again, louder this time and with more frustration in her voice. Reaching into her jeans, she grabbed her phone and dialled Daisy's number. The phone began to ring from inside the room. She spun around, her body shaking, her stomach feeling as if it were somersaulting. It stopped ringing. Chelsy could hear Daisy's voice, so faint, asking the caller to leave a message. She stood back, then called the number again while thumping hard on the door. 'Daisy, what is going on? Open the bloody door. It's me. I need to speak with you.'

Opening WhatsApp, she tapped out another message telling her friend to call her. She opened her social media accounts, Twitter, Instagram and Facebook, copied the message she'd sent on WhatsApp and pasted it in her DM's.

On Daisy's Instagram page, she glanced at her friend's recent pictures and Annette's face caught her eye. She still couldn't believe Annette was gone. The picture was of the three of them in a designer shop, smiling, so happy together.

Chelsy suddenly saw something. A pain darted through her back as her body jolted. She spread her fingers on the screen, seeing it more clearly. They were standing by the shop counter, an assistant folding clothes ready to place in a bag.

A grey figure was perched right behind them. It was tall, ghost-like and transparent. She was positive it hadn't been there before. She scratched the photo with her finger, hoping her phone screen was dirty. Chelsy closed her eyes for a moment, rubbing them with her fingers and looked back to the screen. The figure was still there.

She stepped back, struggling to breathe and peered towards the front door of Daisy's room. A bang on the wood caused her to stagger back. A shadow began to form under the door. Loud groans pushed through from inside the room.

'No. What are you?' Chelsy cried. 'Where's Daisy? Please. Leave us the fuck alone.' She waited, trying so hard to be brave. Chelsy needed to get into the room. Her friend was in danger.

Turning from the door, she raced along the hallway, out to the stairs and to the ground floor.

On the security desk, a sign stated the office was closed. It listed a phone number to call in case of emergencies. Chelsy dialled the digits, listening to the ring tone. After a minute, she dialled again. It gave no option to leave a message.

She moved along the ground floor hallway, furiously banging on doors; when no one answered, she moved back to the desk and sat on the swivel chair by the stairs, taking deep breaths and trying to work out what to do.

Grabbing her phone, she looked at the photo with the shadow figure, terror enveloping her body, her skin hot and clammy. She swiped her trembling fingers from left to right on the screen. There were more photos of her and Daisy, sitting in Chelsy's flat, drinking wine with friends. Food was placed on plates, sausage rolls, burgers, crisps, nuts and other snacks.

What the hell? Chelsy thought. Tapping the screen, she zoomed in, her breath sharp, harsh. The figure was there, behind them in each photo. No one could see it. Chelsy definitely hadn't seen it at the time. She'd remember. She furiously swiped, more photos, the same shadow in each one.

Visions powered through her mind of her mother, the figure she'd said haunted her sleep. The old lady insisting her parents had seen it step out onto the road before they died in the crash.

Chelsy had to know. She had to find out what was happening to her, and to Daisy. It felt like her heart dropped to her feet when thinking about Annette. She had to try something.

Getting off the swivel chair, she moved around the desk and stood in the grim hallway. Holding the phone in front of her, she reversed the camera, pointing it at her face—a selfie. Smiling, Chelsy clicked the side button. She composed herself, ready, waiting and looked. She viewed herself, the hallway behind her and the back wall. Nothing. She sighed with relief—just her in the photograph. She clicked again, an almost identical picture, her head turned slightly, being the only difference. She kept clicking, arranging her hair, some photos with her head back and others to the side.

Hesitating, Chelsy looked again. Nothing. She flicked through the ones she had taken, eventually landing back on

the first one she'd taken a few minutes ago. The one she had
checked and seen nothing but her own face.

Something had developed, like a smudge against the
back wall. 'Shit.' It wasn't there moments ago. She tapped
the screen, looking closer. It seemed like the shape of a
flame, but it wasn't bright. Moving her finger and thumb
inwards, Chelsy pinched the screen, making the picture
smaller again. She swiped, right to left. Her mouth opened
in shock, her stomach aching. In the second picture the
figure had developed. It had formed into a tall, menacing-
looking shadow around six feet from where she stood.
Picture three. The shadow was right behind her. She
screamed, holding her hands tight against the sides of her
head, then turned around, looking at the empty hallway.

Chelsy pounded up the stairs; her adrenalin kicked in,
her mind determined to get to Daisy.

Turning around, she checked the stairs to make certain
they were empty. On the third floor, Chelsy opened the fire
door and raced back to Daisy's room. Her friend had to be
inside.

At her door, Chelsy composed herself, then stepped to
the wall opposite and ran at the door. Her shoulder barged
against it, and her body sprang backwards. *Come on, open,
you bastard.* Again, Chelsy backed up, and then smashed her
body against the wood. She heard it crack. A couple more
times, and it would open. She could see it was flimsy. Again,
she smashed her shoulder against the door, kicking it,
pushing hard against it.

The door sprung open. It was badly damaged and
hanging off its hinges. Chelsy looked along the hallway.
Bloodstains were splashed on the floor. The smell was
unbearable. It seemed to seep into her skin and choke her
lungs.

Aided by the light from a window at the back of the room, she walked along the hallway.

'Hello? Daisy?' Chelsy opened the bathroom door. Something was jamming it. She pushed harder, feeling a heavy object against the door. As Chelsy heaved, she could hear the object slide along the floor. She braced herself for what she'd find. Her body was exhausted, her mind racing and out of control. She was petrified. The last fourteen or so hours had been so stressful. Now visions of Annette flooded her brain, trapped in the taxi and unable to get out. She wiped the tears from her eyes, pleading for Daisy to be OK.

As the door opened, Chelsy placed her jumper sleeve over her mouth and nose to stem the rotten odour. She glanced down at her friend's body. 'Oh my God. Daisy.' She crouched, looking at her face. There was so much blood and it looked as if her eyes had exploded. Pulling her body closer, Chelsy held her. She broke down and screamed so loud her throat became raw.

* * *

Lying on the floor of the bathroom, Chelsy cradled her best friend. She had gone into shock, rocking back and forth and unable to think straight. She wanted to call for help, to ring the police and let them know what had happened. But how did she explain the events of last night? Annette. Being crushed in the taxi after finding out her mother had been buried alive.

Daisy, hearing her grandfather had been responsible for the murder of her grandmother and now lying on the floor, appearing to have bled to death in the same manner.

The horrible shadow figure that haunted Chelsy's mother, now appearing in her photographs. None of this made any sense. Surely, she'd wake and find it was all a terrible nightmare? She lay her friend back down onto the bathroom floor and stood up, still crying, wiping the tears from her eyes.

She had to sort this out. Chelsy needed to go back to the medium, find out what was happening. If she needed to say goodbye, then so be it. Two of her friends were dead.

She'd be next.

It was time to put an end to it.

* * *

She walked out of the bathroom, leaving her friend on the floor. Outside in the hallway, she pulled out her phone and dialled 999, telling the call handler that a woman in a hostel in Islington had bled to death. Worried that she'd get the blame, Chelsy withheld her phone number. It was something she'd have to deal with later, but now, the priority was returning to the old lady. Placing her phone in her jeans pocket, she cut the call as the handler spoke, and then went out to her car.

As she walked around the back of the hostel, Chelsy watched the faces of people she passed, oblivious to what was happening in her life. To them, it was a normal Sunday morning. Time for family, shopping, a coffee or some lunch.

Chelsy got into her car and dialled Darren Fletcher's number. He'd recommended the medium to them, and she needed to talk to him.

'Hey, Chelsy. How did it go? Good, isn't she?'

She took a deep breath; the fear was obvious in her voice as she began to speak. 'They're dead.'

'Who? What are you talking about?'

'Annette and Daisy. They're both dead.'

There was a short pause before Darren said anything. 'Dead? Is this a windup?'

'Look, I don't have time to explain. Last night was fucking awful. It went horribly wrong.'

'How? Chelsy, I'm not with you.'

'The medium. Miriam Yau. She summoned something evil. Something came through during the seance. And something killed Annette and Daisy.'

'Oh, come on. You're bullshitting me. What's going on?'

Chelsy yelled so loud she thought her own eardrums would burst. 'I don't fucking have time for this. Meet me at her address in an hour. Don't let me down. I'm not pissing around.' Trying to compose herself, she raised her voice again. 'Do you fucking hear me?'

'Yes. But I don't understand—'

Chelsy ended the call.

She drove through North London, clueless to everything around her, like she was watching someone else's life, unattached and disassociated with everything she saw. Chelsy kept seeing Daisy, her best friend, lying on the bathroom floor. So much blood. Her mind was plagued with visions of Annette, trapped in the crushed taxi.

It was happening. The tragedies which were part of the women's lives were being played out again; only they were at the helm, in the driver's seat and the starring role.

Following signs for Swiss Cottage, she watched the road ahead. Her mind was occupied, drowning in thoughts and trying to determine what had happened. She needed the old lady to close the box she'd opened; whatever had come through needed to return.

Before it was too late.

* * *

Chelsy turned into the street where last night, she, Daisy, and Annette had arrived, so excited to find out what a seance was about, who they could contact and sceptical about how it would all go.

Now, she felt horrified, too frightened to get out of the car, to go into that place for fear of what might happen. She had to push it from her mind. To concentrate on what needed doing, then somehow move forward with her life. If she got that chance to.

Sitting in the car, she stared across the road.

It seemed so different. The dark, dingy semi-detached house perched at the end of the road looked modern, bright and radiant.

Chelsy watched with her mouth open in shock, unable to understand what had happened to this place overnight.

She opened the car door, walked across the road and stood at the gate. It wasn't the same house. Nothing resembled where they'd visited last night. The place looked completely different.

Bending forward and resting her hands on her thighs, she took a breather. She felt queasy as her world began to rotate. She placed her hand on the wall for a moment to steel herself, then pushed the gate back, walked to the front door and pressed the bell.

A few seconds later, a woman answered, wearing a dark blue pair of dungarees with paint splashes on the front and shoulder straps. She smiled but looked intrigued. 'Hi. Can I help you?'

Chelsy could see she was decorating. A ladder was open, its legs spread on the hallway floor, and a paint tray rested on top. The smell was overbearing but not unpleasant.

Struggling to find the words, she said, 'Hi. Erm, we were here last night. There was an older lady. My friends and I sat in the living room.' Chelsy refrained from mentioning their business here, so's not to frighten the woman.

'I'm sorry. You must be mistaken. My husband and I were here all night. You have the wrong address.'

'No. It's definitely this house. I'm certain. There was an old lady. We followed her down this hallway and into the living room.'

'I can assure you we live alone.'

Chelsy saw the woman become more agitated. She needed to find out what was going on. 'Look. Hang on a second.' Dipping into her jeans, she pulled out her phone and then showed her the address. 'This is it. We got a taxi here. He dropped us off outside.' She held the screen to the woman's face.

'That's my address. But you weren't here last night. As I said, my husband and I live alone. Maybe knock at a few of the neighbours.'

Inhaling profoundly, Chelsy pushed out hard from her lips. 'How long have you lived here?'

Frustrated, the woman sighed, leaning against the door frame. 'Coming up five years I think? The previous owner died, it was a right state when we moved in. An old lady had lived here and we bought the house from her daughter. It looked like it hadn't been decorated in decades.'

With the confusion becoming too much, Chelsy frowned. 'What was her name? The old lady, I mean?'

'The old lady who died?'

'Yes.'

'I can't remember. As I said, we bought the house from her daughter. She didn't want to move in—too many sad memories. Wait, I think I still have paperwork if you're really interested? Stay there a second.' The woman came back a few minutes later, holding an A4 size piece of paper close to her face. She began moving her finger down the page. 'Miriam. Her name was Miriam Yau.'

The colour drained from Chelsy's face like a brick being dropped from a tower block. 'Yau. Are you certain?'

'Yes. I remember now. I had to forward her mother's mail for the first few months. Until the post office sorted it out, but that was her name.'

Chelsy turned without thanking her.

The previous occupant was Miriam Yau.

Chelsy ran into the road, narrowly avoiding a car that managed to swerve around her. On the pavement opposite, she turned back, looking at the house. The front door was closed. *What the fuck is happening? This is madness. How could the old lady be dead? It's not possible. We were with her last night.*

Moving to her car, Chelsy tried to dissect what she'd just learned. Was she losing her mind? Nothing made sense. She'd wait for Darren. He'd be able to explain. He'd given her Miriam's details. He'd hooked them up with the medium. Maybe if she spoke to him, he'd clarify she wasn't crazy. Chelsy had told him to meet her at this address. Once he turned up, it would prove she wasn't going insane.

Peering back over the road, she half expected the house to resemble the dank pit from last night.

It didn't.

Chelsy sat in the car, beyond confused. She watched the clock on the dashboard as seconds turned to minutes. Eventually, she grabbed her phone and searched Darren's number, keeping an eye on the house across the road as she tapped the call button. After eight rings, she heard Darren's voice, prompting her to leave a message. *You arsehole. Pick up the phone.* She dialled again, and on hearing the same voice message, she threw the phone on the passenger seat.

Bending forward in the driver's seat, she placed her head in her hands, pounding her fists on the steering wheel. She yelled, releasing her frustration. More time passed. Chelsy sat, her eyes fixed on the house across the road. She saw the young woman dressed in dungarees coming to the window, then turn as if talking to someone—possibly her partner. Telling him that crazy girl was still outside, probably.

She had to go. It wasn't safe, and if dungaree woman called the police, they'd think Chelsy was a psycho, lurking outside houses looking for people who didn't exist.

Starting the car, she drove, watching the busy streets, the vehicles in front, stopping, starting, bumper to bumper, the frustrated faces in the rear-view mirrors ahead, other drivers heading towards her in their own world, unaware of her problems, entering her life for seconds and then gone.

Realising she had no one to talk to, Chelsy was suddenly desperately alone. Who'd believe her story? Who'd listen to her crazy ass antics? A medium who'd moved on years ago. Annette, crushed on the bridge. Daisy, lying in a hostel bathroom after bleeding to death?

Chelsy followed the A1 across London and drove towards her flat, watching the phone on the seat, praying for Darren to call. The screen was blank; the phone sat in silence. When it was safe, she pulled over and stopped the car. Chelsy grabbed the phone and searched social media. There were more pictures of the crash on Twitter. People posted photos of the taxi crushed against the railing. There were so many comments, some with pity; others were sarcastic with crude, inapt jokes. But it meant she didn't imagine it. The story was there. It happened.

She jumped as the phone rang. Chelsy looked at the screen. Darren Fletcher. Pressing the answer button, she spoke. 'Hello?' Her voice was more forceful than she'd meant.

'It's me. Sorry, I got held up. I'm here. Where are you?'

'For fuck sake, Darren, I waited. Why didn't you answer the phone?'

'I always have it off when I'm driving. I had to help a flat-mate out who was in a crisis.'

'Well, I've left.'

'OK. I'm sorry?'

'She's not there, Darren.'

'Who?'

'The old lady. It's like it never happened. The house is different. A young woman answered. She said the old lady left years ago. I'm so confused.'

'Well, I'm outside now. It's definitely the same place. Are you sure you went to the right house?'

She raised her voice. 'Of course I'm bloody sure. I'm not crazy. What does it look like?'

'The house?' Darren asked.

'Of course the house. What else would I be talking about?'

'It's the same as when I came a few weeks ago. It's dark, distinguished-looking, perched on the end of the road and stands out from the rest of them. Not modern like the others.'

Chelsy gasped. 'Not modern? I don't understand. Take a picture and WhatsApp it to me.'

'Hold on.'

Chelsy heard her friend's voice as if straining while he took a picture. A few seconds later, the photo came through to her phone. She opened it, seeing the house from last night. 'That's where we went. That's where the seance was. But it's not the house I went to earlier.'

'What do you mean?'

'I mean, it's different.' Chelsy pressed a button on the screen. 'Answer Facetime.'

'Hold up. There. Can you see?'

Chelsy watched a picture of the road appear on the screen. 'Yes. Hi. I'm sorry about this, Darren. I'm so confused. I need to talk to you but not over the phone.'

'Is everything OK? You look like shit.'

'I feel worse. Point the camera across the road and zoom in.' Chelsy watched as the live feed showed the house from last night.

'Can you see it?'

'Yes. What the fuck is going on?'

Darren took a deep breath. 'You tell me? Look, I'll come over to the flat. I think you're stressed, is all. You need to rest.'

'Darren. Do me a favour.' She watched the screen still pointing at the old house.

'What?'

'Go over there. I want you to knock at the house.'

'Are you serious?'

'Yes. Go on. I want to prove I'm not crazy. Go over and knock on the door. Please, Darren.'

'This is ridiculous.'

'I know, and I'm sorry. I was there earlier. It's the same place we went to last night. But earlier, the house was different.'

'It can't have been. You must have been at the wrong place.'

'Darren, it was the same address. I know it was. Seeing it on screen now, it's the place from last night. I just need you to go to the house and see who answers.' She watched the screen, hearing the groans coming from her friend. She could hear the car door open and close. She watched the pavement, the road and the house on the other side. The camera was now at the gate, and Chelsy watched as Darren lifted it, the screech noisy and prominent.

'Knock on the door,' Chelsy demanded.

'What am I going to say?'

'You'll think of something.'

Chelsy watched as Darren moved to the front door. He held the camera up with his left hand, and with his right, he tapped on the door.

'This is crazy.'

'I need to see who answers. I really appreciate it,' Chelsy whispered.

'Yeah. Sure. No one is coming. Perhaps she's gone out.'

'Just wait. She's elderly; it may take her time to answer.'

'Wait, I can hear someone. I think she's coming.'

The door began opening. Darren held the phone up and watched as it slowly moved back. It was dark and drab inside. Suddenly the old lady appeared, standing on the right side of the hallway—the same person who'd conducted the medium for Chelsy and her friends.

'Miriam.'

She focused her eyes, struggling with the brightness. 'Yes. Who are you?'

'I came here for a seance a little while back. You probably don't remember me.'

She stepped forward, now standing on the step. 'Oh, I do. I remember you.'

Chelsy watched in bewilderment, trying to organise the events in her head. She'd been to the same house only an hour ago. A much younger woman had answered. She said she knew nothing of the old lady. The house had looked so different, modern, contemporary, and bright. Now it was the shit pit they'd visited last night. Darren was standing at the door with the medium.

Maybe she was losing her mind. Maybe Annette was at home, safe and sound, and the crash never happened. Had she imagined seeing Daisy lying on the bathroom floor? This was too much for her to take. She had to try and understand what was happening. She listened as they both spoke. The medium seemed friendly, genuinely pleased to see Darren.

'Go inside,' Chelsy asked. 'Get her to do another seance. Something is happening, and I need to say goodbye to the spirits.'

Darren turned his face towards the camera. 'I can't. You need to book. Or come over here yourself.'

'Please. So much has happened. I'm begging you, Darren. Tell her that I'm on the phone. That she needs to perform the seance again. I'll explain later, but for now, I need to say goodbye. Please.' She could hear the frustration in his voice. The niggle playing at him.

'For Christ's sake. This is mental. Fine.' He turned the phone on the old lady. 'I'm sorry. My friend is on Facetime. She wants you to do another seance.'

The old lady stepped back into the house. 'She'd be right. Last night was horrid. The evil that came through doesn't happen often. There were stories and shocking events that revealed themselves. They ran from here. They unlocked the demons, setting them free and into our world.'

'Tell her, Darren. She must do another seance. Otherwise, I'm in danger.'

Darren looked at Chelsy on the screen. 'What? Come on, Chelsy. You don't believe all that, surely?'

'Tell her to go to the table. I want her to contact whatever came through last night. Tell her.'

Darren turned to the old lady. 'Can you do it again? She wants you to—'

'I heard what she wants.' She turned and moved along the hallway, then into the living room.

'Go after her,' Chelsy demanded.

'You owe me for this.' Darren pointed the phone to where the old lady had gone, and then walked towards the living room.

Chelsy watched as Darren sat at the table.

The old lady pulled her seat closer, asking him to close his eyes.

As Darren perched the phone on the table, Chelsy debated whether to drive over there, but she knew there wasn't enough time. She had to hope that whatever they'd brought through last night would show up again, and that saying goodbye over the phone would be enough.

She watched as Darren sat high on the chair, his back straight and his expression serious. The old lady grabbed his right hand; she faced the camera while Darren faced the back wall.

She began talking under her breath, muttering. Chelsy struggled to hear what she was saying. Pressing the volume button on the side of the phone, she realised it was already at maximum. She couldn't interrupt. She watched the old lady's lips, trying to make out the words.

Suddenly she pushed her neck back; her eyes screwed tightly shut.

Chelsy watched on, her body cold, tired and worried about what would happen.

'Someone is with us.'

Chelsy listened as the old lady spoke. Her voice was clear, piercing.

'I see a man; he's tall, wafer-thin. He's here with us. He's beside us. Who are you?'

Chelsy sat still, her mouth open and eyes glued to the screen.

'I asked you who you are?'

Did the table move? Chelsy could see Darren's head turning to the side. He looked alarmed.

The old lady continued. 'I'd like to know who you are? We mean you no harm. Please feel at ease with communicating. Let me know what you're doing here?' The old lady began moving on the chair; her eyes closed so tight, her face pale. The sidelight shone towards the table and began blinking.

Chelsy jumped as someone started to speak. The voice was deep, husky and sinister, like a cassette tape playing backwards. Leaning forward, she watched with intense fear. Her body twitched as she saw the old lady moving her lips. The voice was coming from her mouth.

'I still watch her.'

'How do you mean? Watch who?' the old lady asked. 'Please talk. Who are you? Who do you watch?'

Chelsy sat in her Fiat 500, parked on a side street a couple of miles from her flat, listening intently. The voice continued.

'I'm watching her now.'

Staring towards the quiet street, Chelsy tried to be as silent as possible. She didn't want to interrupt the seance. Fighting the terror rising up in her, she hoped the voice was something else. But she knew. Chelsy knew it was the shadow figure. The monster that used to visit her mother.

Was it watching her now? 'Please make it stop,' she whispered under her breath.

'You must go now. The girls that were here last night. They want to say goodbye.' The old lady's voice was back to normal. She waited, listening, her eyes now open and staring ahead. 'They are saying goodbye. You must go back. Cut yourself out of their lives. Do you understand?' She raised her voice. 'Do you understand?'

Suddenly, the screen went blank. Chelsy jumped in the driver's seat, tapping buttons on her phone. She called Darren's number, hearing his voice message.

'It's Darren. You know what to do.'

'Darren. Call me back. Is it over? Did the shadow figure go? Please call me.' She rang again, leaving another message, then looked at the last pictures on her phone, desperately searching for the shadow figure. She saw Daisy, Annette, the restaurant, and other pictures where the shadow figure had appeared. Now, it was only them in the photos.

Overwhelmed with relief, Chelsy pushed a deep breath from her mouth. This was good. It meant they'd said goodbye.

She got out of the car, the fresh air a welcome relief as she paced back and forth along the pavement.

Sitting back in her car, Chelsy grabbed her phone and called the old lady, then Darren. Her face felt hot, and her body was tired.

She pictured Daisy, Annette. Her friends had died so tragically. She couldn't go the same way.

Chelsy wouldn't let it happen. Darren had to have sent it back. He'd gone to visit Miriam and had another seance. Whatever had come through, whatever had been channelled, she prayed it was back in its box.

Sitting in the car, she waited in anticipation, worried for her friend. When she had called Darren's mobile and the old lady again, receiving no answer from both, she pulled away from the side street and onto the main road.

Chelsy drove towards Swiss Cottage along the quiet London streets, passed the shops, the pedestrians, the neon glow beaming from the traffic lights and the cars moving towards her becoming a blip in the rear-view mirror.

She turned into the street and searched for a parking space. She drove slowly, looking for Darren. A car pulled out, and Chelsy thanked the Universe for its help. Quickly, she undid the seatbelt, opened the door and raced down the street.

'No. No, no, no. What the fuck is going on?' Chelsy felt the chilly air push into her face. Rubbing her hands down her numb skin, she saw the house where she was this morning. The bright lights inside, the white walls in the front living room, the style, so lush, so chic.

The woman is fucking with my mind. That's it. She has me in some kind of trance, like a time warp. She's hypnotised me or something and screwed with my head. Chelsy debated for a moment, knocking on the door and speaking to the woman from this morning. To explain what was happening. She couldn't. Dungaree lady already thought she was strange, if she went back she would most certainly call the police. Then she'd have to explain everything, including the body of her friend left lying on a bathroom floor.

She stood at the gate, hidden behind a bush to the right side of the house. Suddenly a person came into view and she pulled back further into the branches. The figure moved across the living room floor and stopped at the window, looking out. Could the person see where Chelsy was standing? The figure appeared dark, dreary looking, and for a moment Chelsy felt a stab of fear that this could be the figure stalking her. It didn't look anything like the blonde lady from earlier. Chelsy needed to know.

Slowly, she pulled one of the branches sideways, peering at the figure standing in the window. It turned slightly and the light hit their face. Chelsy brought her hand to her mouth and gasped.

It was the old lady who'd conducted the seance.

Miriam Yau.

Chelsy tried in desperation to understand what was happening, but her brain was addled and confused. Now, the house was modern, contemporary, and so stylish. Last night the place looked tired and decrepit. The two versions of this place and these people were now colliding.

Chelsy stood, watching the old lady at the window. She seemed to glance towards where she stood. Chelsy ducked, too frightened to move. She needed to confront this woman and ask her what was happening. Either she was losing her mind, or the old lady was fucking with her. But either way, her two friends were dead, and she needed answers.

Chelsy composed herself, moving her body away from the bush and stood.

The old lady was watching her now.

Then she disappeared.

Spinning around, Chelsy looked behind her. It sounded as if someone was approaching. She backed away, staring towards the empty window. *Where did she go? What next? Her friends were dead. Daisy, Annette.*

Terrified, Chelsy raced back to her car, her eyes stuck to the now empty window at the front of the house. She jumped into her Fiat, slammed the car door shut, and locked the doors, sobbing with fear. Eyeing her reflection in the mirror as she pulled her hair in frustration, it seemed she'd aged thirty years in the last day.

Chelsy stemmed her tears and took deep breaths. *Ok, you need to pull it together. There has to be an explanation for all this. It can't be happening. The old lady was here last night. She conducted some sort of spell, a trance we never fully left. This is all that's happening. You're not going mad. Maybe Daisy and Annette are alive. Maybe it's all in my mind—a mass of confusion. The chemicals unbalanced in my brain. That's it. That has to be it. Maybe she used scented candles, a type of relaxant, to force us into a meditative, deliberate state.*

Pulling the phone from her pocket, she connected it to hands-free. Eyeing the wing mirror on her right, she pulled out onto the road.

It was quiet; the sky was dull with thick clouds, and the car windows were slightly frosted.

She dialled Daisy's number, pictures of her lying in the hostel bathroom pushed through her mind. Last night in the pub after the seance, Daisy's eyes had streamed with blood. The same way her grandmother had died. Chelsy shivered in the seat and her teeth began to chatter together. The loud ringing tone played out over the speaker. Then Daisy's voice, asking to leave a message.

She hung up and dialled Annette's number. Again, the sound of her phone ringing out over the speakers. Earlier, a policeman had answered, telling her that her friend had died in a road accident. She needed proof. Proof that all this was her state of mind, a trick of the brain, an unbalance due to the seance. She had to find out.

Pulling over to the curb, she opened Twitter and typed in the search bar.

Taxi crushed on London Bridge.

She screamed in horror as pictures came up. It was still trending.

Trolls were mocking it; others were saying how sorry they were.

Her phone ringing through the speakers caused her to jerk.

Darren's name was displayed on the screen.

She pressed the answer button. 'Oh, thank God. What happened to you?'

'We lost signal. Christ, it was weird. She started talking in a crazy voice. I left.'

'What do you mean you left?'

'I walked out of there. It was freaky. I wish I never recommended her.'

Chelsy watched the road ahead. 'You can't. You don't understand. You can't just leave. Darren, are you listening?'

'Yes. Where are you?' he asked.

'I've just left the house. I don't get it. I went back to the address, but the old house wasn't there. Only a modern version. I saw her in the window. The old lady. She stood, watching me, then disappeared.'

'Look, turn back,' Darren instructed. I'm outside. I'll drive us home, and you can collect your car in the morning. This shit is getting out of control.'

Relieved, Chelsy touched the accelerator with her right foot and carried out a U-turn.

She drove, her eyes fixed on the road. 'Are you still on the line?'

'Yes. I'm outside the house.'

'Darren, can I ask a question? How does the house look?'

'Exactly how it did earlier. I'd think it was abandoned if I didn't know better.'

Slowly, Chelsy turned onto the road, unsure of what she

would see. The house came into view; it was old, run-down and battered looking. 'How can this be? How can it change? It's like I'm back in time. Like she's distorting my brain.' Chelsy hit the accelerator as Darren waved from the pavement. She was desperate to speak to him, to have a friend with her in this crazy mess, and to get out of here in his car while they figured the whole thing out. She spotted a space down the end of the road and sped towards it. But as she was about to draw level with her friend, her eyes flicked to him again. He seemed to warp. His body all of a sudden looked like smoke. He was tall, transparent, his face was distorted, and his mouth wide open.

All at once, Chelsy knew it was the figure that had haunted her mother for so long.

Somehow, whatever had happened in the house, the old lady had brought it back through. Darren was gone, possibly possessed by this figure, and she was the last survivor of the friends.

The woman's voice echoed in her mind. What she said as they left last night.

You didn't say goodbye.

Chelsy wailed in the driver's seat.

The figure who was once her friend drifted onto the road in front of her.

She turned the steering wheel to avoid hitting him.

And drove straight into a tree.

The End

THE HITCHHIKERS

5

Nate watched through the windscreen as his Grand Cherokee Jeep swallowed the road ahead. In his peripheral vision, he saw only darkness. The full beams lit a few yards of the road at a time. The rain lashed against the glass, and he observed the windscreen wipers, fighting to clear the water as it landed.

Reaching to the left, he placed his hand on his wife's lap, watching as she pushed strands of her long, black fringe from her face. Her skin was flushed with the heat pumping from the grills. He glanced at her beautiful brown eyes, wet from the warm air. 'You OK?'

Becca smiled. 'Yeah. I'm just tired.' Leaning forward in the passenger seat, she wiped condensation from the windscreen. 'Christ, Nate, couldn't we have come a different route? This place is so desolate.'

'Well, there's the main road, but it's double the journey. This route cuts straight through, more or less. We'll be fine.'

'You better hope we don't break down.' Holding her phone in the air, Becca saw the empty signal bar. 'It was good seeing Christopher. He seems to have settled in well.'

Becca suddenly felt guilty. Her son had moved to Nottingham University a month ago, and they hadn't been to see his place until now. 'I miss him.'

'Oh, come on, Becca, we Facetime every day.'

Smiling, she said, 'But it's not the same. Being there, seeing him.' Tears formed in her eyes, and she battled with the lump building in her throat.

'Right, you are the most incredible mother ever. You've devoted every moment of your life to making him shine. This is *your* time now. Don't feel sad. He's living *his* life. Bloody hell, look how happy he is!'

Becca looked at Nate; his strong build, forearms bulging as he gripped the steering wheel, his chiselled face and his short, cropped hair. He always found the right words to say. For a second, she wanted him to pull the car over and dive on him, making love in the seclusion.

'I didn't like his girlfriend.'

'Oh, what?' Nate started laughing. 'Go on. What's wrong with her?' He prepared for the barrage of abuse aimed at Tilly.

'Well, her eyes are too close together and go in different directions. I didn't know if she was talking to you or me.'

'Her eyes? OK, what else?'

'How she looked at me. She just stares, like there's nothing there.'

'Oh, Becca, you mean when you were speaking? What did you want her to do, turn her back and sit facing the opposite direction? You make me laugh.'

Playing with her seatbelt, she pulled it off her body to stem the boredom of the drive. 'I'm just saying; she's not good enough for Christopher. She's not his usual type.'

'And what's his usual type?'

'Not Tilly, that's for sure.'

'Becca, he's happy, he's studying law, the subject he's always loved, his grades are amazing, he has accommodation, a social life and a nice girlfriend. Let's be happy for him.'

'I am happy; she's just weird, is all.'

Nate slowed the car as they approached a sharp bend. Easing the brakes, he gently glided the vehicle around the corner and pressed the accelerator.

'Are you sure we're going the right way?' Becca asked.

'What? You don't trust me?'

'It seems like we've been in the car for hours.' She watched the road ahead; although the full lights were on, piercing through the gloom, it still seemed bleak and lifeless. They hadn't seen another vehicle for ages; there were no lights in the distance, and their phone's route calculators were on the blink after losing connection.

As Nate watched the road, shadows formed in the fields, positioned in the full lights, the mass of bleakness in the distance. They needed to get off the road and find civilisation. He couldn't admit to Becca that he was lost. He'd planned the route from London to Nottingham. There was a straight road along the M1, but the average speed check put so much time on the journey. He'd missed the turning on the way home, wanting to drive along the A40; now, he was clueless as to their location. It seemed like they'd been driving for hours. Nate was nervous they'd end up back in Nottingham. Turning to Becca, he asked, 'Shall we get a hotel? I'm tired, it's dark, and I need to rest.'

'Erh, hotel? Do you see one anywhere?'

Nate smiled. 'I mean, as soon as we see one, let's stop. We've got nothing to rush home for; we'll see it as a mini-break.' He eyed the clock on the dashboard. It was gone 10pm.

'We'd be lucky to find a vacancy at this time of night.'

Nate was hopeful. 'Surely they'll be a main road soon.'

'So, you admit it? We're lost?' Becca sighed heavily.

Nate chose to ignore her remark. 'I'm sure this is the way. We'll find a main road soon. Just relax; nothing is going to—'

'Nate. Watch out!'

The seatbelts cut into their bodies as Nate slammed the brakes. A car was lying in the ditch. The headlights gleamed off the metal, and a sense of anguish drenched their bodies.

Nate checked the rear-view mirror and eased the Jeep over to the side of the road. 'Bloody hell. I'll go and check if they're OK.' Opening the driver's door, he listened as Becca undid her seatbelt. She joined him a moment later. With trembling hands, he grabbed a torch from the boot and shone it along the road.

'Do you think they're dead?' Becca asked. 'Look at the state of the car.'

The vehicle was stationary, the engine was on, and the bonnet was badly dented.

'I hope not. But it doesn't look good; the car's in a right state. Hun, stay here. I don't want you to see anything. We're obviously the first people to stumble across it. Please, will you wait here?'

Nodding, Becca watched as Nate walked to the car. He stopped at the passenger seat and then moved around the vehicle, careful not to touch it. The rain was still heavy and it pushed against his face.

'Are they alive?' Becca shouted. She watched as Nate climbed the ditch, shining the torch into the front.

'It's empty.'

'What? How is it empty?'

'I don't know. There's no one inside. Maybe they left the

scene. Weird they didn't turn the engine off though?' He looked at Becca. 'I bet it's a drunk driver.'

Becca moved along the road and joined her husband. 'How the hell did they get out?'

With a tad of envy, Nate stood back and glared at the Porsche badge and then pointed the torch towards the passenger side. 'They must have climbed out here, then made off. At least they're OK.' He removed his mobile phone from his jeans pocket, searching for a signal. Nate thrust the phone around in the air, swinging his right arm while glaring at the screen. 'I say we get help when we reach the main road.'

'Nate, I think someone is there.' Pointing towards the fields and aided by the lights from the Jeep, Becca thought she could see a figure. 'Hello?'

Stepping to the side of the road, Nate shone the torch, scanning the area. 'I can't see anyone.'

'I don't have a good feeling about this. Can we just go? Please, Nate.'

'Hold on a second.' Nate pressed his body against the bushes, the torch in his hand, seeing a shadow crawl along the grass through a gap. 'Hello? Who's there?' Turning towards his wife, Nate said, 'It could be someone from the Porsche, but why hide? Maybe they're injured.'

'They're creeping around, trying to hide.' Stepping back towards the Jeep, Becca pleaded with her husband. 'Nate. We need to get out of here. I mean it. I don't feel safe.' Rain pelted against her body; her bones felt soaked.

After another scan with the torch, Nate joined his wife.

Someone sneezed.

Becca grabbed the Jeep door, her body trembling, panic building in her stomach, rising, washing over her. She stepped into the Jeep.

'I'm going to call the police. Do you hear me?' Nate instructed. 'I don't know what the fuck you're playing at.' Again, the figure seemed to charge around in the field, swiftly moving one way, then the other. Feeling the need to get away, Nate grabbed the handle of the driver's door. If it was someone from the Porsche, why crawl around and not say anything? It was obvious they were hiding. He felt confused, under threat and had to leave.

As he joined Becca in the Jeep, Nate closed the door. 'Let's go. As soon as we get reception, we'll call the police. It's suspicious. I don't like it.'

'Drive, Nate. Get us out of here.'

As Nate released the handbrake and pressed his foot on the accelerator, a hand slammed against the glass of the driver's door.

The fright caused Becca to scream.

Nate hit the brakes, feeling like his heart bounced in his chest.

A woman stood by the side of the Jeep, pleading for help. Moving to the front, she thumped her fist on the bonnet. Extending her arm and waving her thumb around, she mouthed, 'Can you give us a lift? Please don't go. You have to help us.'

'What's happened?' Nate asked, cracking the window slightly and feeling suspicious that she was hiding in the field.

Stepping back to the driver's door, she calmly announced, 'We've had a crash.'

Nate grabbed the torch from the footwell and shone it towards her. She looked in her mid-thirties; her blonde hair was tied up, and she wore a short dress with a long coat over it. Her pale face was damp from the rain and smudged with make-up. She was soaked, her body shivering, and appeared desperate to get warm.

Breathing a sigh of relief, Nate was suddenly aware of what had happened and why she was standing on the road. He opened the door and got out. 'Christ. Are you OK? What happened?' Nate spun around, pointing the torch towards a rustle in the bushes. Another figure walked towards them. He was much taller than the woman and wore a dark black hoodie under a brown jacket. His jeans were ripped, and he appeared bewildered. Nate watched as he approached.

'We've had an accident,' he said. 'An oncoming car took the bend too fast. I had no choice but to swerve off the road. I hit the ditch and smashed into the rock wall. The bastard drove off.'

'Oh my goodness. Are either of you hurt?' Nate asked.

'We're OK. We could do with a lift, though?' the guy said. 'I'd like to get checked out. I think my ribs may be cracked.'

'Sure. Come on; we'll give you a ride.' Nate opened the back door, watching Becca's face as he helped the strangers into the car.

Her eyes gave a concerned look, as if she wasn't happy.

'Thank you. We really appreciate your help.' He had a broad North of England accent and winced with pain as he spoke.

Nate closed the back door and moved into the driver's seat. 'Did you get the registration of the other car?'

'It happened so quickly. I remember them hurling round the bend; I had seconds. Then my car was in the ditch.'

'There are some idiots out there. How long does this road go on for? I think we're lost,' Nate asked, avoiding his wife's eyes as he finally admitted it.

'I'd say another twenty miles, give or take. Where are you headed?' Again, his voice was strained.

'London,' Becca replied. 'But at the moment, we seem a million miles away, thanks to this one.' Sarcastically, Becca rubbed the back of Nate's head, and then turned to the couple. 'I'm Becca.' Signing towards her husband, she said, 'This is Nate. So, where do you live?'

The guy spoke fast as if expecting the questions; his answers seemed unnatural, like he'd prepared or rehearsed, making Becca feel uncomfortable.

'We have a place further along this road. We were visiting my sister when the accident happened.'

'You're lucky to be alive. I imagined the worst when I saw the vehicle. You should thank your lucky stars,' Becca added.

Nate thought about the couple in the back. Although it was rude to judge, they didn't seem like the type to own a Porsche.

'We're known as JJ. Jules and Jack,' the woman said eagerly. She spoke with a midlands accent, possibly Birmingham. Her voice was high pitched and enthusiastic. She seemed pleased to be warm and out of the rain.

Becca watched the couple shifting in the seats, their hands clasping each other. Jules had a pleasant face. Her forehead remained still as she smiled, giving the impression she'd had botox. Jack was more weathered looking, at least ten years older. His stubble was dark black with a hint of grey underneath, at odds with his short blond hair, and his eyes were a deep brown colour aligned with heavy wrinkles that circled them.

'We're so grateful you stopped. God knows how long we could have been out there.' Jules was giddy.

'It's no problem,' Becca insisted.

Nate watched the couple through the rear-view mirror; they seemed comfortable. Picturing the Porsche in the ditch, he knew how lucky they were to get out in one piece.

Suddenly the smell of weed filled the Jeep. Becca turned, watching the couple pass a joint between them. She wanted to say something but didn't have the courage. Now she was uncomfortable. Turning, she faced Nate and watched the dismay on his face.

'Jesus. What are they like?' he whispered.

'You both want a drag?' Jack asked from the backseat.

'No. We're not into that. I'd rather you didn't do it in the Jeep to be honest.' Nate turned slightly, watching as Jules took a long drag, the end of the joint illuminated for a moment.

'It's just weed. I need it for my nerves. I'm sorry,' Jules added.

'Don't apologise; it's not their thing is all.' Jack reached for the joint, inhaled hard, then blew the smoke in the direction of Nate.

'Guys, come on. I'm trying to concentrate on the road. If the police stop us, we're in trouble.'

Jack laughed as he spoke. His voice became slurred. 'You can take a left further down. The road is much longer, but we'll be safe. No cops that way.'

Feeling awkward, Becca said, 'Look, we'll drop you off, then we need to get on our way. How far did you say your house was?'

'Did we say? I don't remember.' Again, Jack laughed; this time, it was more of a growl.

Nate watched as the couple began whispering to each other; they kissed, and then they took another drag of the joint. He turned towards Becca, his voice low. 'We need to get them out. Let's keep driving; try not to engage.'

'So. What did you say your names were?' Jules asked.

Becca took a deep breath. She was distressed and the smell of weed caught in her throat. She began coughing. 'Becca. This is Nate.'

'Becca and Nate. Sounds like a sugar brand. You two need to mellow out a little. You're uptight.' Jack unwound the window and tossed the remainder of the joint out, leaving the window open.

Jules began laughing, then reached her hand forward, kissing her partner's neck.

Becca watched in the mirror. She saw Jack slouch on the seat, moving his body further down. Suddenly, Jules put her hand down into the groin of his jeans. Becca closed her eyes. This had quickly turned menacing. They'd given these people a lift, helped them after the crash, and this is how they were repaid. She was always told never to pick up hitchhikers, but they were alone and vulnerable. They couldn't have left them. Now they were off their faces, and she wanted them out. She watched as Jules' hand began to move back and forth. Jack smiled and looked straight at Becca. All of a sudden, she lost it.

'Can you fucking stop?'

'Whoa.' Nate hit the brakes. 'What's going on?'

Immediately, Jules removed her hand from her partner's jeans.

'Chill, man. What's wrong?' Sitting up on the seat, Jack smirked and closed the window.

'You know perfectly well,' Becca hollowed.

Nate turned. 'Where's the house?'

'Just a little further up. We can't thank you guys enough. Seriously. I'm sorry if we've made you uncomfortable. It's not our intention.' Jack offered.

Pressing the accelerator with his right foot, Nate turned to his wife. His voice was hushed. 'What happened?'

Becca shook her head, not wanting to answer at the moment. The couple in the back were taking the piss, and she wished they'd left them on the road. 'I'll tell you later,' she whispered. 'Keep driving.'

Earlier That Evening.

'We're the two JJ's. Jules and Jack.' She smiled towards the elderly couple sitting at the next table. They'd been stood at the bar, Jules sipping a gin and tonic, and Jack a beer. As the elderly couple arrived, he'd watched them settle, removing their coats and warming by the open fire. Jack waited, patient, diligent, and then walked over to them. Jules followed him, and they sat.

'Well, it's good to meet you both.' The older man reached his arm out, introducing himself. 'I'm Albert; this is my wife, May.'

Jack sat, watching them, not offering his hand back. He eyed Albert, the way he dressed, his expensive taste, his demeanour and the keys to the Porsche they'd pulled up in, lying on the table. He remained silent while Jules spoke to the couple for the next half hour, finding common ground with politics, current affairs, and passion for old films.

Looking affectionately at his wife, Albert seemed so gentle, attentive and in love. Buttoning his jacket, he swiped a hand through his long grey hair and pushed it out of his face.

May removed a scarf from her handbag and placed it around her short black hair, tying it tight at the back. 'It's good to meet you both. We're off now though. Enjoy the rest of your night.' She was well-spoken, much shorter than Albert and extremely elegant.

Standing, Jules placed her arms around May and then Albert. 'Drive safely. Great to meet you both.'

'Likewise,' Albert answered. Slugging the last of his lemonade, he held May's hand, and they walked outside.

Jack watched, his eyes following them as they left the pub. He turned to Jules. 'You ready?'

'Jack. No. They're lovely. We can't—'

'Finish your drink, and let's go,' he snapped.

Bringing the glass to her lips, Jules fought the dread in her stomach, the nervousness which built every time Jack had one of his plans. She downed the last of her gin and tonic. Jules watched as Jack stood, making his way out. Bracing herself, she placed the glass on the table and followed.

Outside, it was dark. The only glow was the neon light of The Harbour Inn public house along the quiet stretch of road. The moon provided enough light for Jack to see towards the car park. He saw the full lights turn on and quickly hid behind a bush, grabbing Jules and pulling her beside him.

'That's them. You know the plan. Same as before. We've done it many times,' Jack commanded. 'I'll get close to them. When it's safe, I'll overtake, get enough distance between us, and then pull over. You ready?'

Rife with anticipation, Jules nodded. She hated this, and it wasn't what she'd signed up for. Listening to the car approach, she placed her hands over her eyes to stem the bright lights.

They waited until the elderly couple had pulled out onto the country road and then raced towards their Ford Mondeo.

Jack started the engine while Jules placed her seatbelt around her waist. As she buckled it into the clip, she conceded she didn't want to be here. Not with Jack, not doing what they did. They robbed houses and stole cars. Jack could break into any older model and have it started within seconds. The newer ones were tricky. He'd break into properties late at night, find the vehicle keys and move them off the drive.

To him, it was better than sex.

Jules worried; she knew one day it would go wrong, the cards would tumble, and they'd be caught. Jack would speed, he was always high, and people's lives were at risk. He didn't care; it was all a game to him. She'd tried to leave him, but he'd always talk her into going back.

Jules had to get away from him.

The next attempt would have to be the end.

For now, she had to follow his orders.

* * *

In the distance, Jack watched the lights disappear around a bend; he slammed his right foot on the accelerator. 'Let's do this. They're fucking minted, these two. Did you see the car they were driving? A fucking Porsche Jules. Are you listening? They have money, baby—lots of it.' Jack turned to Jules. 'You know the drill. We'll take the car first. Leave the bastards stranded. Then pocket the phones, make them surrender their address and empty the house.' Pushing back in the seat, Jack watched the road, his arm outstretched, cool as you like. This was his time, his moment to shine. He knew Jules was hesitant, that it frightened her, but the money they'd made paid for her outfits, expensive restaurants and a nice apartment.

He was sure of himself.

Jules would never leave him.

Seeing the lights in front, he felt a buzz of excitement. 'There they are. Easy money. Right, keep watch. Make sure no one is behind. I'll find a way around the vehicle. If it comes to it, I'll honk the horn, whack the full beams on and force them to pull over.'

Holding the handrail, her heart racing, Jules thought about opening the door, hurling herself out and running. Watching the road as Jack sped, the ground moving under the car at great speed, gazing at the vehicle's lights, she felt sick. Albert was in the driver's seat; May sat next to him. After enjoying the chat in the pub, she felt sorry for them and was peeved with her partner for what he was about to do. 'Jack. Please slow down. You know how I worry.'

'It's all good. Just keep a lookout. If you see anyone, shout.'

Feeling the tension rise in her stomach, Jules felt nauseous. Like the blood was charging around her body, her heart struggling to pump it.

After a joint he'd had before going into the pub, Jack was stoned and began laughing to himself. They'd waited patiently for the right people to come in the door. Then they made their move. Once Jack had seen Albert and May, he knew they had money. Albert had told them about his business, how he and May had worked together. How they'd retired due to technology, not able to keep up with the online retail business, and they'd managed to sell the company at just the right time.

Jack knew this could be a game-changer. The flashy car was only the start. He intended to take it, change the number plate, and sell it on, after ransacking their house. *Happy days,* he thought to himself.

'Jack. Slow down. They'll see you. You're getting too close.'

'It's all under control. Just Chill.' Jack attempted to move around the vehicle. As he pulled out, forcing the steering wheel anti-clockwise, Albert moved with him. 'Shit. You son of a bitch. Oh yeah. You want to play that game, huh?'

'Please slow down, Jack.'

'Keep your mouth closed and watch behind. I hate the constant moaning' Stabbing the accelerator, Jack began flashing the lights. The full beams caused the car in front to swerve. He listened as Jules began to panic; the loud whimpering noises penetrated his mind. 'There's a bend up ahead. As soon as we're around it, I'll overtake them. I'll get some space between us before hiding the car and standing out on the road.'

Albert was watching the car behind as he approached the bend. 'What is wrong with this lunatic?' Concerned that the driver would ram them, he sped up. As he approached the sharp corner, he lost control. An oncoming car swerved out of the way. Albert stamped on the brakes.

The oncoming car managed to gain control, rounded the bend and drove on.

Albert was still furiously grappling with the steering wheel, trying in desperation to control the Porsche. Then he slammed into a rock wall.

* * *

Grappling with the steering wheel, Jack narrowly avoided the Porsche. 'I need to park the car out of sight and go back and grab the keys.' He saw an airbag inflated as he passed the vehicle, concerned for the elderly couple.

Jules was too frightened to speak, muted by the shock of

the crash. Jack was out of control. It was foolish to go back, but no amount of pleading would persuade him otherwise.

Steering the Ford Mondeo onto a narrow country lane, Jack parked the vehicle in front of a rickety-looking gate blocking access to the field. It was secured with a robust lock and a sign reading, *"Trespassers will be prosecuted."*

He and Jules got out together in silence, and Jack grabbed a torch from the backseat. As they walked to the road and approached the vehicle, Jules saw the motionless bodies in the car and began to sob.

'Oh my God. What the fuck, Jack? What have you done? They're dead. You've fucking murdered them!'

'It wasn't my fault. How was I supposed to know they'd meet another vehicle? They should have pulled over earlier!' Jack grabbed Jules by the arm and began shaking her. 'You're part of it. You'll go down too. I swear. I'll bring you with me if anyone finds out?' Driven by greed and a clouded mind, Jack said, 'Help me find the keys to the house. Check their pockets.'

'No,' she screamed. Across the fields in the distance, Jules could see lights. Possibly a couple of miles away, heading in their direction. 'Jack, we have company.'

Turning, he saw the dazzling beams. 'Oh, shit. We're fucked. Quick, help me get them out. If they see the bodies, we're finished.'

Sniffling, Jules watched as her partner undid the seat-belts, fighting with the airbag and pulled May from the vehicle, her legs thumping on the ground. The lights were gaining on them, and Jack thought he'd have a heart attack. His skin burned with anguish, and his eyes became blurry. With his hands under May's arms, he dragged her through the bushes and placed her on the grass. Running around to the driver's side, his legs pressed against the car, he pulled Albert out. His body was slighter heavier, and he ordered Jules to help. 'Grab his legs. Quick, Jules, we don't have much time.' They dragged Albert's body into the field, leaving him with his wife and ran.

The lights rounded the bend.

'Get down; they'll see us.' Turning, Jack watched as the vehicle stopped.

A torch pointed in their direction, and they tried to evade it, to duck, crawling one way and another, desperate to avoid being seen.

As the couple walked back to their car, Jack's world came crashing down as Jules raced towards them.

Present Time.

Becca and Nate sat in silence. The smell of weed was still strong in the Jeep.

Becca felt disgusted that they'd picked up Jack and Jules. The two JJ's, as they'd announced. They'd lit up a joint, then began to fondle in the back seat. What were her and Nate thinking, giving these strangers a lift?

Watching the road, Nate felt anger festering inside him, building. He needed them out of the Jeep and was worried for Becca. She hated awkward situations. Unable to cope. It stressed her out and brought on panic attacks.

Watching to his left, Nate hoped he'd see lights, a house, but there was nothing. Just miles of darkness, endless shadows and a multitude of bleakness. 'Where's the house, guys?' Nate asked impatiently.

Jack laughed. 'A little further up. We can't thank you both enough for stopping, really. You've helped us out of a hole.' The old couple from the pub had told Jack where they lived. He was certain the house was a little further along the road. Maybe they'd have another car, and he and Jules could drive back, pick up the Mondeo and get out of here.

Jules was high from the joint they'd smoked. Moments ago, she'd placed her hands in Jack's underwear. She'd been hoping to catch Becca's attention then give her a signal, catch her eye and somehow instruct them to pull over and get Jack out of the Jeep. It was a chance that came and went. The joint had caused confusion, and she was desperate. Somehow, she needed to get the message across for the couple in the front to help her. She sat, feeling Jack's breath on her, disgusted by how he'd acted earlier. Dumping the bodies, then threatening her, telling her she'd go down with him. It was too much. She had to get away from him. This was going to be her chance to escape. She'd play it cool, wait for the opportunity and then run.

A new life.

A new beginning.

'Stop,' Jack shouted, causing the other three to jump.

Jules darted a look towards her partner as the Jeep came to a halt.

Becca and Nate turned around and watched Jack.

'I feel sick. I'm so stoned I can't focus. I need to get out for a second.'

Jack knew the house was close. He needed to stand out on the road and search for lights. Opening the Jeep door, he stood out on the quiet country lane, scouring for the old couple's house. He leant back into the Jeep. 'We're fine from here. Thanks for the ride. Come on, Jules.'

Apprehensively, she undid her seatbelt; fear scratched at her body as she looked at Becca in the front. This was her moment, her last chance. Suddenly, Jules leant over, slammed the back door of the Jeep and screamed, 'Drive!'

Nate turned his body around, facing the back of the Jeep as Jack pounded on the window with the palm of his left hand.

'What's wrong?' Becca shouted.

'Please. I beg you, drive!' She broke down, tears spilling from her eyes. 'Please.' Jumping to the middle of the seats, she watched as Jack began punching the glass with his fists.

As Nate pressed the accelerator, Jack removed a knife that was tucked into his sock and stabbed the back tyre.

* * *

'What in the name of Christ is wrong with you two?' Watching the road, Nate listened to the cries from the woman in the back.

Becca had her shoes on the seat, her body curled tight, stunned by the events taking place in their Jeep.

'We should have left you on the side of the road,' Nate continued.

Struggling to compose herself, Jules said, 'Sorry. I need to get away from him. You have to help me. He's a fucking mad man.'

'I can see that.' Nate was furious. Pounding his fist on the dashboard, he caused the Jeep to swerve. 'I can't believe you brought this shit to us. How dare you.'

Jules was crying; her hands covered her face for a moment and then dropped to her lap. Looking between Becca and Nate, her eyes were so full of self-pity and fear. 'I had to get away from him.' She reached forward and placed her hand on Becca's shoulder. 'Please help me.'

Becca shrugged her off. 'You're just as bad.'

Jules didn't answer.

Nate watched the road, searching for a place to stop and get help. His phone was still showing no signal.

Suddenly the Jeep began dropping on the right-hand side. He opened the window, listening to the loud hissing noise. 'Oh no. No, no, no. Not now.'

Placing her head in her hands, Becca screeched, 'This isn't happening.'

Now a flapping noise was evident. The tyre pressure was dropping rapidly.

Nate pulled over, steering the Jeep close to the ditch to allow any other vehicles to pass. Grabbing the torch, he got out.

'I'm so sorry,' Jules offered.

'Don't talk to me. I don't want to hear from you,' Becca snapped.

Standing by the driver's door, Nate stated, 'It's buggered. I think the bastard stabbed the tyre as we drove off. I have a spare in the boot.' As he moved around the vehicle, he could see a flashlight in the distance. 'Oh shit. Guys, out of the Jeep. Quickly. I think he's coming. We need to move.'

Becca opened the door and got out. Jules followed. They looked along the road. A speck of light danced in the bleakness around a half-mile from where they stood.

'Please. He's going to kill me. You have to help.' She smashed her fists on the roof of the Jeep in fear. 'He can't get to us.'

Becca turned towards Nate. 'If he has a fucking knife, he'll use it. We have to run.'

'Where? Run where?' Nate turned, looking around him. It was pitch black; their headlights illuminating just a few feet around where they were standing. Turning off the lights and removing the vehicle's keys, Nate stated, 'He'll see us. We need to keep hidden.'

Becca gasped; dread gripped her skin, and her body was cold and numb from exhaustion.

Nate removed his phone from his pocket, instructing Becca and Jules to do the same. 'Keep the torch low to the ground. Don't lift the light under any circumstances. We can't risk him seeing us.'

Jules began wailing.

Walking towards her and covering the woman's mouth, Becca whispered, 'I swear to God I will whack you and leave you here for him to find you. You've brought so much shit to our door. Don't fucking test me. Not now.' She shone the light on Jules' face, watching her nod.

'Come on. Follow me.' Nate kept the torch towards the

ground. Pushing the bushes back on the side of the road, he made a gap for Becca and Jules to move through. Once they were in the field, he pushed his way through, cutting his arm on the sharp twigs.

Nate led the way, listening to Becca's sharp breaths beside him and Jules snivelling, wiping the mucus from her nose and trying to keep up.

They trampled the wet grass which reached their knees, willing their bodies to keep going.

Turning, Nate glanced behind, checking if the torchlight was close. He couldn't see anything. He carried on walking, pissed off with the situation they'd been dragged into and fearful for their lives.

Suddenly they heard a voice.

'Jules! I'm going to fucking kill you. Do you hear me?'

The three of them stopped, too frightened to take another step. They all held their breaths. The voice was distant, but they were frightened he'd catch up if he knew what direction they had gone in. Jack was high; he had a knife and was obviously a very violent man.

'Keep quiet,' Nate whispered. 'He doesn't know we've come into this field.'

'He'll work it out. Our Jeep is on the road. He'll see the gap in the bushes,' Becca pointed out.

Nate had forgotten about their vehicle.

'Please help me,' Jules said in a strangled whisper.

Again, the voice in the distance. 'Jules. I'm coming.' The horn blared on their Jeep, indicating how close Jack was.

Nate realised he'd left it unlocked. 'We need to run. Quick, hold my hand.' Nate could feel his wife's icy skin. He turned to Jules. 'We have to get out of here. I need you to be quiet. Don't make a sound, understood?'

The three of them raced across the fields, traipsing through the damp grass, turning behind to watch for lights.

Nate was kicking himself for stopping on the road. He should have listened to Becca and kept driving. His chest began to wheeze as he moved through the field, his lungs tight as he gulped the cold air.

They ran together, the lights from their phones bouncing on the ground, flicking left, right, their heavy breathes filling the night. The rain had stopped, but it was so cold, and mist pushed in their faces causing their skin to ache. The moon was partly visible through the heavy clouds, and only bleakness surrounded them.

Becca turned, seeing a light behind them, it jumped wildly like someone was racing towards them. 'I think he's behind us, in the field.'

Spinning around, Nate watched as Jack gained on them. He turned back, now able to make out a silhouette in front. 'I think that's a house. Look.' Nate pointed ahead as he ran.

'Oh please, God,' Becca panted.

Running towards the shape, they watched it enlarge; a speck of light now appeared towards the back of the building.

'It's definitely a house. Come on, keep moving,' Nate insisted. 'Are you OK, Becca?'

She forced an answer. Her face was sore from the cold, her lips ached, her body was giddy with adrenalin, and she struggled to keep moving.

Finally they burst out of the field onto a small lane, and raced towards the gates of the house. As the three of them reached the front of the house, Nate banged on the front door.

'Help! Is anyone here? Please help us.'

'Help us, please.' Becca joined her husband and

slammed the palm of her hands against the wooden front door.

'He's right behind us,' Jules screamed. She could hear Jack crashing through the fields, getting louder and closer every second.

Nate turned the doorknob, astounded that it opened. He shone the torch along the empty hallway and then helped the two women inside. 'Hello? We need help. We've been attacked. Is anyone here?' Nate shouted. Locking the door, he listened for an answer, then searched the downstairs rooms. Finding no one on the ground floor, Nate darted upstairs. After a few moments, he called out as he ran back down towards the women. 'No one is home.' From the glass in the front door, he could see the light moving closer through the fields.

After they searched the rooms for a house phone and a quick check that the windows were locked, Nate ordered, 'We need to hide.'

Becca leant forward and kissed her husband's cheek. 'It's a good job we don't go to see Christopher every week.'

Nate jumped as the doorknob began to twist behind him. Shining the torch towards a small sofa chair, he pushed it against the front door. He could see the large shadow through the window. 'Quick, upstairs.' Backing away from the door, he could hear Becca and Jules racing up to the first floor. Turning, he followed them, listening as Jack began thumping the glass.

The three of them stood at the top of the house.

'It's not going to be long before he gets inside. I'm guessing the bathroom is the safest bet. We can lean against the door and try to hold him off.' Nate shone the torch along the upstairs hallway. 'Let's go.' He moved behind Becca and

Jules, watching the stairs. He had to be ready if Jack came up before they reached the bathroom.

He could hear Jules, the fearful gasps, the agitated, frantic state of her mind. Becca, panting, frightened and trying to be courageous.

If only they'd taken the M1 home.

There were loud thumping noises coming from below, then the sound of glass shattering onto the floor.

Jules screamed, 'He's going to kill me. You have to help.'

They stood by the bathroom door; Becca went in first, Jules next and finally Nate. Slamming the door, he slid his body to the ground, pressing his legs against the back wall.

The two women sat on the edge of the bath.

They were silent, only their chests moving and controlled breaths pushing gently from their mouths.

'What the fuck is it with this guy?' Nate asked more to himself.

'I'm so sorry to drag you both into this mess,' Jules whispered.

Becca watched her face, aided by the phone torch, wanting to punch her, pull her hair and drag her to the ground. She refrained from acting on the violent thoughts. 'We should open the door and feed you to the lion.'

Nate looked at his wife with a concerned expression, disappointed with her comment. Turning, he placed his left knee on the floor and his right leg pressed against the back wall, his palms firm against the bathroom door, needing to be ready if Jack tried to get inside.

The torch was placed beside him.

'So, what now?' Becca asked.

Heavy footsteps began thudding up the stairs.

Grabbing Nate's wrist with her hand, squeezing tight, Jules pleaded, 'Please don't let him in here. I beg you both.'

Nate's voice was hushed. 'Just keep silent.' He shone the torch towards his wife, then at Jules. 'We can do this.'

Listening to the loud steps across the floor, the women huddled together, preparing for the attack.

Opening doors and slamming them shut, Jack moved between rooms, calling their names.

Nate, Becca and Jules remained still, muted and motionless, wide eyes peering in the same direction.

The door handle twisted. Jules gasped.

A tap on the door.

They held their breath, too scared to move, too anxious to make a sound.

Another tap.

They watched, the three of them staring towards the door. Suddenly, a stabbing sound, like a knife going into wood. All Nate could think of was *The Shining* as he leapt away from the door.

Leave me alone,' Jules screamed.

Becca jolted, pleading with Jack to stop.

The three of them stood against the back wall, listening as the knife continued into the bathroom door. They could hear the heavy sighs, the knife being drawn back and driven at the door.

Raging, Jack pounded the door, shouting and punching the wood. Drawing his neck back, he slammed his forehead against it. Exhausted, the weed affecting his mental state and the rage he felt, his body cumbersome, Jack backed away.

The hallway became a blur; his eyes were starting to cloud over, his body jolting with palpitations, and he wanted to vomit. He dropped the knife and stepped backwards towards the stairs.

Jules listened to his stumbling legs, dragging across the

floor. She reached for the bathroom lock, aided by the torch and opened the door.

'No, Jules,' Becca ordered.

Breaking away, Jules watched as Jack held his head, still staggering. He stared at her, his arms outstretched.

Racing across the room, visions powering through her mind, the torment, anguish and misery this person had caused her, she pushed him down the stairs, screaming like a maniac as his body fell.

Jack landed by the bottom step, mangled, his head twisted, and his neck broken from the fall.

Jules raced down the stairs and out of the house.

Moving out of the bathroom, Nate grabbed the torch and stood at the top of the stairs shining the light on Jack's body.

'What's happened?' Becca asked.

'Don't come out here. He's dead. She must have pushed him.' Nate moved towards his wife and held her; then, she cried into his chest.

* * *

Nate and Becca sat in the bathroom for almost ten minutes, stunned, exhausted and completely drained. They held each other tight, not wanting to let go. It had been the night from hell, and they swore they'd never pick up hitchhikers again.

Nate called the police and told them what had happened, then gave them the address which he'd found on a letter in a kitchen drawer.

Jules had escaped, but it wouldn't be long until the police caught up with her.

As Nate and Becca stepped over Jack's dead body and

stood at the front door, they watched the blue lights illuminating the night, the loud sirens ringing out as the police made their way to the house.

Turning to Becca, Nate placed his arm around her waist. 'You OK?'

'Yeah, just don't ever pick for hitchhikers again.'

Two deafening cracks rang out through the house. Nate's body dropped to the floor, followed by Becca's. The bullets from the handgun had ripped through their skulls, killing them instantly.

* * *

Albert had driven his battered Porsche up to the house, hoping he'd find the couple who'd murdered his wife. Earlier, he'd gained consciousness, saved by the inflated airbag. May hadn't been so fortunate. Hers hadn't worked.

As Albert gained consciousness and woke in a field, he got off the grass, shaken and disorientated. Shining his phone torch, he found his wife's mangled body lying a few feet away. Hysterical, he dropped to his knees and sobbed. Cradling his beautiful wife, he swore he'd get revenge. As he drove to the house, ripped apart by grief and full of vengeance, he passed a Jeep, parked by the ditch and abandoned.

As Albert pulled onto the drive, he saw a shadow in the hallway.

Getting out of the car, he walked along the side entrance into the garden and hid in the back office.

His life with May, the only woman he ever loved, had now ended. Stricken with grief, he moved to the gun cabinet. Albert braced himself. He'd enjoyed shooting in the past and being a member of a local gun club.

Now, he'd enjoy it again.

They'd ruined his life.

Albert was going to ruin theirs.

Walking across the grass, he stepped into the unlocked kitchen at the back.

They'd never had a reason to lock the place before.

Albert saw the figures in the hallway, two of them, a man and woman, holding a torch. Assuming they'd come to empty the place after killing his darling May, Albert lifted the gun, pulled the trigger twice and watched the couple drop to the floor, satisfied he'd taken revenge.

As sirens rang out around him, he turned the gun on himself and pulled the trigger again.

The End

ANYTHING

6

Vinnie Cartwright stood in the hallway of his first-floor flat, stunned from the conversation he'd overheard on the bus. He'd been shopping in Camden, a bustling town in North West London, and strolling around the world-famous market, eating a pack of twelve doughnuts, half strawberry and the other half raspberry. Enjoying them so much, he'd almost sucked the skin off his fingers to get the last remnants of sugar.

On the way home, he'd overheard a conversation. Two elderly gentlemen were sitting at the back of the bus, their voices low, leaning into one another. One of the men had said that he'd found 'the shop'. His friend had asked which shop he was talking about. The first man went on to explain that the shop was difficult to find. After visiting Camden quite a few times, he'd finally found it. He described meeting the owner, following him along the pavement and entering the shop through the back door. The shop owner had moved around the counter, asked what he'd wanted, and the wheels were set in motion.

Vinnie had wanted to talk to him. He'd heard about the shop, but he couldn't miss his stop. The next one was almost a mile along the road, and Vinnie didn't fancy walking back. He was tired, and the carb and sugar overload from the dozen doughnuts was taking effect.

Now, as he eyed the full-length mirror, his face plump and heavily rounded, his brown eyes sunk into his head, the spare skin under his chin and his black hair wild and chaotic, disappointment washed over him, and he thought about 'the shop.' He'd tried, Christ; he'd wanted to shed the weight.

Vinnie had signed up to an online class and paid over three hundred pounds for a twelve-week course. Strict with himself, he woke at 6.30am, squeezing into an extra-large vest top and baggy tracksuit bottoms to work out in the living room.

Thirty minutes of cardio, light at first, then as the course progressed, he pushed harder. Racing around the living room, he'd charge back and forth between the walls, burpees, star jumps, squats, running on the spot, the dreaded plank.

He ignored the thuds on the floor coming from the neighbour below. The ceilings were high, and Vinnie imagined Mavis Harper using a broom to poke the ceiling.

This was his time.

Vinnie disliked the gym. He hated the smell, the posers curling twenty kilos in front of the mirror, the tempting protein bars lodged in the machines with their neon lights, people watching him, the smirks on their faces, the subtle nudges to their friends.

Vinnie Cartwright was over twenty-five stone. He was five feet nine, and his body fat was treble what it should be.

For the first month, he'd kept to the program, exercising thirty minutes every day, often followed by a brisk walk. Yes, he should have kept to the diet—low carb, plenty of veg and at least three litres of water a day. He did try, but Vinnie did have the odd bag of crisps, a couple of takeaways at the weekend and a handful of chocolate bars during weekdays. He had to. It was the only thing that kept him going. But he adhered to the fact that working out would cancel the junk. The exercise was regimental. Vinnie stuck to it. He'd put so much effort in.

This morning, when he'd checked the scales on day twenty-eight, he'd gained three pounds.

Picking up the scales, Vinnie began slamming them against the bathroom wall as pieces of glass dropped by his feet, then he hurled them across the living room.

Now, he stood, seeing the large overhang of his stomach, his droopy man boobs and his flushed, rounded face.

Tears began filling his eyes. He'd always been over-weight. The kids at school mocked him and pointed as he walked to class. The names they screamed at him were despicable. He ate to cope with the stress. His mother and father reassured him that the weight would drop in his adult life, that God makes us all shapes and sizes.

In his teenage years, Vinnie had never had a girlfriend, or even kissed a person of the opposite sex. The bullies made it too difficult with their sarcasm and cruel jibes. His confidence and self-esteem were non-existent.

When Vinnie left school, he moved to London and trained to be a chef. His love of food drove him to make a career in it. He was going to master flavours, dishes, spices from around the world, and be surrounded by his one great love. Food. Finger dipping with the cake mixes didn't help though. When no one was looking, he'd dunk his forefinger into the bowl of ice cream, icing sugar, chocolate. Whatever was left over, Vinnie Cartwright would eat it.

Waste not, want not.

The motto he lived by.

Now, he stood, feeling sick with shame, his mind returning once again to that overheard conversation. The two men had been sat in front of him, discussing the shop called Anything.

'Where is it exactly?' One of the men had asked.

'It's difficult to find. The shutters were down. You have to knock and hope the owner hears. I'm told he doesn't advertise, has no phone, no way of outside communication. But I got lucky. I waited for ages; it was a friend of mine who'd first told me about it.'

The other guy leant forward. 'But what is it? What happens in there?'

'It's all your dreams wrapped into one. You can get *anything.*'

'Anything?'

'Yes. Anything.'

Vinnie regretted not asking, but he didn't have the courage. He knew the shop was in Camden, but he'd been there many times and never found it. He'd heard of it from a friend of his who was having marital problems; he'd stumbled across the shop as if it had appeared from nowhere, then knocked and waited.

The old man had answered, then brought him inside.

Vinnie's friend, Martin Kessler, had asked for financial help after splitting up with his wife.

Once Martin had done something for the shop owner, it happened. Vinnie wasn't sure he'd believed Martin at the time, but that conversation on the bus suggested he may have been telling the truth.

Looking in the mirror, Vinnie wondered if this shop really boasts *anything*. If it did, Vinnie was going to find it. He was going to lose the weight.

Vinnie swept up the glass in the bathroom, and finding more shards where the scales had landed in the living room. He wanted to hurl them out the window, to run down to the street and stamp on them until they became unrecognisable. *Now, weigh that, you piece of shit. Show me what I weigh now.* He imagined people walking past, laughing, applauding him.

Best thing for them, mate. Mine haven't worked for years.

Good on you, son. Who needs them anyway. Live and let live.

But instead, Vinnie picked up the scales, placed them back in the bathroom and took a shower. Standing under the hot water, he held his stomach, kneading it, then he began lifting his midsection and bouncing it in his hands.

It needed to change. Vinnie couldn't go on like this.

After washing his hair and body, he turned off the shower and dried himself. His skin was raw, a bright red colour from the heat of the water. He could feel himself sweating, moisture seeping from his skin as he dried it. He could spend all day like this. Dry and soak, dry and soak. His weight couldn't continue to be a problem like this.

Dressing in an oversized T-shirt, jumper, and baggy jeans, Vinnie took a bus back to Camden.

He walked along the High Street, past the market; the smell of food hung in the air, and he wanted so badly to stop, to eat more doughnuts or a burger, a half-pounder with cheese and loaded with onions. Stopping for a moment, Vinnie pondered whether to do just that. *No. I am here to change my life. The first day and all that. It starts now.*

He pictured himself grabbing a bull by the horns, the animal bowing down to him. Everyone applauding and asking for photos.

Vinnie wanted that.

Slim was the new him. Slim him. That's how he'd roll now.

Walking along the side streets, he looked at the shops, the assistants welcoming customers, talking, showing them around. He passed cafes, restaurants, nail parlours, tattooists, florists, E-cig outlets and newsagents. Everywhere was open. Every shop welcoming the public to come in, look around and spend.

He walked for hours, circling Camden over and over and thought about asking people, but what did he say? *Oh hi. I'm looking for a shop. A specific shop. You can buy anything. Anything your heart desires. But it's closed. The shutters are always down, and there's no way of contacting the owner. Have you seen a shop like this?*

Why hadn't he asked the men on the bus? His friend Martin had said you have to look and be lucky. But look where? Vinnie had combed every inch of Camden. Aware he looked crazy, Vinnie had to keep walking, searching; it was here somewhere.

He strolled past families with small children and over-sized buggies, tourists standing on pavements, taking photos, selfies and large, overenthusiastic group hugs, planning where to visit next. Vinnie was becoming frustrated; he'd walked miles, round in circles, over the same, familiar ground, passing the same people. Christ, he was going to thump someone in a minute.

It was getting dark, and Vinnie was hungry. He could get something to eat, come back tomorrow or the next day. He'd keep coming here until he eventually found—

Suddenly, Vinnie saw a small, grey building with the metal shutters down and a piece of boarding over the front window. It hadn't been there earlier. He was certain. Standing on the pavement, he eyed the place, confused and bewildered. He'd been here many times today. There'd been a wall with barbed wire, a locked gate and a sign instructing to keep out. But now, here it is. The place he'd heard about.

Anything.

Moving along the road, Vinnie eyed the place. The grey stone was crumbling and in need of repair. Tarpaulin hung over the flat roof, and a cracked waste pipe spilt water onto the pavement. The edge of the window was besieged with a fungus or mushroom substance, and it stank. A metal shutter was pulled over the main entrance with a large chubb lock securing it.

Vinnie hesitated. The building looked dark and menacing. There were no signs or welcome cards and nothing instructing what was sold inside. It could have been an abandoned building. But Vinnie was certain he'd found, 'Anything.'

As he stared at the dark, decrepit building from the pavement, he wondered how the guy made money. How could he run a business like this? Vinnie was in two minds. His inner voice told him to go home. To leave and never return.

Confident that the shop had appeared out of nowhere, it seemed like it knew he was coming. And something that did, couldn't be good news. The other voice instructed him to brave it out and pursue his dream.

Glancing behind, feeling paranoid, he then moved further along the pavement, unsure what to do next.

As Vinnie walked forward and tapped the knuckles of

his large hand against the metal shutter, the vibration startled him. Standing back, he waited for a reply. Vinnie hesitated, partly wanting to go home, his heart racing. He damped the sweat on his forehead with a handkerchief, not knowing what to expect. The longer he waited, the more convinced he became that the shop was empty.

He banged the shutters again, the noise drawing attention and causing people to look at him. *Come on. Open the bloody door. Where are you?* Vinnie wondered what he'd say if the guy did open the shop. How would he feel, describing what he wanted? Admitting defeat. *Oh, I can't lose weight. But hey, you're the guy who sells everything, right? So bloody make me skinny. I'd love to have a sexual encounter at least once in my life. To walk through a door without turning sideways. To get off the sofa with ease, majestically sweep up and drift along the floor. Are you getting me here, mate? Make me fucking skinny.*

Vinnie imagined grabbing the guy and shaking him as he shouted his demands. He laughed to himself. Easy at first, then he burst into hysterics. People watched, concerned looks on their faces, wondering what was wrong with the large man banging on the shutters.

Vinnie couldn't do this. The more he thought about it, the more ludicrous it sounded. Anything. What the heck? This is bonkers. *Yeah, mate. You sell anything, right? Anything I want? So get me an evening with Elvis. A one-time private concert. Just for me. Or a night with Judy Garland. Here's one, Let me walk along the yellow brick road and meet the famous wizard. Or a lead in Angels With Dirty Faces. See how that sounds—what a load of shit.*

Moving away, he began walking back towards the high street. But then he heard someone behind him.

'Can I help you?'

Vinnie turned. A man appeared from nowhere. The first thing Vinnie noticed was the hat. It was a bowler type, weird looking and dated. He was old, maybe early to mid-seventies; his grey beard was thick, long but neat and met in a sharp point at his chin. His eyes were dark brown, almost black. He was small, under five feet, and he wore a black waistcoat with matching coloured trousers. Vinnie had never seen such a peculiar looking character, and if it were a dark alley, he'd turn back. Eyeing the man suspiciously, he asked, 'This shop. Is it yours?'

The man stared right through him. 'Whether I own this establishment is neither here nor there. I trust you were looking for it. Either that or you're lost. But I doubt the latter as you've been circling for hours now. A man with such determination and conviction is headstrong; he knows what he wants, to change, modify, and face the goals head-on. No, you're not lost.' The man stepped forward out of the darkness. 'So, what is it I can help you with?'

'You seem to have all the answers,' Vinnie fired back. A strange mist seemed to surround the stranger, which made him appear sinister, cutting a mysterious figure on the side road.

The noise from the high street behind him had deadened, and it seemed they were alone.

'I don't have all the answers. That would be a ludicrous way of thinking. A man with all the answers doesn't ask questions. To question is to learn. Only someone ignorant and naive would think they know everything. That person would look down on others, disrespect them and frown upon one who wants to learn. I never disrespect anyone. So, I'll ask again, what is it you want?'

Vinnie was tongue-tied. The old man spoke with such

confidence, like everything that spilt from his mouth was a life lesson. He had to admit he was impressed. 'I heard you can help people.'

Smiling, the old man turned. 'Follow me.' Walking along the pavement to the side of the shop, he removed a key from his trouser pocket. He opened the chubb lock and pushed open a door leading to the back of the shop. Once there, he removed another key, unlocking the chubb and lifting the metal shutter.

Vinnie watched in shock. It didn't make a noise. Nothing. Like it had been muted. The old man opened a glass door, pushed it hard, and then stepped inside. Vinnie followed.

The lights came on, and Vinnie looked around the shop floor. There were jars everywhere. Objects floated in a watery substance and were labelled. Each one had a number, no wording. Walking forward, he stared in awe. There must be hundreds.

It looked like a biology lab. Vinnie wanted to ask what he collected, but he wasn't sure if he'd like an answer.

The old man moved behind the counter and turned to Vinnie. 'I'm guessing one of two things. Someone recommended me. That's why you're here. I don't advertise, the shop is never open, and I never promote my business. So, I'd assume it's someone I've already helped. I'd also assume that whoever recommended me is a close friend. They trust you and are pleased with the service, hence, the recommendation.'

The old man was correct. Vinnie's friend Martin had told him about the place.

'The second assumption is, of course; you overheard a conversation.'

Bang. The old man was right on both counts. Who the hell is he? Vinnie thought. He looked at him, wondering if he knew about the bus journey this morning and how he'd overheard two men talking about this place. His friend Martin had been here after recently splitting with his wife. It had hit Martin hard, and he was near bankruptcy. He'd contemplated suicide before he'd heard about this place. He'd confided in Vinnie after finding a stash of money.

Vinnie had been convinced he'd stolen it and that the shop, Anything, was a fabricated story.

But after listening to the enthusiastic conversation on the bus this morning, Vinnie had to see for himself.

The old man continued. 'By your appearance, I'd say you don't need food.'

Vinnie blushed. Was he being rude? Or just straight with him? He couldn't tell.

'You have a nice flat, a good job, no recent split with a partner. You have no children, and you take pride in how you look. I see you've shaved this morning, you smell pleasant enough, your hair is styled back, and your clothes are acceptable. So, how come you can't lose weight?'

This guy was good, Vinnie thought. He'd been watching him. He knew about his life and where he lived. It's like the old man knew he was coming. Vinnie looked around at the shop; the jars were so odd-looking. He wondered what was inside each glass container.

With a deep breath, paranoia pushing through his body and a fear of judgement, he announced, 'All my life, I've suffered from weight problems. I've tried. I've spent so much of my life on fad diets, everything you can imagine. I don't like exercise, but I'll do it if it works. I like food too much. That's the problem.'

Smirking, the old man said, 'What if, Vinnie, I could give you something that would make you never worry about your weight again?'

Vinnie watched the man behind the counter. He hadn't told him his name. 'OK. I'd like that. It would be a dream come true.'

'Would you do anything to lose weight?'

Hesitating for a moment, Vinnie answered. 'Yes. Yes, I would.'

'Has the problem got out of hand?'

'Yes. It's taken everything from me. It's robbed me of the life I deserve. It's taken my confidence; I can't get a girlfriend because I'm painfully shy. I can't think of anything worse than striking up a conversation in a bar or chatting to a woman in the park. So, I avoid it. I'm so fucking desperate and lonely.'

The man took a deep breath. He could hear voices outside as people passed the shop. 'Vinnie Cartwright, I have something for you.' He reached to a drawer by his knee, pulled it open and moved his hand over the boxes. Then he pulled one out and held it in the air. 'This is it.' He looked at Vinnie, stood in front of him, his face sweaty, his cheeks large, swollen and bright red. He could see the effect his weight had on his life. But things were going to change. And change they would. 'Don't ask me what's in them; I won't tell you anything about them. You don't need to know, and I have no desire to explain. You will follow my instructions. One a week, every week, on the first day. If you fail to do this, the weight will come back at an alarming rate. You'll balloon.' He handed the box across the counter. 'There are thirty tablets here; if you do as I say, the weight will drop off at a furious rate and even out over the course of the treatment. You will take all thirty over the next seven or so months. So, are you ready to change, Vinnie Cartwright?'

With his mouth wide open in astonishment, Vinnie stated, 'It sure sounds amazing. One a week, every day on the first day. I'll balloon if I don't take them all. Am I right?'

'Correct. Your metabolism will be like nothing you've ever experienced. Anything you eat will burn off. It will be like the food never touched your lips or went inside your stomach.'

His eyes wild with antisipation, Vinnie announced, 'That's insane. How the hell—?'

The man held up a hand. 'We don't ask questions. I've already told you that.'

Vinnie gave an embarrassed look. 'Fine. How much?'

'How much?' the old man echoed. 'I don't want money.'

Like a fish jumping out of the water, a swirling sound caused Vinnie to look around the shop. He was certain something moved inside one of the jars next to him. He felt his heart pound for a moment. 'Well, what do I owe you?'

The old man handed over a carrier bag, and Vinnie placed the box inside.

'Taking these tablets means you've signed the contract— a gentleman's agreement. I will let you know what you have to do. Once you take the tablets from the shop, you're bound to my rules. Now, I'll be in touch. Go, start your new life, free yourself from this burden and be happy, content in how you look for the first time in years.'

'I'll do anything.' Vinnie smiled. 'But I still don't know what you want me to—?'

'As I said, I'll be in touch.'

Backing away, Vinnie watched the old man as he watched Vinnie.

Then, the shop owner moved around the counter, opened the shutters, and Vinnie left.

* * *

On the journey home, Vinnie couldn't stop thinking about the shop owner. It was like he'd appeared in a puff of smoke, like a genie from a child's story. In a way, the things he'd promised were very much in the same vein. Pulling the tablets from the carrier bag, he looked at the plain white box. There was no writing, no label, nothing to indicate what they were. Twisting the cap, he spilt a few of the tablets onto his hand. They were tiny, much smaller than the standard headache tablet; they were white and, again, no markings. Vinnie stared at them, wondering if they really could change his life.

Getting off the bus, he thanked the driver and walked along the road towards his flat. His mind was occupied with the contents of the jars. What had the old man kept in them? Something had moved. He was sure. The objects were large and weird-looking, like a collection from a freak show in the olden days. The scenario ran over in his mind. The old man, asking him for a favour. He said he'd contact Vinnie, but surely a man that can get anything would want for nothing. It didn't make sense.

Upstairs, Vinnie sat on his sofa, on edge, starting to become fearful of what the old man wanted from him.

He picked the tablets up, wondering whether to take one now or tomorrow. *Sunday is the start of the week, there's no time like the present,* Vinnie thought. Again, he twisted the cap and

emptied a tablet into the palm of his hand.

He got off the sofa with much effort and grabbed a glass

of water. Then he held the tablet in the air, eyeing it, bracing himself and popped it into his mouth, swallowing it with the water.

Waiting, he thought he'd hear a drumroll or see a puff of smoke, and suddenly he'd be four shirt sizes smaller. He expected his waistline to shrink and his trousers to fall to the floor.

Nothing. Nothing happened. Struggling with the anti-climax, it was as though the effort wasn't worth it.

He rushed to the mirror in the bathroom, pulling at his double chin, grappling with his overhanging stomach and running his hands over his enormous man boobs. *This isn't good. Not at all,* Vinnie thought.

Eying the broken scales which he'd placed against the wall, he wondered if he'd ever hear from the old man at the shop again. Perhaps it was all a game to him. Maybe these pills did nothing, and he never asked for this mystical 'favour' in return. How would the old man even contact him? He hadn't asked for his phone number. But then again, how did he know so much about Vinnie? His single status, address, and time he'd spent trying to lose weight? He knew Vinnie was coming. He knew he was looking for the shop. Vinnie had pounded the streets of Camden for hours, trudging through the crowds of people out shopping on a Sunday afternoon. He'd passed that area many times, circling the streets, searching. Then it suddenly appeared.

And so did the old man.

What the heck was in those jars?

* * *

Vinnie spent the evening in front of the telly watching re-runs of old game shows on a plus one channel. At just gone

8pm, he ordered a pizza, drank three cans of beer to wash it down and went to bed.

On the way to his room, he brushed his teeth, had a wee and took another glance in the mirror.

'Bloody anything. What a load of shit.'

* * *

Vinnie woke at just gone 6am. Something had rattled out in the hallway. Pushing the blanket back from his body, he moved across the room and put on his tracksuit bottoms. As he walked towards the hallway, he could feel them slide down his legs. 'What the fuck?' Vinnie looked down. His overhang had shrunk. But how? He pulled the tracksuit bottoms back up and over his waist. He could pull them out; they were looser. Usually, his pants cut into his stomach.

Elated, Vinnie tied the string tight, something he hadn't done for years. This was good.

Out in the hallway, an envelope rested on the doormat. Vinnie bent down, feeling more flexible, lighter. How could this happen overnight? It's impossible. He looked at the envelope, addressed to Vinnie Cartwright. No stamp. Hand-delivered.

He knew who'd sent it.

Walking into the kitchen, Vinnie sat at the table, anticipating what was inside. He opened the envelope, removed the letter and began reading. The writing was small, and hard to read with stylish joined-up writing. That was the first thing he noticed.

Vinnie.

It was good seeing you yesterday.

I trust the first tablet has started to take effect. You won't believe how quickly the results show.

So, onto pressing matters. You mentioned your friend recommended me to you. For that, I am grateful. He had problems of his own. He went through a bitter separation. When he came to my shop, bless him, he was in bits. He didn't know where to turn. His wife, sorry, ex, had consumed most of his money after he'd agreed to pay the mortgage and all the spending money she needed. With the hefty sum he'd paid every month, the bills on his new property and his children's education quickly adding up, it soon drained his bank account. He came to me and I helped him. It had to be somewhat discreet. If I wired money or gave him something which he'd need to declare, he'd pay tax. So, I planted a suitcase in a park late at night. He found it after my instructions, and the rest is his business.

As I stated, and you'll already know, this isn't a free service. I want something in return. You must understand I'm not a charity.

So, I've thought long and hard; it kept me awake. But I've worked out what I want.

Your friend has moved on; he's still bitter about the split; it wasn't amicable. But he's getting over it. At least, I hope.

I want you to bring her dead body to me. Refuse, and I'll have you killed. This is not a threat.

Kill her, then bring me the body.

You have one day, Vinnie.

Do not let me down.

Vinnie sat on the chair, feeling his world come crashing down.

This must be a joke, he thought. It has to be. What's wrong with this lunatic?

He sat, stunned into silence, then read the letter a second and third time.

Steph Parnell, Martins's ex-wife? Vinnie couldn't do it; the thought was ludicrous.

Since high school, Vinnie and Martin had been friends; he'd been the only person never to insult Vinnie or laugh at him.

Vinnie knew Steph through her marriage with Martin. He adored Steph.

They'd been married for over ten years. Vinnie had been there to pick up the pieces when it all went wrong. So how the hell could Vinnie murder Steph? Yes, he'd lost contact with her since they'd split, because Vinnie had owed Martin. He couldn't keep in touch with her, knowing how broken his best friend was.

But there was no way on earth he'd *murder* her.

This had to be a joke. The old man was on a wind-up, surely?

But taking the tablets had sealed the agreement. Wasn't that what he'd said? A gentleman's agreement. He'd have to drop them back. There was no other way.

Moving into the bathroom, Vinnie stood, dumbfounded, staring into the mirror. It was like a different person. After one tablet, he didn't recognise himself.

'What the fuck is happening?' he whispered. 'How is this possible?' Glaring down at his body; the paunch overhang had dissolved like pieces had been cut from a steak, the fat trimmed away. He was far from skinny, but it seemed he'd lost over half a stone during the night.

Despite the letter, Vinnie felt excitement bloom in him. He hadn't looked this good for over a decade. It had taken effect on his face too. His features were more striking, his cheeks less puffy, and the skin around his chin was tighter.

He stared at this stranger, this man he didn't recognise.

* * *

Vinnie walked into the bedroom, grabbed his phone from the bedside unit and called Martin. He picked up on the third ring.

Sounding half asleep and his voice croaky, Martin said, 'Hi, Vinnie. Wow, it's early.'

'I found the shop,' Vinnie stated.

'Oh, you did? When?'

'Yesterday afternoon. I need to talk.'

There was a brief silence, and then Martin spoke. 'OK. But not on the phone. Meet me at Dale's cafe. Say in an hour?'

Ending the call, Vinnie moved to the bedroom window. He looked out over the park; the deep grey clouds and the chilly autumn morning produced a gloomy appearance. He watched as the leaves danced and rose into the air, the parents pushing young children on the swings, and a couple of women spoke with babies strapped into pushchairs.

Then he thought about the letter and the old man asking him to kill Steph.

* * *

A bell rang as Vinnie opened the door to the cafe, seeing his friend at the counter.

Martin turned, struggling to hide his astonishment. He began to speak, watching Vinnie in amazement. 'Tea, is it? Still one sugar?'

Vinnie held up his thumb, watching as Martin paid for the drinks and brought them over to the table. Wearing a black suit with a freshly pressed shirt underneath, Martin looked well-groomed, his face clean-shaven and his black hair short and held with gel. Martin looked like a man who didn't have a care in the world.

'Christ. I don't need to guess what you asked for,' Martin said.

Vinnie spoke, keeping his voice hushed. 'How the hell did this happen to me? I went to bed last night and woke like this. It's mental.'

Martin sat, sipping his tea, pushing Vinnie's across the table, careful not to spill the hot contents. 'I know. It's bonkers, isn't it? A friend told me about the place. I had trouble finding it.' Although excited for his friend, Martin kept secret the shop's location, knowing the consequences could be fatal if the old man chose that route. He hoped he hadn't.

Vinnie sipped his tea, watching the surprise on his friend's face as he struggled to stem his astonishment.

'I can't believe the contrast,' Martin continued. 'You look completely different.'

'You look good yourself. New haircut, the glint in your eyes. What's going on mate?'

Bracing himself, Martin announced, 'I have some good news.'

'Go on?' Vinnie asked.

'Well, I can't help my feelings; God knows it may be the wrong choice. Perhaps I'm mad, going back there, the path I thought I'd left behind. But I'm getting back with Steph. We're going to try and work things out. It's not just for the kids; I still have very strong feelings for her. I'm still in love with her.'

Lifting his cup, Vinnie's hand trembled so intensely that

the tea spilt over the edge. He placed the cup back on the saucer. 'You're what?'

'Steph and I. We're... giving it another go. Please be happy for me before you start going off on a rant.'

The room began to spin, and Vinnie thought he was going to pass out. He sighed deeply as he watched the smile on his friend's face. He wanted to be pleased for them, but he couldn't be. 'I need to ask you something?' He watched as Martin tensed, his face became serious, and his eyebrows drew closer together.

'What?'

'The old man. What did he ask you to do?'

'Don't. Don't go there. You have what you want. Your dream is now a reality. It's happening, Vinnie. Do what you have to do. Don't ask questions.'

Sat, open-mouthed, Vinnie inquired, 'And if I don't?'

'Then you're making the biggest mistake of your life. *They'll come for you.*'

Vinnie sat in his flat, thinking about the conversation with his friend earlier. Martin had refused to say any more on the subject after telling Vinnie to do his task, no questions asked. He'd said they'd come for him. What did it even mean? Could Vinnie go back, find the shop and ask the owner to change his mind? After all, the shop is called Anything.

He stood, moving towards the window, his body feeling tired, drained and wanting to go for a lie-down. His shift started in a couple of hours, and he wouldn't be finished until late. Although his only saving grace was the restaurant would be quiet this evening, being a Monday. It wouldn't be too taxing. He would have time to think.

Looking out of the window, Vinnie noticed something. He stepped back, his heart almost leaping from his chest. Two large, menacing-looking men were standing in the middle of the road and staring at him.

'Shit. What the fuck?' Moving to the side of the window, Vinnie ducked. His breathing became fast and erratic. He wanted to run, but where? They had to have come from the shop. This was getting out of hand—a crazy situation.

Martin had said they'd come for him if he didn't follow the order. But how could he follow the order?

How could he kill Steph?

Lying under the window ledge and facing the bathroom, Vinnie saw the broken scales leaning against the wall. He'd lost so much weight overnight. His dreams had come true. All those years of diets, and exercise, only to pile on the pounds. But this madness had to stop. What the shop owner was asking was ludicrous. A favour for a favour. What kind of man was he to ask such things?

Turning his body, slowly rising, he drew his eyes from the wall, looking out the window.

The men were gone.

Vinnie waited, peering along the road, watching the parked cars, searching for shadows. He couldn't see anything. Turning away, he stepped to the side and out of view. He waited a few moments, then turned back. Relieved to see the road was empty.

He thought about what Martin had said when he'd questioned what would happen if he didn't do as the shop owner had asked. *Then you're making the biggest mistake of your life. They'll come for you.* They were his exact words.

They'll come for you. What did Martin do in return for his wealth?

Vinnie debated whether to go back to the shop. He could return the tablets. Wash his hands of this terrible mess. Then forget all about it.

Yes, that's what he'd do. Go back. Bring the tablets and walk away.

* * *

Walking along Camden High Street, Vinnie recalled how he'd traipsed the streets for hours yesterday, searching, desperate to change his life. To take control. Then, he had been dubious but excited. Now, he just felt complete terror.

He walked, peering into shops, watching people saunter in and out, the smell of food drifting from restaurants, and cafes, clinging to the air around him. He wanted to eat but, for the first time he could remember, he wasn't hungry. Vinnie wondered if it was an effect of the tablets or of fear.

Reaching the corner where yesterday he'd found the shop, he stopped in astonishment. It was the right place. The exact spot where he stood the day before. Now, a brick wall stood in its place. Bewildered, Vinnie moved forward, his mind racing, addled and confused. Placing his hands on the wall, he hoisted his body upwards, gripping the top with his fingers, the rough cement digging into the tips. There was nothing but wasteland. A couple of workers were standing by a skip, watching another man operating a small digger as it lifted soil. Vinnie let go of the wall and dropped to the ground.

He stood, leaning against it, furiously wiping sweat from his cheeks. His vision became blurred, and he was suddenly weak.

As he moved away from the street corner, his phone rang. Dipping into his tracksuit bottoms and removing his phone, the words, 'No Caller ID' appeared across the screen.

'Hello?'

'You're looking good. I must say I didn't think the tablets would take effect so quickly.'

Vinnie's body jolted. He spun in a circle, watching everyone around him. People were walking across the road, a couple with a buggy, an elderly woman and a group of teenagers. Turning back, he faced the wall. There was no sign of the old man. 'What is going on with you? You're a lunatic.'

'Well, that's gratitude for you. I go to the effort of helping you, and you speak to me like that.'

With his voice raised, Vinnie asked, 'Where's the shop?'

'You're looking in the wrong place.'

'No. I'm in the right place. How did you move it?'

'You tell me. You were so determined to find the place. I told you the rules. Now, time is running out.'

'You didn't tell me I'd have to kill someone.'

'My laws, remember. You came to my shop; you took my product. I'm changing your life for the better, so I make the demands.'

'You're sick. I can't do it. I can't kill my best friend's wife.'

'Ex-wife,' the old man stated. 'They split up, remember?'

'Whatever. I'm not doing it. So take your tablets back. The deal is off.' Removing the box from his pocket, Vinnie dropped them on the floor. 'There you go. Take them. Fuck you and your shop.' Vinnie ended the call. Suddenly, he sensed doom, like a car would come hurtling towards him or a tree would land where he stood.

Walking back onto the main road, he watched behind and started to jog. Vinnie had never felt so fit, but at what cost? He'd shed over half a stone overnight; more had dropped off today. He felt alive, and vibrant but what the old man wanted was absurd.

As he moved along the road, he wondered how far this person would go? It was obvious he was serious about the threat. Martin had warned him too.

But Vinnie couldn't commit murder.

* * *

He flagged a bus down halfway home, his body aching and his face was damp with perspiration. Vinnie sat at the back, slumped down on the seat and kept hidden. As he exited the bus, he continually glanced over his shoulder

There was no sign of the old man or the two people who'd visited earlier.

As he approached the front door of his flat, he saw it was open. Slowly, he moved towards it, pushing the door back, now able to see into the living room. 'Hello? Who's here? Leave me alone. I'm going to call the police.' Stepping across the wooden floor, he eyed his bedroom, imagining the door opening, the two people from earlier charging towards him.

Vinnie reached the sofa and knelt on it. Slowly, he edged his body forward, his heart racing and his body trembling with fear. The floor behind the sofa was empty. Pushing himself off, he moved to the bedroom. Vinnie kept his eyes focused, staring ahead. The door was closed. He stepped backwards, too frightened to turn around. Standing outside the room, he watched the brass handle, counted to three, and forced it down, pushing the door open. He looked towards the bed, the small table beside it, the digital clock blinking its neon lights and displaying numbers.

The room was vacant.

In the bathroom, Vinnie moved the shower curtain back with visions of Hitchcock's Psycho playing in his mind. The bath was empty, with no sign that anyone had waited there.

Once he was certain the flat was empty, Vinnie moved to the window. He stared onto the road where the men had stood earlier.

No one was there.

His phone rang, causing Vinnie to jump. Again, 'No Caller ID' displayed along the front.

'Hello?'

'Quite the fright you must have got. This was just a warning. The next time we visit, we'll kill you.'

Vinnie broke down. His body began to shudder, and he sobbed. 'Why are you doing this?'

'Do you seriously imagine I do it for nothing? Everything in life has a price, Vinnie. This is yours. You came to me in your time of need. I helped you. I told you that I'd want something in return. The people who visit me, take from my shop, have tasks and rules they must obey. I'm sorry. Perhaps I'm getting impatient in my old age. You have until midnight to do as I've asked. If by that time, Steph is still alive, you won't see morning. That's a promise.'

Dropping the phone onto the floor, petrified, Vinnie screamed. He collapsed on the sofa, crying uncontrollably. Still hearing the old man's voice, Vinnie got off the sofa and lifted the phone to his ear.

'I have a little something to show you.'

Hands shaking, Vinnie looked at the screen and tried desperately to keep the phone still. 'What? What is it you want to show me?'

There was silence for a moment. Suddenly the phone beeped. Vinnie had a new WhatsApp message. Tapping the picture, he zoomed in. It showed his friend, Martin, sitting at the kitchen table with Steph. Vinnie knew the house. He'd been there many times but not since they'd split up. Vinnie could see the pictures in the background, held in thick white frames, the words written in black ink, recipes from around the world. Vinnie had often commented on them, laughing that his friend should just write them in a notepad. To the left of the photo, he could see the spice rack and the Italian coffee maker further along the sideboard.

The old man began to speak. 'This was taken a couple of minutes ago.'

Another ping. Vinnie looked at the photo, again, tapping the screen to see it more clearly. His eyes were wild, and he thought he was going to pass out. An elderly couple sat on a sofa. The picture had been taken from the hallway, through the gap in the living room door. As Vinnie zoomed in closer he could see it was his parents. The picture had just been taken. He listened to the voice.

'You know what you have to do.'

Terrified, his stomach in knots, his face damp from fear, Vinnie walked, trance like to the front door of his apartment. Switching the lights out, he moved into the communal hallway. Thankfully it was empty. He didn't feel like having a conversation with a neighbour. His body was numb, robotic as he moved to the stairs, slowly walking down towards the apartment block's front door.

Outside, the wind was harsh, and it whipped into his face. He turned, realising he could feel the cold more now that he'd lost weight. His frame felt lighter, his clothes looser, and he could breathe easier. He enjoyed the feeling. But at what price had it come? How could this madman justify his requests?

Martin had warned him. His voice reverberated in his mind again.

They'll come for you.

Who the fuck were these people? How had they managed to camouflage the shop for so long, making it almost impossible to find? Vinnie had so many questions. The picture of his dear parents sat on the sofa in their living room haunted him. Someone was there. Perhaps someone was there with them now.

Vinnie had no choice. He knew if he called the police, his parents were dead. And besides, he'd give them an address for the shop, but they'd never find it.

It was like a mirage, a portal to a cruel world, waiting to be found.

Anything.

What was the deal with that place?

And what was in those jars?

* * *

Walking along the main road, Vinnie listened as vehicles passed and shutters were pulled down as shopkeepers finished work for the evening. He kept his head low, wondering if he was being watched as he made his way to Martin's house.

He had no choice.

He watched the cracks in the pavement, the lights shining from the street lamps overhead, as he plotted how to murder his best friend's ex-wife.

Martin had sat in the cafe earlier, so pleased to be back with Steph. His eyes were enthusiastic, full of anticipation for the future.

Now, Vinnie was going to take it from him.

He reached a side road just off Chalk Farm High Street. Rather than CCTV capturing his bus ride, Vinnie walked, careful to monitor any cameras on the way there, keeping his face covered with the hood of his coat.

Standing outside, he glared at the four-bedroom semi-detached house. He hadn't been here since Martin had moved out. But now he was back. He debated whether to knock on the door, barge in and race towards Steph. Strangle her, watching until she took her last breath.

As he walked towards the front door, a message pinged on his phone. Vinnie wanted to ignore it; he wanted to leave it there, festering in cyberspace. Reaching into his tracksuit bottoms, he removed the phone and read the message.

I'm watching. Go around the back of the house. Martin and Steph are upstairs. I suggest you wait until one of them leaves.

Your mother and father are comfortable.

Keep it that way.

Frustrated, Vinnie wanted to smash the phone on the ground and stamp on it until nothing was left. The old man had ruined his life in twenty-four hours.

Approaching the front door, he listened for any movement inside the house. Then he crept around the back, checking for cameras as he walked along the side entrance.

Vinnie stood in the cold; the sky was dark and starless, and the garden was bleak. Staring into the blackness, he wondered if someone was there, watching him. How else would the old man know he'd arrived? He wanted to run, to race from the back of the house, along the High Street and keep going until he collapsed.

Vinnie was terrified. He thought about his parents and then quickly cleared their images from his mind, knowing he had a job to do.

Stepping backwards, careful not to fall over, he peered towards the top of the house. Vinnie could see them, standing near the window. The old man was right about them both being in there.

Martin was holding a glass of beer; Steph had red wine. They were talking, oblivious to anything around them. They toasted, clinking the glasses together and throwing back the alcohol.

Vinnie watched as they placed the glasses to the side. Martin began undoing his white shirt, his body pale and lean, and he dropped his trousers. Reaching forward, he removed Steph's jacket and nibbled on her neck. 'No, no. For Christ's sake, stop. Not now. What are you doing? Remember how this lady treated you? Take things slowly, you prick. I have a fucking job to do.' Vinnie kept his voice low so's not to be heard. He needed to distract them, not wanting to be out here all night. Crouching, he turned on his phone torch, pawing on the ground, and then crawled on his hands and knees. Vinnie found a large stone. Quickly, he grabbed it, stood and took aim, hurling it towards the top window and hitting the wooden frame. 'Shit.' He saw the worried faces.

Martin spun, his naked body at the window, his face against the glass. Vinnie watched as his friend undid the latch and lifted the window.

'Who's there? I'm calling the police. Do you hear?'

Damn it, Vinnie thought. He watched as Martin placed his clothes back on and moved out of the room.

Steph was still there.

This was it. The next few minutes would determine the rest of his life. If Martin called the police and made good on his threat, the old man would most certainly kill Vinnie's parents; then, he'd kill Vinnie. If Martin came down and searched for the intruder, Vinnie would get into the house and Steph would die.

Waiting in the garden, he held his breath, his heart racing, his stomach flipping under his clothes. At the last second, he raced along the side entrance and hid around the front of the house. Crouching behind a bush, he watched the front door open.

Martin walked out, still buttoning his shirt, his bare feet moving along the steps and then he moved around to the side entrance.

This was it, Vinnie thought. He had seconds. Watching the light show through the crack of the front door, he walked towards it.

Vinnie stood in the hall. The light was on in the kitchen at the end of the house. He could see a shadow. Martin moved past the window outside.

Vinnie could hear Steph above, her footsteps moving across the ceiling. Peering up the stairs, he braced himself and then began to move upwards.

Steph began speaking. 'Can you see anyone, Martin?'

His friend's voice sounded from the garden, too distant for Vinnie to hear the words.

'Just leave it then. Come back inside. Martin, are you listening? Leave it.'

As he neared the top of the stairs, Vinnie feared Martin would walk into the house, spot him and ask what he was doing. Why he'd thrown a stone at the window and crept up the stairs. His stomach was churning, his legs unstable, and he wanted to leave. But it was too late. He'd come here to kill Steph. The picture of his mum and dad, sitting on the sofa spurned him on. It was either them or her.

Vinnie had no choice.

Standing against the wall at the top of the house, he could hear Steph talking, insisting that Martin come back inside.

So what now? Does he charge into the room and hope to strangle her before his friend comes back, or use a sharp object to stab her in the chest? He realised in his desperation that he had no weapon, no plan on how he was going to do this. And no escape prepared. This wasn't him. Vinnie wouldn't harm anyone. But he'd been driven to this. The threats were real. He had to do it.

As he stood, leaning against the wall, he heard footsteps moving towards him. Vinnie closed his eyes, his heart racing, punching through his chest. Steph was standing close to him on the other side of the wall. He held his breath, worried she'd see him, call Martin, and a fight break out. Christ, he wanted the ground to open up and swallow him whole.

Steph came out of the bedroom and moved along the upstairs hall. She opened the bathroom door, then closed and locked it.

Pushing out a heavy sigh, his body tense and nervous, he was relieved she hadn't seen him. He stepped into the bedroom. He had seconds before Steph came back.

Martin shouted from downstairs. 'There's no one here. I'm coming back up.'

Shit, shit, shit. What now? Vinnie thought. He moved to a large wardrobe as the toilet flushed. Then a tap turned on.

Fighting the tears of terror which threatened to spill from his eyes, Vinnie scanned the room. He'd never been more scared. As the bathroom door opened, he stepped inside the wardrobe. He could see Steph moving across the bedroom, looking out of the window. She wrapped her arms around her body, trying to warm up. Vinnie watched; there was no time now. Martin was on his way up; he could hear him on the stairs.

Steph turned, and the two of them spoke.

The space was tight, and Vinnie tried to keep as still as possible. Luckily, the wardrobe was relatively empty, and there was more room now he'd lost weight. He ducked, trying to get comfortable and knowing he couldn't stay here all night. How long were Steph and Martin planning to stay? A few minutes ago, they'd clinked glasses and embraced; now what?

He watched as they both came into view. Steph was holding him, kissing his cheek.

Martin returned the gesture and started undoing his shirt.

No. Don't do this. I can't breathe. Please don't do this. He had to get out; feeling claustrophobic, hemmed in, and trapped, Vinnie needed an exit. He stemmed a sneeze as his body began to jolt.

Martin was bare-chested; he began removing his trousers, standing in his underwear. Reaching forward, he removed Steph's clothes, the two of them kissing, embracing passionately and right next to where he hid.

As they moved towards the bed, someone came charging into the room.

Vinnie gasped as he watched a man holding a baseball bat smash Martin over the back of the head. He dropped to the floor as blood began to seep from his head. He hit him over and over.

Turning away, Steph listened as the reins fell hard on her ex-husband.

Vinnie watched in terror as Martin's body bounced; his legs were trembling and then went limp.

'Christ, what took you so long?' Steph asked.

Throwing the bat on the floor, the guy turned, smiling at Steph. 'I didn't expect him to leave and go outside. I was waiting in the end room. I had to time it right.' With a curt grin, the guy moved across the bedroom, grabbed a can of petrol from the cupboard and began pouring it all over the carpet. Straightening his back for a moment, he poured the remainder of the petrol over Martin's limp body. He turned to Steph, holding the empty can in the air. 'This will hide what happened. The police will know it's arson, but they won't have the evidence to pin it on us.' Leaning forward, his hands on his knees, he tried to catch his breath. 'Christ, We've done it. Are you OK?'

The shock on Steph's face was evident. The bat slamming down on her ex-husband played in her mind like a chilling video clip. Nodding, she said, 'I feel so bad. But as you say, it's the only way.'

Rubbing his hands together, excited, his breaths harsh, he stated, 'The money will come through on this place, and we'll make a better life for ourselves. We've been patient; it's a good thing.'

'Are you sure they won't suspect us?'

'Absolutely. Why would they? You've been separated for a long time; the fact that you never got around to the divorce will work in your favour. It will appear that you really did still love him.' Turning, the guy looked at Martin's dead body on the floor. 'The poor bastard's one mistake was telling you about the recent money he'd come into. You begged him, Steph. You asked him for more, but he wasn't willing to share it. This was the only way. Getting back with him, pretending you still loved him and leading him here. Now, all of it is ours. No one will suspect you.'

'Then what?' Steph asked.

The guy moved towards her. 'Then, we wait for the life insurance. And enjoy the rest of our lives together.'

Vinnie watched in horror as the guy produced a lighter and set the carpet on fire. The blaze became an inferno in a matter of seconds. Through a slight gap in the wardrobe door, he saw the guy reaching over and holding Steph's hand, and then they left the bedroom.

Vinnie tried to open the wardrobe door, but Martin's body blocked him from getting out. Trapped, the room already blisteringly hot and the flames so intense, he desperately shoved his body against the wardrobe door. Pounding his fists on the wood, he could feel his skin burn as if it were melting. 'Help. Please, someone. Help me. Help me.'

His cries rang out over the house.

Then there was silence.

The old man sat in the shop, listening to the radio. It cut to the news, and the person began with a shocking murder in West London.

An elderly couple have been found dead in their home after an intruder broke in late last night.

Simon and Paula Cartwright were sitting in the living room of their home in Fulham, West London, when the intruder broke in at just after 11pm.

Police are appealing for witnesses and have said the attack was a callous, appalling act of wickedness on two innocent people.

The couple were both in their seventies, and neighbours are shocked.

The old man stood, then moved towards the shelves. In one of the jars was the charred remains of a finger belonging to Vinnie Cartwright.

He liked to keep memories—trophies that reminded him of the game he loved to play.

He thought about Vinnie as he stared at the jar and how he'd come to such a wicked end.

Moving to another jar, he thought about Martin, and how he'd first found the shop. He'd called in over a month ago, questioning the old man, asking if it were true that he could get anything. The old man smirked as Martin asked to get back with his ex-wife. He'd explained the rules and that Martin would need to do something in return.

The following morning he'd posted a letter through Martin's front door.

Martin, Thanks for coming to see me yesterday. I've thought long and hard, and all I ask is that you tell your best friend about my shop. Vinnie is struggling both physically and mentally. I will help him. Once you do this, Steph will be back in your life. I can't guarantee for how long; the rest is up to you. Now we have a gentleman's agreement; you must carry this out. It's an under-standing between both parties, you and I.

P.S. Oh, tell him anything, anything at all regarding this letter or how my shop works, and I'll have you killed. They'll come for you. This is not a threat.

Now, the old man pondered the situation and how it had all panned out. He didn't expect the twist of fate, greed, lust and all the other evil emotions that people can be capable of.

He loved the game; he'd devised ways of helping people, but he couldn't control the outcome. That was down to them.

You may question the old man's morals. His integrity and principles. Some may think he's as evil as the people who visit his shop.

But in this life, everything has a price.

Again, he looked towards the jars, needing more of them. Always needing more.

He stood, hearing footsteps outside. Someone tapped on the shutters.

Moving around the back of the shop, he stepped out onto the quiet street.

A middle-aged man stood in front of him, well dressed, his eyes full of excitement and anticipation. He turned around, checking briefly behind.

'Hi. Is it true you can get anything?'

Smiling, the old man instructed, 'Come this way.'

The End.

AFTERWORD

Thank you for choosing my story collection, The Macabre.

Like Vinnie Cartwright, If I found the shop, 'Anything,' I'd ask for every single reader to leave a review.

😂 😂 😂

I'm unsure though what the old man would want in return.

If you enjoyed, The Macabre, please write a review on Amazon and Goodreads.

Even one line is absolutely amazing and will honestly help me so much.

ABOUT THE AUTHOR

Stuart James is an award-winning psychological thriller and horror author and his books are constantly top of the Amazon charts.

His thriller, The House On Rectory Lane, recently won The International Book Award in horror fiction.

Make sure to click the link below and sign up to my newsletter to keep up to date with everything I'm working on.

https://www.stuartjamesthrillers.com

Books by Stuart James.

The House On Rectory Lane.
    Turn The Other Way.
    Apartment Six.
    Stranded.
    Selfie.
    Creeper.
    The Macabre.

ACKNOWLEDGMENTS

Thank you so much for choosing The Macabre and I hope you enjoyed it.
You can sign up to my mailing list and keep up to date with other projects I have planned.
Just go to:
https://www.stuartjamesthrillers.com

I'd like to say a huge thank you to my family for your extreme patience and listening to my ideas constantly.
Ha ha.
I feel you know my thrillers as well as I do.
The short story collection is something I've had planned for a while and I absolutely loved writing them.
I will do more shortly.

Firstly, a huge thank you to everyone on my Facebook arc group for your ongoing support. I can't thank you enough.
We have almost 130 members and I'm so, so grateful to you all.
Please get in touch if you'd like to be a part of it.

Special thanks to the Facebook groups who continually promote my works and support me so much.
The Fiction Cafe.
Tracy Fenton and her wonderful book club, TBC.
The Reading Corner Book Lounge.

UK Crime Book Club.
Donna's Interviews, Reviews and Giveaways.
Mark Fearn. Book Mark.
Also to the incredible book bloggers who have supported my journey so much and to all you wonderful readers and authors.
Also massive thanks to Adam Croft, Alan Gorevan and Lindsay Detwiler.
A huge thank you to my neighbour, Doctor Vikas Acharya for your help on my first story, The Intruder, and your invaluable insight with the hospital scenes. You sir, are an absolute gentleman.
And lastly, special thanks to Zoe O'Farrell, Chloe Jordan, Kate Eveleigh, Donna Morfett, Emma Louise Bunting, Emma Louise Smith, Michaela Balfour, Kiltie Jackson, Mark Fearn and all the readers who requested an arc of The Macabre.
Your support is forever grateful.
You really are amazing and I can't thank you enough.
Thanks to my wonderful family for all your patience and support. I love you all so very much.

Make sure to keep up to date with projects I'm working on and sign up to my mailing list at:
https://www.stuartjamesthrillers.com

Also, you can follow me on social media.
I love to hear from readers and will always respond.
Twitter: StuartJames73
Instagram: Stuart James Author
Facebook: Stuart James Author.
TikTok: Stuart James Author

WS - #0194 - 220724 - C0 - 203/127/16 - PB - 9781804673829 - Matt Lamination